Abernathy

To Gordon

[signature]

Claire Patel-Campbell

Stairwell Books

Published by Stairwell Books
70 Barbara Drive
Norwalk
CT 06851 USA

161 Lowther Street
York, YO31 7LZ

www.stairwellbooks.co.uk
@stairwellbooks

Abernathy © 2017 Claire Patel-Campbell and Stairwell Books
Cover © 2017 Natalie Dixon and Stairwell Books

All rights reserved. No part of this publication may be reproduced, stored in or introduced into a retrieval system, or transmitted, in any form, or by any means (electronic, mechanical, photocopying, recording, e-book or otherwise) without the prior written permission of the author.

The moral rights of the author have been asserted.

Softcover ISBN: 978-1-939269-56-0
Hardcover ISBN: 978-1-939269-71-3

Cover design: Natalie Dixon
Layout design: Alan Gillott
Printed and bound in the UK by Imprint Digital

For Thomas,
always loving, always encouraging, and always ready with tea or gin, as circumstances require.

When you hit the farm that used to be the Weiler farm, you know you're here. You know you've hit the last cornfield, after miles and miles of nothing but cornfields. There's still another mile to go before you hit the main street, such as it is, but that's the boundary. The faded red barn and the ancient silo mark the gateway. That's where it begins. You see the wide, flat streets and the wide, flat storefronts. That's when that familiar feeling hits you. It starts in your hands and feet and runs all the way through you like a current in a wire as you get closer. It settles deep in your gut, a ball of pulsing electricity. You know this town. You've been here before, or maybe you never really left. Everything about it is lodged inside you.

It's home.

They stand there in silence for a long time, looking at her, the winter wind whipping across their backs. The little hairs on the backs of their necks are standing up and they both shiver. It's not just the weather. It's that nasty, cold feeling you'd get in your gut when you were a kid, and something gave you the creeps. Like a little change in the way the world turns that nobody notices but you. Like somebody walking on your grave.

She's lying face up in the fresh snow, half hidden under it, her feet and her breasts poking up out of it, stray strands of dark hair blowing across her face. Still – unnaturally so. There's no breath there to make her chest rise and fall, no blood to make her skin pink. It's early December and with that comes the kind of cold that cuts through clothes, through skin, right to the bone, but they barely feel it. She seems much colder than that to them – colder than anything they've ever known. Dead. She makes the world around them seem dim and far away. It's as if the three of them exist in a tiny bright bubble all their own. The snow is so gleaming white, it burns their eyes, but they can't look away. They're transfixed. No one will breach this cell. No one will rupture the skin of this. There is no piercing the surface, no breaking the tension. They're alone with her.

It's taking everything they have just to comprehend what it is they're seeing. She's like a riddle. The solution seems tangible, on the tips of their tongues, but they can't quite reach it. She's tiny, but she seems huge to them. The enormity of what must have happened to her is giant. It spreads out all the way to the trees to the south, and across the snow to the east and west, and over them and behind them, back to the town to the north. She's like a doll, stretched into something vast and grotesque, but still beautiful somehow. They take her in, piece by piece, trying, failing to make sense of her. Nothing makes sense to them right now. The power to speak at all, let alone explain anything, is beyond them. They've been staring at her, uncomprehending, for almost an hour, and neither one of them has said a thing. It's as if she's taken away all the words that would give her some context, some meaning. There was no warning, no sign of her before they found her here. They came up on her without any idea what it was they'd stumbled on, and now, here she is, just…staring at them. Empty-eyed, broken. Her lips are slightly parted, as though she wants to say something, and they both find themselves waiting for her to speak first – waiting for her to explain herself.

"What sh'we do?" Gallagher asks at last, his voice creaking, like a door long shut, whose hinges have become rusty through disuse. Murphy swivels his head slowly to look at him, squinting as the early morning sun grows brighter. He's been staring at her so long that he can still see her ghost when he turns away, filmy and translucent, floating in front of Gallagher's face.

"Don' know. Sh'we tell Abernathy, you think?" Gallagher looks back at him, screws up one eye and sucks his cheeks. He sways back and forth on his heels for a second, and then he remembers the hole in his boot and stops as the snow starts creeping in. It tingles as it seeps through the lining and reaches the sole of his foot.

"Hm. Don' know. Don' know, don' know," Gallagher says, casting his eyes over her again. Murphy looks scared. He's never seen a dead body before – only on TV, and Gallagher knows that's always been more than enough to give him the willies. For his own part, he's seen enough death not to be afraid of it. He knows what it is to look at someone when they're no longer someone. Just a body. Just a shell. He feels bad for Murphy. He's shaking, and he knows it's not because he's cold. The strangest part is that she looks peaceful, though. She's all blue-white and unmoving – if you didn't look too close, you'd almost think she was asleep. Except her eyes are open. There are little dark smudges of make-up ringing them, and a slash of deep red lipstick on her mouth.

Or maybe it's blood.

Gallagher feels himself shiver again. It's a chill right inside him, under the skin, under the muscle, starting in his chest and working its way out. It passes all through him as he lets that thought roll around in his mind.

"We can't jus' leave 'er…can we? What if…what if somebody else finds 'er?" Murphy asks, timidly. Gallagher tongues the broken tooth at the back of his mouth meditatively. Kowalski punched him in the jaw a couple of nights ago, he remembers. He'll have to see to him later.

He sighs, wishing he could stop himself from thinking what he's already thinking. But it's too late for that.

"She's not goin' anywhere, and there's nobody else comin' out here this morning. We might could maybe think about it and decide later," he replies. If he were being honest, he'd tell Murphy all he wants to do is run – to turn around and hightail it through the woods and the frozen drifts and never look back. The terrified kid in him is there now, rising up from a place inside him he'd thought long gone. It's the same feeling he got, alone in his grandmother's basement, when he was nine. He wasn't supposed to be there, but his sister had dared him to do it. Then the door slammed shut behind him and he thought he'd wind up a pile of bones before anybody found him. It's also the same feeling he got when he sat down with his parents, at twenty-one, to tell them the truth about himself. Now though, he pushes down the swell of fear in his stomach, squeezing it down tight inside him, trying his best to hide it for his friend's sake.

It's been a strange morning already and he's been unsettled ever since they passed the edge of town. There was a ripple in the surface of his otherwise imperturbable core – a little spike in the graph, usually untouched. No highs, no lows. But today, something felt off, even though he couldn't quite say what at first. He half thought about turning around at the time. Now, she's making him wish he had.

They'd planned on heading out towards the river while it was quiet to get some shooting in before breakfast, but the deer didn't show their faces at all. Nothing did, in point of fact – not so much as a possum – and part of him thinks that should have tipped him off. Maybe they know. Maybe they can sense something's horribly, irredeemably wrong. He's always thought there's something about the trees and the air and the animals out here – some part of them that can tell when an aberration like this takes place. Something's out of whack, off kilter. Someone's committed the gravest of sins, disturbed the delicate balance of things: there has to be something left behind, some sign of it out there in the universe.

"Seems kinda mean," Murphy says, kicking at the snow. "She's pretty, don'cha think? You recognize her at all?" he asks, knocking Gallagher off his train of thought. He has a way of doing that, without even knowing it – of dragging him back to earth whenever his thoughts tend down tracks like these. He peers at him searchingly, looking, hoping for a sign that he knows more than he's letting on.

Gallagher turns away from Murphy, and looks out to the dark, jagged tree line, where the spindly, spiky branches bite the ice-blue sky, and then back at her again. He's trying to imagine what she would look like if she were flesh-colored and upright, but he finds he can't do it. He can't make his mind bring her back. She's stuck as she is now.

"Hard t'say. She looks sort of like John Callaghan's girl, but…I don' know, I never thought about what she'd look like dead. How long's she been here, you think?" Gallagher says. John Callaghan was a friend of his father's, who'd lived out in California for a while. Mary, his daughter, was already in her mid-teens when the family moved back to town, but she was a few years younger than him, and she was always shy of him, covering her face behind her hair whenever he stopped by their house. He hasn't seen much of her since then and he's having a hard time picturing her now. The last he heard, she was living in her grandmother's condo in Ashland, and by Callaghan's account, had picked up some asshole on-off boyfriend. She comes back every now and then to see her father, usually when the boyfriend isn't around, although it's rare to see her around town and even rarer to see her without Callaghan. She always seems to be hiding somehow, even when she's in plain sight, and it's bothering him now: he can't quite remember her face because he's never really seen it. Maybe it is her. It could be her. She looks older than he thinks she ought to, but then he could still be picturing her as a kid. And then there's the nose. That doesn't look right, either. There's a little hitch in it, like it's been broken and reset.

He breathes in slowly through his nostrils and lets it out in a stilted half-whistle through his teeth, trying at least to remember what Callaghan told him about the boyfriend. To the best of his recollection, he'd made it sound like the guy was a real lowlife, but it never occurred to Gallagher he might be violent.

Murphy takes off a glove and scratches at his straggly brown beard, then digs his hands deep into the pockets of his faded, moth-eaten overcoat. It makes him look like a child, that outsized, old-fashioned coat. He's a head shorter than his friend, dark and wiry, with sharp, angular features, where Gallagher is broad and bluff and blond. He's built like a brick shithouse, as Murphy likes to remind him, and descended from Irish chieftains, or so his mother told him. It's a fact of which he's intensely proud: he takes his Gaelic stock very seriously. He's trying to hold on to that chieftain blood now, trying to be strong and stoic.

"That's what I was tryin' t'figure out. It's awful cold, and I don' see any footprints or tracks or anything. Could've been days. I didn' hear anything about anybody missin', though. Did you?" They know they're getting nowhere, asking each other these questions, but still they both silently hope one of them might just be holding out on the other. They're dancing around the reality of the situation in ever-tighter circles, and they both realize it, but with every half-answer and delaying tactic, it becomes harder to admit.

"No. Callaghan's girl had a boyfriend, though, I remember that. Didn' he say he was trouble?" Gallagher can't be sure because he's not looking right at him, but he thinks he sees Murphy give a little twitch when he brings up the boyfriend. Somewhere inside him, it sets off an alarm. It's the smallest shift, but it's there. He turns to look him in the eye, waiting for it to happen again. But then Murphy nods, firmly – as firmly as he ever does, at least – and Gallagher lets himself dismiss it. He imagined it. They've been staring at her too long.

"You think that's what it is?" Murphy asks, swallowing hard. "You think the boyfriend done it?" Gallagher makes a face, twisting his mouth to the side. He's eighteen months older than Murphy, and, he likes to think, a little smarter.

"I don' know, though. It don' look like a…a crime of passion, 'r whatever they call it. I mean, she looks so…posed. Why lay 'er out like that? Why not jus' toss 'er in the river? That's some eerie-ass shit right there. 'Sides, we're not even sure it is Callaghan's girl."

"Ok. Well, maybe we oughta head back t'town and jus' ask around a little. You know, 'fore we go tellin' Abernathy," Murphy says. He wrinkles his long, narrow nose, looking up at his friend with eyes full of fear. Gallagher nods. The fact is they're both a little afraid of Abernathy, and rationally or not, they're scared of finding the blame laid at their feet for this. Neither of them dares say it out loud, but Gallagher is pretty sure their thoughts are mirroring each other right now. If they don't tell him, if they just let the inevitable fall of new snow hide their footprints, then nobody ever needs to know they were even here. They can go home. They can forget all about it, or at least try.

"Yeah. I think that's smart. No sense gettin' mixed up in this 'fore we know what it really is."

Aside from anything else, part of Gallagher thinks maybe this is something more than just eerie-ass shit. He's read stories in the newspaper about things like this: pagan sacrifices. Girls with their throats cut, left out in the woods, killed to satisfy a bloodthirsty demon god. The problem with that is that she doesn't have her throat cut, of course. She looks like she could just wake up and walk away, except for her unlidded eyes and her blue skin. Her hair is smooth and dark and unruffled, and there are no bruises on the pale, bloodless flesh that he can see – nothing that looks like the way he'd imagine a satanic symbol might look, and for that matter, no marks of any kind. From what he can see above the snow, she's wearing some kind of plain white dress – not fancy like a wedding dress, it's shapeless and way too flimsy for the time of year – but it doesn't look ripped. It all looks so perfectly planned. He's glad he doesn't know what that plan was. He doesn't want to imagine what kind of terrible mind would think to leave her like that. If he ever killed anybody, he imagines it would eat him up. He'd be so torn up inside that he'd want to do something to make it better. He'd want to give back something of what he'd taken away. It's a thought that's crossed his mind before. The way he is, the life he leads – he's a man who turns to fighting more often than not, and his self-restraint can evaporate in the blink of an eye, or the swing of a fist. It's possible there will come a time when he really will have to decide what to do. But this…whoever did this had no heart, nothing inside to make them repent for stealing the life right out of her. They just left her here, completely exposed, not even giving her the questionable dignity of throwing her in a shallow grave. It's like they wanted her to be found. Like they were proud of what they did.

It was her perfect dark hair, in fact, that gave her away that morning. It's fanned out around her head, like a splash of ink on the frozen ground, and they spotted it pretty quickly, even if they didn't know what it was right away – a dark stain in a vast, virgin sea of white.

Gallagher studies her for a minute more, trying to decide whether she looks in any way like the pictures that accompanied the stories he's read before he gives up. He can feel Murphy staring at him, waiting for him to make a move, but he finds he's temporarily mesmerized. Then his friend tugs at his arm and he almost jumps out of his skin, suddenly ready to round on him. It's reassuring in a way. Always fight. Never flight.

"All right," he says. Finally, he forces himself to tear his gaze away. "Let's go get the truck."

The silence in the truck as they drive back to town is heavy, almost palpably so. It hangs around them like a dense, toxic cloud and Gallagher feels like he's choking on it. More than once, he has to stop himself from swerving off the road when it threatens to overwhelm him. He feels agitated, jumpy. Murphy, meanwhile, is tight-lipped and ashen faced, hardly even blinking. He just sits there, staring vacantly ahead, and it's doing nothing to help Gallagher calm down. There used to be a light in his eyes, a genial, puckish spark that lent his narrow face a certain charm – but it's gone now. Something extinguished it, irretrievably.

If he thinks about it, that little spark has been gone for a while. After everything Murphy's been through, it's not surprising. It put out the light in him. But this is different: it's much worse than that. Now, there's something else in its place. There's a pure terror he's never seen before – not even when he knew he was about to get the crap kicked out of him back in their school days. It was where the pattern to their daily lives first began to form: Gallagher is the one to stay steady and strong in the face of trouble, and Murphy is the one who freaks out. This is the way it's always been. He looks out for Murphy, who was always going to be nervous after a lifetime of being bullied by the bigger, brawnier boys they grew up with. He's always been the one to keep his friend from going to pieces, and Murphy, for his part, has always been resolutely loyal. Gallagher is playing his part now, just like always. But just this once, he wishes it could be the other way around.

It's still early when they hit Main Street and the only people out and about are the devout and the ones who haven't been home yet. It's not unheard of for the men who've lost their jobs in the last few years to pass out in Mawhinney's and stumble out the next morning. It's pretty much inevitable, in fact. The choice they have now is God or booze, and none of them ever pick God. These are the men whose hope is wholly dead, Gallagher thinks. It's the way Murphy's life is going, too, he realizes with a jolt. He tries to cast the thought off, physically shaking himself to knock it loose, and leans forward over the dashboard to look up at the sky. The brilliant blue is rapidly turning grey and it looks as though another storm is on the way. If it's anything like the storms they've had lately, Gallagher thinks guiltily, it'll swallow her whole and no one will find her until spring.

As they get out of the truck midway along Main Street, Gallagher looks down at his friend, suddenly full of sympathy. His slight frame isn't up to the cold and his teeth are chattering. Arms clasped across his chest, Gallagher can see he's beginning to wish he'd listened to his wife when she tried to make him wear the itchy red long johns she bought him the winter before. He'd joked about it that morning, imitating the way she fussed over him, clucking like a mother hen. Gallagher had laughed, but a little piece of him felt bad for it: he likes Sally.

"What sh'we do now?" Murphy asks. Gallagher visibly starts at the sudden break in the silence, and it's so out of character in a man who makes it his business to be steady as a stone, that any other day, under any other circumstances, Murphy probably would have laughed at him.

"Let's get some coffee and see if Hal's heard anything," Gallagher growls, embarrassed, turning towards Elm Street. It's where the town's one and only coffee shop is, right next to Mawhinney's, the town's one and only bar. It's also the only business open at this hour on a Sunday, its bright yellow awning fluttering in the rising wind. Nothing in the little coffee shop is less than fifty years old, but somehow, Hal has always kept it pristine, blazing summer to blazing summer, bitter winter to bitter winter. The mismatched furniture is always polished and his green-and-white linoleum-tiled floor gleams in what's left of the morning sun. Next to Mawhinney's, with its broken, buzzing neon sign and cracked, faded paint, it looks like it belongs in a Norman Rockwell picture. It's the only splash of color in an otherwise unremarkable patchwork of slush-grey sidewalks, slick black roads, and houses all in shades of white and brown.

"All right. But let's be careful about it." Gallagher nods. He's known Murphy a long time and he's sure he's never seen him this spooked. Right from when they were kids, all the way through high school, when the guys on the football team or the hockey team or the basketball team would pound seven shades of shit out of him, Gallagher's been the protector. Now, out of nowhere, he finds he feels like he's let him down somehow.

"Mornin', Hal," he says when they get inside, as casually as he can manage. A blast of hot air hits him in the face from the heater above the door, stinging his freezing skin, making his eyes water. He looks at Murphy meaningfully, telling him wordlessly not to say anything, not to let Hal know anything's not right. If he speaks, he'll give them away in a split second. They sit down at their favored table, shotguns stowed outside in the truck. It feels weird to be empty-handed all of a sudden. Gallagher has always liked the weight of his gun, liked how safe it makes him feel. He feels naked without it now, exposed and vulnerable. The table is one of three in the wide bay window, where a little of the sun's warmth remains, and they absorb it for a minute before they ask for some coffee, trying to settle their rattled nerves.

"How yous guys doin' this morning?" Hal asks, filling up their cups. Murphy looks at Gallagher before he replies, wondering how much he should say.

"Not so bad," he says, cautiously. "No shootin' t'be had, though." Hal shakes his shiny bald head and smiles, sympathetically. He only has three teeth left – two on the top and one on the bottom – and a protruding dome of a gut that makes him look a little like a friendly goblin. There's no way to tell how old Hal is: most people agree you'd have to split him open and count the rings. He's always been there, though, longer than pretty much anybody else, and, thinks Gallagher, always will be, or some other version of him. The town needs a Hal. When he goes, someone just like him will be along to replace him. Nobody will even know the difference. He'd put money on it.

"That's too bad," he says. "You want some breakfast? I'm right'n the middle o' makin' pancakes. The missus has a hankering." These days, 'missus' might as well refer to his round, taut belly: his wife's been dead twenty years. He refers to her in conversation from time to time, though, as if she might still be around somewhere, keeping an eye on things. Murphy nods.

"Sure." He looks over at Gallagher as Hal shuffles back to the kitchen. It'll be a while before he's back.

"How d'you think we should do this?" Murphy asks. Gallagher purses his lips and takes his gloves off. They're ancient, cracked black leather, lined with sheepskin that's almost worn through, but they were Billy's and he doesn't want to part with them.

"Don' know. Maybe jus' ask him how Callaghan's doin'?" he ventures. Murphy nods, though he still looks nervous, chewing his lower lip the way he used to when he was a kid and thought he was in trouble for something. He doesn't say anything more before Hal comes back, twenty minutes later, with two plates piled high with fat, golden-brown pancakes.

"Pfannkuchen!" Hal says, ceremoniously. The German word is a rarity. Usually, he only lets slip his heritage if he's upset or worried about something and he's not thinking hard enough. Maybe he does know something, Gallagher thinks. He eyes the old man warily, but he can't find anything in his expression to give him away. Hal lays the plates down with a flourish, and waits, wanting to watch them taste his handiwork, which is unnerving enough in itself. Gallagher forces a smile and licks his lips, silently willing him to stop staring like that and just go away. But the most important thing, he thinks, is to act as normal as possible – to do nothing that might invite too many questions. So he says nothing. He lets the old man stand there, hovering over him while he eats, even though he's starting to feel like he could throw up every meal he's had in the last week.

"You fellas hear about Callaghan's girl?" Hal asks. Murphy flinches visibly and Gallagher kicks him under the table with his holey boot.

"What about 'er?" he says, trying to stay calm.

"Only gone and got herself knocked up. Her old man told me. That no-goodnik she's been dating don' believe in usin' protection, I guess." Murphy chokes and sprays coffee all over his breakfast, prompting a laugh from Hal. It's always the same throaty wheeze, like that dog from the cartoon, Gallagher thinks, and saved only for occasions of high mirth.

"Didn' know you were such a prude, boy!" he guffaws, slapping him on the back. "I'll getcha summore."

"'S ok," Murphy mutters, coughing. He swallows hard and wipes his mouth with the back of his hand. Still wheezing away to himself, Hal wanders back into the kitchen, dismissively waving a gnarled old hand behind him.

"I don' think he knows anything," Gallagher whispers, eyeing Hal's hunched back as it disappears behind the chain-link curtain. "Guess it's not Mary, though."

"Guess not," Murphy says, craning round to make sure the old man isn't coming back. "Say…you think we sh' go over to Joe's maybe?" Joe's, or St Joseph's as it's otherwise known, is the Catholic church over on Peach Street. It's the biggest parish in town, and it's also where Gallagher's cousin, of whom he's no longer especially fond, is the priest. He narrows his eyes.

"What for? You wanna confess or somethin'?" he asks. His friend's eye twitches a little – that same twitch he thought he saw back out by the woods – and he swallows hard, shifting around in his seat. Gallagher looks at him a second longer, suddenly wondering if maybe there is something on Murphy's mind. "You don't, do ya?" he presses. Murphy swallows again and laughs uncomfortably.

"Come on! What…what would I have to confess?" he says, his voice suddenly high and strange. Gallagher leans forward a little, looking at him closer than he ever has.

"You tell me," he growls.

"Nothin'! I got nothin', I swear!" Murphy squeaks.

"What do you wanna go over to the church for then?"

"I just…wull…don'cha think maybe Father Daniel'll have some thoughts on the situation?" Murphy replies, still hesitant. Gallagher folds his arms and sits back again in his ancient vinyl chair, which creaks a little worryingly under his weight. Something's off with his friend, but he can't figure out what. He sighs and lets his mind shift toward the priest. Father Daniel is his mother's sister's boy, and they'd been good friends as kids, closer even than he and Murphy are – but a lot has changed in the years between then and now. Too much has changed.

"He prob'ly will. Don' mean we necessarily wanna hear 'em." Murphy blushes. Gallagher knows he still looks up to him, even after more than twenty-five years of friendship, and his cheeks burn red under the heat of his friend's eyes, nostrils flaring involuntarily under his scorn.

"Fine. You think of something," Murphy says, dropping his gaze. Gallagher sighs. He knows that look: he's sulking now, and that won't do anybody any good.

"All right. We'll go over there. But I'm not stayin' for mass. We'll go when they're done with all that."

They sit in silence a while longer before Gallagher gets up to pay. He's well aware of Murphy's shaky financial status, compared with his own relatively comfortable position. Gallagher was finally made production manager up at the machinery plant in Ashland a few months ago, after more than ten years of hard grind. Gradually, methodically, he'd worked all the way up through the ranks. His father had helped him get the job when he was a few months out of school. He might as well forget college, the way his grades were, but this was a good job, he said. It was an honest living and that was a fine thing for a young man. He's never been remotely academic, but he has a good brain, or so his boss tells him, and he likes the feeling of having found his place there. The promotion is titular more than anything else, but it affords him a slightly better salary and a little office above the factory floor. Now, it gives him a small sense of satisfaction to be able to pay for his friend without thinking twice, even under the present circumstances.

"That'll be fifteen even," Hal says. Gallagher quickly hands him a couple of crumpled bills before Murphy has a chance to make a move for his wallet. He smiles tightly at the old man.

"Ya know, if you keep gougin' people like this, they won't come back," he says. He tries to make the words come out jovial and light-hearted like usual, but his voice cracks, and he's pretty sure he missed and hit nervous and twitchy. If Hal notices, though, he doesn't say anything. He grins and takes the money.

"C'mon now, I gotta make a livin'," he says, with a shrug. It's their bit. Hal hasn't changed his prices in ten years or more, but Gallagher always kids him that they're too high. If he didn't do it now, Hal would figure something was up for sure. He looks over at Murphy, who's slouched down in his seat, avoiding his eyes. At least part of this is probably because Gallagher had to pay for him again, and he knows he's embarrassed. After Murphy was laid off from his construction job the year before, Gallagher knows how tough it's been for him. His wife works at the high school library, but her salary just barely covers their bills, and money has been getting tighter and tighter. Lately, the little spare cash he does have has been going pretty much solely on beer at Mawhinney's, to the point that Gallagher isn't sure he can go much longer without saying something about it. Murphy's had to drive as far as Madison to find work in the last few months and it's been rare that he's been able to keep the same job for more than a couple of weeks. If he'd just cut back on the damn booze, things might be different, he thinks. Gallagher's even offered more than once to find him something at the plant, but whether through pride or stubbornness or both, he's always turned him down. Lately, he's been getting harder to be around, too – moody, evasive. Gallagher takes a deep breath, brushing away the little swell of irritation he suddenly feels for his friend, like a bug in his peripheral vision.

It's snowing again when they get outside. The fat, wet flakes are beginning to settle on the freshly plowed streets and they unconsciously pick up the pace, despite Gallagher's reluctance, to make it over to the church before the storm gets any worse. It's already darker, and they've spent a long time outside today as it is. The church is a relatively new building by the standards of most of the town's establishments, constructed hastily in red brick in the early part of the twentieth century to accommodate the growing Irish and Polish populations. Gallagher's own family was among them – his mother's and his father's side. His mother's great great grandparents came to the town with her infant great grandmother in 1902, when the town, though growing, was still really only a loosely associated collection of farms, gathered around a little wooden church. A section of his father's family, most of whom had established themselves forty years previously over the Minnesota border in the nascent Saint Paul, arrived in 1903, and they all stayed put thereafter. If you come to this town, you stay. One way or another, you stay. That was what he'd been told his whole life. It's burned into his consciousness. You find someone from a good family, you get married, you have kids, the cycle repeats, over and over and over. He's the fifth generation of his family to have been raised in the town, and if things were different, he would have been raising his own kids here by now. He was the first one to break the chain and that paved the way for his sister, two years younger, who upped and left for good as soon as she graduated from college. She and her husband are in Duluth now. Free.

Father Daniel is still standing outside as he always does, despite the deteriorating weather, shaking the hands of the few parishioners who've ventured out. He's red-nosed and smiling, bundled into a thick quilted coat and a long blue scarf, although the smile looks a little strained. Standing there, buried under all that fabric, he could still almost be the funny, slightly nerdy kid Gallagher remembers. Almost. He's a slender, sandy-haired man – not as skinny now as he was when he was a teenager, but still maybe half Paul's size – with mild grey eyes behind round, plastic-rimmed glasses and a witty, self-effacing demeanor. Gallagher had liked that about him when they were kids. Now he finds it grating.

"You sure you're ok doin' this? I mean, after everything that happened with..." Murphy whispers, as they approach. He doesn't need to finish the sentence. Gallagher shoots him a look, clenching and unclenching his fists inside his gloves.

"This was your idea," he says, through gritted teeth. It's more than five years since he's been anywhere near the church – right after Billy died was the last time – and it's all he can do not to turn on his heel and never look back. They're here for a reason, though, and while he won't admit it, the priest has been known to be useful in a crisis. But then of course this is a lot worse than hiding spray paint or empty beer cans, he thinks, and even the idea of forming the words to explain what they found makes him feel sick.

"Jimmy!" Father Daniel calls, spotting Murphy first. "It's been a while since we've seen you here. Anything I can…" He breaks off when he sees Gallagher coming up behind Murphy, jaw set, brows knitted, much as he'd looked the last time he was here.

"We need some advice," Gallagher says, flatly. The priest nods silently, face suddenly blank, and gestures at the church door.

"All right," he murmurs. They follow him into the little chapel, drawn in by a blast of warm air. It's almost unchanged, but for the installation of two big industrial heaters, for which even Gallagher will admit to being grateful.

"So," Father Daniel says a little more forcefully, quickly shutting the door behind them. "What can I do for you?"

"Something…happened. Something real bad," Murphy begins, crossing himself absent-mindedly as he sits down in one of the low, rough-hewn wooden pews. He's long since stopped believing in an all-powerful creator, able to save him from all his troubles, but it's hard to break the habit, even now.

"Are you in some kind of trouble?"

"Not exactly," Gallagher puts in, before Murphy can speak again. "See…we were out by the river, and…well…to cut a long story short…we ran across a dead body." There it is, bald and blunt. All the color slowly drains from the priest's face, and it gives Gallagher a nasty little thrill to see it.

"Have…have you told Abernathy?" he falters. They both shake their heads.

"No," Gallagher says.

"So…why are you telling me?" Gallagher laughs grimly.

"Don' know. Thought maybe you could give us some divine inspiration on what we oughta do." Murphy looks at him a little reprovingly, but he doesn't say anything. Gallagher has good reasons for losing his trust in the church – better ones than Murphy's, though he'd never say it – and his attitude isn't going to change.

"Well...who was it? Did you recognize them?" the priest asks. Gallagher shakes his head again, but he's surprised to see Murphy doesn't do likewise this time. He looks away from the priest for the first time, whom he's been eyeing warily since they arrived, and stares at his friend.

"Jimmy?" he whispers. Murphy lets out a long slow breath and puts his hands behind his head. That means he's hiding something and he's deciding whether or not to say anything. Gallagher's seen him do it too many times to think otherwise.

"I...I wasn' sure 'til we figured out it wasn' Mary Callaghan, but...I...I knew her..." They're both staring at him now, and he shuts his eyes tight, turning his face towards the cracked plaster of the ceiling.

"It was...it was a couple-three days ago. Remember, the night you came to Mawhinney's with me?" he begins, turning his eyes from the ceiling to his hands, which he twists together in his lap. "You were outside, goin' six rounds with the Mitchell brothers, and...she...she came in and sat beside me. I remember thinkin' how much she looked like Mary...I think I even said so to 'er..." It's a jolt to hear Murphy describe that night with the Mitchells in such bald, almost mundane terms, and it shakes Gallagher. To him, it had seemed heroic. He was defending his friend in a way nobody else would. He was visiting righteous fury on Andrew Mitchell until his fists were bloody and raw. He was doing what he should, and he would have kept right on doing it if Brian Kowalski hadn't sucker punched him. But the way Murphy tells it... Gallagher eyes the priest, looking for reproach, but he doesn't find it.

"And?" Father Daniel asks.

"And she said her name was Sarah McIntyre. Apparently, we went to high school together, but...I don' know, I thought maybe she was spinnin' me a line. She said she moved to Illinois when she was in her junior year, but she always remembered me because…because she had this big crush on me…" His voice drops as he stops speaking and he keeps his gaze firmly on his lap.

"Oh Jimmy. What did you do?" Gallagher whispers.

"Nothin'! Nothin', I swear. I mean, I knew she was flirtin' with me, but I told 'er no thanks! I love Sally. For chrissakes, Paul, you know that! C'mon, you were my best man!" Murphy says, indignantly. He meets Gallagher's eye for the first time since they set foot in the church and there's something wild, desperate there. Something he's never seen before. He waits for Murphy to blink, but he holds his ground until Gallagher finds himself capitulating.

"I know," he says, trying to steady his voice, which comes out shaky and small. "But I also know how hard it's been for you and Sally lately." He's being as gentle as he can, ignoring the fact his heart is starting to pound in his chest. There's an uncomfortable empty moment, and Father Daniel takes a deep breath, looking from one to the other.

"Did she…did she say what she was doing in town?" he asks, swallowing and pushing his glasses up the bridge of his nose. Sweat is starting to bead there, Gallagher notices.

"She just…she just said she had somethin' to take care of. I didn' ask what it was," Murphy mumbles, looking down at his hands again. He's picking determinedly at the cuticle on his left forefinger and he can see it's on the point of bleeding.

"And then?" Gallagher presses, only just stopping himself from reaching out and grabbing Murphy's hand to keep him from tearing the nail away altogether. He tilts his head down, trying to scrutinize his friend's face, which is half in shadow. He's looking for some sign that he might be lying and at the same time, hoping, even praying not to find one.

"And then she left and I don' know where she went. She never came back," Murphy says, a little more steadily as he finally stops scraping at his nail. He turns back to Father Daniel, who was in his class in high school.

"Do you remember any Sarah?" he asks. There's a different note in his voice now – something colder, harder. "She was real pretty, like Mary – dark hair, blue eyes, but skinny, like she'd been sick, and kinda…kinda intense lookin'?"

"Maybe," Father Daniel says, slowly. "I mean, I wasn't exactly a big hit with the girls, but…yeah. Yeah, I guess that name rings a bell." The first part of this isn't true. Gallagher remembers how many girls were in love with Daniel in high school, how many hung on his every word and waited for him after class and surrounded him in the cafeteria – so many that even he got a little jealous once or twice. He looks at him for a second, wondering if he just doesn't remember or if he's doing that damn self-deprecating thing again. There's another empty moment – almost painfully so – and the priest scrubs a hand over his still-smooth face. In point of fact, except for the dog collar, he's hardly changed since high school. Murphy's always envied him that – he's said so to Gallagher a few times. His own face bears the deep lines and ruddy complexion of a life lived mostly outdoors, without much in the way of indulgence or luxury.

"Look, I really think we ought to tell Abernathy. The fact is, whoever she was, this girl's dead, and the person responsible is still out there," Father Daniel says. He's trying to sound authoritative, but it comes out a little schoolmarmish, and Gallagher allows himself a small inward smile.

"All right," Gallagher says. "We'll tell him." He'd never say it out loud, but he finds himself a little disappointed that the priest didn't have more advice to offer.

Father Daniel nods, and gets up to show them out. He looks even more spooked than Murphy did, Gallagher notices – pale, trembling, almost sick – and he hasn't even seen the body. Fucking pathetic, he thinks, letting his anger get the better of him for a second.

The snowstorm has lessened a little when they head back outside, but the sky is still leaden with clouds, and the wind is vicious. The streets are empty now, and they'll stay that way until Mawhinney's opens in the evening. Something holds Gallagher back, though, and somehow, he finds he can't quite tear himself away from the church just yet. He looks from the little brick building to his friend and back again.

"You comin', or no?" Murphy asks.

"Tell me the truth, Jimmy. Did *anything* else happen that night?" He looks him straight in the eye, putting his hands firmly on his friend's shoulders. Murphy breathes in slowly and lets it out through his teeth.

"I kissed 'er, ok?" he snaps. Still holding his gaze, Gallagher notices there are tears in Murphy's eyes, which he roughly wipes away. "I was so tired and so drunk that night, I…I think maybe I just needed a little human contact, but…look, I swear I didn't hurt 'er. I'd remember that…wouldn' I?" Gallagher loosens his grip on Murphy's shoulders, trying to be as reassuring as he can.

"All right. Well, let's think about this," he says, evenly. "If you were that hammered, you can't hardly have been in any shape to do much damage to anybody, let alone drive a dead body out to the woods and lay it out in the snow like that. C'mon. It's gonna be ok. Abernathy's boys'll figure it out, and then we can go back to normal."

Murphy is silent for a moment more, and Gallagher notices he's shaking.

"But…what if I put 'er in the way of gettin' killed? What if I coulda done somethin' to help 'er?" he asks, looking up at his friend, that same frantic, desperate expression on his face.

"You didn' kill 'er, Jimmy. But you probably were the last person t'see 'er alive – so we gotta go tell Abernathy now. Ok?" Murphy nods, a little reluctantly, visibly trying to pull himself together.

"Ok."

Just as there's always been a Hal, there's always been an Abernathy. All the way back to the town's very first beginnings, almost a hundred and sixty years ago, before it was even a town, the family's been there, and one or other of them has always been in charge. From the first farms to the formal founding in 1924, all through the ensuing decades, it's been like this. The line has meandered along the way, and some have been more distantly related than others. A brother. A cousin. A son. A second cousin twice removed. A grandson, a great grandson, and once, even a great-great granddaughter, all the way down the family tree, until the present Abernathy – Francis Abernathy III – who also happens to be the chief of police. They can all trace their roots back to the very first Abernathy, whose portrait hangs, austere and ever watchful, on the wall in the hallway of the tiny, yellow-painted town hall. He was an imposing, somber old gentleman and there's something of that in the man who holds the position now.

His predecessor was his father, who owned the grocery store and the drugstore and the launderette, and when he died of a heart attack ten years back, his son stepped in before anybody knew there'd been a change. Nobody ever leaves this job. They always die in harness. That's just the way it is. His own children have all moved away from the town, but it's tacitly understood that his oldest son, a high school principal in Milwaukee, will be the next to take the position when the time comes. No one's ever questioned it and no one's ever opposed an Abernathy, or at least not successfully. There have been one or two challengers along the way, but they've never been able to hold a candle to the respectability and the power of the name. They tried valiantly, but inevitably, it was in vain. For show more than anything else, there's an election every few years, but of course the results are a foregone conclusion: everybody knows the way it will go. This is the Abernathys' town and that's the way it will always be. There isn't even a name for the office. They don't need one. It's a tradition that's never steered them wrong and no one's really ever felt the need to change it. You can always trust an Abernathy – everybody says so. It might as well be the town motto.

Murphy and Gallagher pull up outside the police station as the afternoon creeps in and it's already dark. They've circled the town a few times until Murphy feels calm enough to go through with it. He's still shaking a little as they get out of the truck, but Gallagher is starting to lose patience. They pause outside for a moment, and Gallagher looks his friend hard in the eye, wordlessly imploring him not to back out. He nods to let Gallagher know he's ready and they finally head up the steps to the station. It's a tiny breezeblock building, smaller even than Hal's place, with just enough space inside for a single jail cell and five officers including Abernathy. It looks strangely inviting in the gathering gloom, casting a dim yellow glow out onto the snow and the leafless shrubs. Inside, a very young, very skinny woman, with frizzy blonde hair scraped back into a high ponytail, sits at the front desk, in a uniform that looks too big for her. She looks up from her crossword puzzle, startled, as they walk in, wrinkling her small snub nose.

"Hi Shelly," Murphy says, trying to muster a smile. "Got the short straw, huh?" He remembers when Shelly Eriksen was born, and it's decidedly surreal to see her here now: she looks like a little girl, playing dress up, except for the gun strapped to her bony hip.

"Yeah, I guess," she replies, cheeks flushing. "Can I help you with something?"

"Yeah. Yeah, we need t'talk to Abernathy real quick. Is he here?" Gallagher asks.

"No, he's down in Sheboygan with his brother this weekend and he's not gettin' back 'til late tonight. Anything I can do?" Shelly asks, smiling timidly. Gallagher and Murphy exchange a look, each knowing the other is thinking the same thing. It means delaying a day, but they can't lay this on her: she's just a kid. At the back of his mind, a little voice berates him for it. It's just an excuse, it tells him – a coward's way out – but Gallagher ignores it.

"No," he says. "No, we'll come back in the morning. You have a good night now."

"What d'we do now?" Murphy says, forgetting to whisper, as they turn to leave.

"Keep your voice down!" Gallagher hisses, grabbing him by the arm to hurry him outside again. "We go home. We lay low 'til tomorrow, and we try again then. I'll take the day off from work, and meet you right here first thing. Think you can do that?" Murphy nods, and swallows hard. He almost looks like he might cry, Gallagher thinks, like a little kid who's been caught doing something he knows he shouldn't. He immediately feels guilty for snapping at him, and slings his arm around his shoulder to comfort him.

"Look. There's nothin' we can do now. We just gotta try'n get some sleep. All right?" He already regrets the decision to leave without saying anything, and he's finding it harder and harder to keep his cool. Murphy nods again, shrinking out from under his friend's arm and out of the syrupy light.

"You think I should talk to Sally?" he asks, voice trembling a little, face half-hidden in shadow. Gallagher shakes his head, starting to feel sorry for his friend again. Murphy is weak: there's nothing he can do about that.

"Maybe better not – not yet anyway. You don't wanna make her worry too soon," he says, gently. "Come on. I'll take ya home."

Murphy and his wife live in a little brown wood-sided house on the western edge of town, one story, without much in the way of a yard, or external appeal of any kind. Gallagher knows they've been thinking of trying to start a family, but he struggles to see how they'd fit one in there. There's one real bedroom – although Sally Murphy somewhat optimistically refers to the large closet adjacent to it as the "guest room" – one tiny bathroom, and everything else is crammed into a single room at the front of the house. It's stuffed to the gills with sagging, mismatched furniture – cast-offs from Murphy's parents, who died in a car-wreck when he was barely out of high school – and always smells like cigarette smoke and cheap air freshener.

Gallagher's own house, on the other side of town, is larger, brighter, prettier, but it's lonelier too. It's more than he needs now that Billy's gone, if he's honest – and the fact of the matter is the emptiness gets to him sometimes. At night, when Mawhinney's is closed and he's alone at last, with only the TV for company, all he can hear is his own breathing. There's no one there to complain to or laugh with, or even just sit with to make the silence comfortable. The quiet now is heavy, painful even. For all Murphy's struggles, at least he has the chance to have a family, to make a life with Sally, and much as he wishes it didn't, it makes Gallagher quietly jealous.

Alone at his kitchen table, staring at the empty space where Billy would have sat, he turns the events of the day over in his mind, a fifth of whiskey beside him. The dead woman's face is burned into his memory and he can't shake the feeling he knows the name Sarah McIntyre – he just can't place her. On top of that, he has an uncomfortable knot in his stomach, somewhere between nagging guilt at leaving her out there, and fear at the thought that his friend might somehow be mixed up in whatever happened to her.

You never know what you'll do when you're faced with death, he thinks, and the last time he had to worry about it was almost five years ago. It had been different then, naturally, because it was so much closer to home. It caught him completely by surprise when Billy died, like a sack of bricks to the gut – he didn't leave his house for two full weeks right after it happened – and now he wonders if maybe he's just gotten used to death. His mother died a few months after Billy, and his father a year after that. Stubbornly, and against his sister's wishes, after what happened with Billy, he'd refused to have them buried in the Catholic cemetery behind Joe's. Instead, just like with Billy, he went up to Ashland and had them cremated. Jenny, his sister, had tried to convince him to relent, but she was already settled out in Minnesota by then – she's been there six years now – and after she moved, she was always a few steps removed from his life and from their parents'. She could have fought harder if she'd wanted to, but deep down, he's always suspected she understood why he did what he did. The pain was too big. There was too much he couldn't forgive.

All three of them now reside in an otherwise empty closet in the third and smallest of the bedrooms upstairs, usually locked, but full of keepsakes – photos, mementoes, odd items of clothing – that he very occasionally allows himself the indulgence of looking at. The only clothing of Billy's that isn't locked away is the gloves. Billy found them in a thrift store and had immediately decided he had to have them, even though they were far too big for him. He liked to pretend he was a pioneer or a lumberjack, putting on a ridiculous deep voice every time he wore them. Now, Gallagher likes to try and pretend he can still feel the warmth of his hands in them and sometimes, he can kid himself that it brings him comfort.

Since their deaths, he's worked hard at protecting himself, at keeping himself from feeling much of anything at all. Jenny calls once in a while to check on him, make sure he's still functioning, and he always tells her he's fine. It's not really a lie. He's still holding it together, at least on the outside. He has his routine and that's ok. He gets up, he goes to work, he keeps moving. But the only thing that makes him feel anything is getting into stupid bar brawls with the meatheads he went to school with – guys he might have called friends once, but who wasted no time in turning on him when they found out about Billy.

Now, though, cracks are starting to appear in his carefully constructed armor. He's been so numb for so long that he'd started to forget the reality of death – the horror and fear and anguish that comes along with it. Now, here it is, right at his door again. His mind drifts back to Sarah, mentally rifling through the hazy images of his adolescence for some sign of her. He tries to slot her into the hallway or the cafeteria or the auditorium, but he can't make her look the way she would have then. Instead, her lifeless body hangs like a ghost, chasing the other images of his former friends and classmates away. His memories of high school mostly revolve around the football field, and aside from Murphy, he never had much time for anybody outside his own class. He'd hung out with Daniel a little, or Danny as he was then, most often at the beery parties his football buddies would throw, but at the time, he was part of a very different crowd – poets, wannabe actors, singers, dancers, musicians – and now that he thinks about it, he doesn't really know how he ended up as a priest.

There's a twist in that road somewhere, a kink in the tale, and now he finds he can't quite make all the pieces of that puzzle fit.

He doesn't know why it never occurred to him before, but it never did add up. He even has a vague recollection of there being a girlfriend at one point – but something sometime around Daniel's junior year and his senior year changed him. He found God and he found him in a big way: he dropped all his old friends, stopped going out, cut his hair, even changed the way he dressed, and Gallagher has never known why. He started going to mass two or three times a week and he started talking about the seminary even before his finished his junior year. At the time, still a good Catholic boy, he'd admired him for it: it wasn't until a lot later that the rift opened up between them.

If he ever had anything to do with Sarah back then, he knows he doesn't remember it now. All he can think about now is Daniel, and all the hurt he caused. He sighs and drains his glass. He considers digging through some of the stacks of old photos in his attic to find some from that year and look for some clue, but it's getting late, and he knows he needs to try and get some rest at least. Most nights now, he sleeps on the couch, preferring it to the wide, empty expanse of his bed. Tonight, though, he steels himself to make the trip upstairs, wobbling a little with the whiskey. He closes his eyes and trails a hand along the wall, guiding himself. In that quiet instant, for just a fraction of a fraction of a second, he imagines Billy is up there waiting for him, just like he used to. But as quickly as the image appears, it vanishes – and he dies all over again.

He sprawls out on the bed without undressing. When he got home, he'd changed into his old high school sweats, hoping they'd make him feel better, hoping they'd bring back something of his old, oblivious self. He's dreading the day ahead: he knows they'll have a lot of explaining to do when they come to tell Abernathy what they found, and more importantly, why they waited. He finds now that he can't easily come up with the words to explain it to himself, let alone someone else. It makes him feel like a teenager again, trying to explain to his high school principal why it was he thought it would be funny to set fire to the dumpster behind the cafeteria. Shivering, he crawls under the covers, pulling them right up to his chin like a child.

The whole thing keeps spinning inside his head and he can't hold his thoughts steady enough. The whiskey isn't helping: he's polished off more than half the bottle over the course of the evening and he's starting to feel sick. He wants to sleep, but when he closes his eyes, he can still see her, lying there in the snow. Worst of all, he's angry with Murphy all of a sudden – really, truly angry, for the first time in years. It's not for lying to him about recognizing her at first or what happened between them that night, but for not being able to hold his liquor. If he could just remember a little more about the night, everything would be so much easier. He sighs and thumps his head against the pillow, clenching and unclenching his fists.

"Shit," he murmurs aloud. "Shit…"

Gallagher wakes up some time before dawn to the sound of someone furiously pounding at his door. He'd been dreaming of Billy and, coupled with the inevitable hangover now worming its way into his brain, just the act of opening his eyes, leaving that warm, pleasant world behind, is physically painful. He thuds down the stairs, hating whoever is at the door as his head starts to throb, to find Murphy standing there, red-faced and shaking, his ragged breath hitting the freezing air in little puffs of water vapor.

"Jimmy!" Gallagher exclaims, startled. "I thought we were meetin' at the police station?"

"They…they found 'er," Murphy says, still breathing hard. "Somebody fuckin' found 'er." Gallagher can feel the blood draining from his face, and involuntarily, his hand shoots out to grab the doorframe, as his stomach lurches and his knees threaten to buckle under him.

"How do you know?" he whispers, swallowing thickly.

"Abernathy's callin' an emergency town meeting. He's got Shelly and that Hausmann kid roustin' everybody out of bed. We gotta get over to the church – now."

"You don' think…Daniel…?" Gallagher murmurs.

"I don' know. Maybe. Look, jus' get your coat, would ya?" Murphy snaps. He's agitated, scared, and Gallagher nods silently, taking a long, stuttering breath.

"All right," he says, trying to force himself to calm down. "All right. Let's go." Hastily, he jams his feet into his holey boots, glad of his thick woolen bed socks, and reaches for his overcoat, forcing it on over the sweats he'd ended up sleeping in all night. Murphy grabs his arm with surprising strength, tugging him out of the house, almost dragging him over to the truck.

"What's with you?" Gallagher asks, as he climbs into the driver's seat. He's not convinced he's really sober enough to drive yet, but Murphy doesn't seem to be in any shape to get behind the wheel in his place. "Look, we already talked about it – you didn' do nothin' wrong. Guys get drunk and kiss girls all the time. You didn' kill 'er." Murphy is silent. His whole body appears tense, his shoulders hunched up to his chin, and he keeps his eyes steadfastly away from his friend as they head for the church for the second time in two days. Gallagher has the feeling there's something else bothering him, but he doesn't press him. His mind is already racing away from him, afraid of what Abernathy is about to say.

When they pull up outside Joe's, which is the only building in town big enough to accommodate more than fifty people, there are already maybe a few hundred of their friends and neighbors crammed together inside, bemused-looking and shivering. A lot of them are wearing their coats over their pajamas and their nightgowns, disheveled and only half awake. They look small, Gallagher thinks, like children who've stayed up too late. They shuffle inside behind them, and elbow their way inside. There's already a buzz of conversation among the crowd like the hum of insects, asking each other what's going on, sharing speculation. The two of them squeeze in at the back, hoping Abernathy doesn't spot them. Gallagher closes his eyes for a second, trying to steady himself. He isn't sure how much longer he can keep himself from throwing up, and the warm, damp air, full of stale breath and dust, isn't helping.

Abernathy is one of the few who've managed to get dressed, but he isn't wearing his police uniform, and he looks strange without it, Gallagher thinks – less powerful somehow. He's standing on the altar, behind the lectern, wearing a big black ski parka with fake fur around the hood, over jeans and a sweater with a reindeer pattern, waiting for the last of those he was able to turn out of their beds to arrive. He looks completely different, dressed like that, and Gallagher almost doesn't recognize him; he can't remember the last time he saw him in plain clothes. The unmistakable salt-and-pepper moustache is still there, but he looks smaller, frailer. Abernathy is past sixty, but Gallagher's never thought of him as old before.

"All right!" Abernathy shouts over the hubbub. "Settle down!" He waits another full minute for everyone to be quiet before he begins. It gives Gallagher and Murphy just a little more time to sweat, and they both shift uncomfortably from foot to foot.

"Now. I know it's early and most of you probably wish you were back home in bed. But a crime has been committed, and as your chief of police and your leader, it's my duty to tell you, so that rumors don't spread and I don't have a panic on my hands." His voice has that same deep, resonant tone that lends it so much authority, but it sounds wrong without the uniform. It's as though the real Abernathy, all dressed in dark blue, is behind a door or a curtain somewhere, throwing his voice, letting this other man, this impostor represent him. He pauses, looking around the room, and Gallagher is sure his gaze settles on him and Murphy longer than anybody else.

"As Officers Eriksen and Hausmann may have told you, the body of a woman has been found out near the river. This woman." He pauses for a moment, and holds up a large, color photograph of a girl, letting the crowd take a good look at her. It takes Gallagher a second to realize the person in the photo is Sarah. The picture must be at least ten years old because the girl in the picture is clearly in her teens. She's smiling at the camera – a warm, bright smile, full of hope and innocence, her big blue eyes speaking of a happy, carefree existence. Alive.

A ripple of noise rises up in the crowd again. Abernathy raises a hand, silencing them in an instant – an ability Gallagher has always found impressive.

"We have reason to believe this woman is Sarah McIntyre, based on preliminary information. We have yet to identify her formally and we're not aware of any next of kin in the area. It's understood she lived here as a child, but she left town with her family some years ago. We don't yet know why she was back here or whether she had any friends nearby, but it looks as though someone must have known she was coming." He stops again for a moment, surveying the frightened faces in front of him before he goes on. "Now, we're working as fast as we can to find out what happened and who's responsible, but if anyone has any information at all, please come forward immediately. In the meantime, I urge you all to remain calm. There's no reason to believe anyone else is any danger for now and I ask that you all let us do our jobs." He steps down from the altar, without waiting for anyone to ask questions, and skirts quickly around the edge of the crowd to the back of the church, head down, apparently ignoring the growing commotion around him. Before they realize what's happening, he's right on top of Murphy and Gallagher.

"You two – a word, please," he says, through gritted teeth. He ushers them a little way away from the building as quickly as possible, and they almost trip over one another as they stumble out into the bitter cold.

"Officer Eriksen tells me you two came into the station yesterday, looking for me – care to tell me why?" he asks, once they're out of earshot of everyone else. His tone is patient, measured, but they still look at each other nervously, neither willing to be the first to say something.

"Well?" Abernathy says, impatiently, a flash of his usual stern, commanding manner appearing. Gallagher clears his throat and looks at Murphy one more time before he speaks. His friend is wide-eyed and ashen but he nods for Gallagher to go on.

"We, um…we found 'er first," he mutters, clearing his throat again as he feels his face start to burn. He can feel Abernathy's steely eyes on him, silently reprimanding him.

"And just why the hell didn't you say anything? Do you know how that looks?" he hisses. Gallagher swallows hard, finding his mouth suddenly dry, his tongue like cotton. He stands a good head taller than Abernathy, but he still remembers the hidings he used to give them both when they were kids, usually at their fathers' behest, and the fear of that pain and humiliation has never really left him. He's still pretty shaky, too – he feels feverish and agitated, his head pounding, sweat laced with whiskey starting to bead on his forehead – and he knows it wouldn't take much to knock him down right now.

"We're…we're sorry," he whispers, feeling sure his cheeks must be scarlet by now, lit up like a beacon for everybody to see.

"Look, you're gonna have to come down to the station so we can take your statements. Now, are you gonna do that voluntarily or are we gonna have to do it the hard way?" Logically, they both know Abernathy doesn't have much on them other than their own stupidity, but such is the power of memory, that they obediently follow him on foot back to the police station without a word.

Shelly Eriksen is already at the front desk as they troop in, and glances reproachfully down at the floor as they track dirty grey remnants of the snow behind them on the aged linoleum. She stares, craning her neck as they follow the chief towards the tiny bullpen, wishing she had some idea of what's going on. She knows about the body they found out near the river, but beyond that, the chief hasn't told her much. He ordered her to stay at the station while the town meeting was going on and now her curiosity is killing her.

"Murphy, you go with Officer Legler," Abernathy says, pointing at the uniformed officer behind him – a broad-shouldered, charmless ox of a man, not native to the town. He has a mean look on his face as he gets up to take him into the station's one and only interrogation room, which in fact doubles as a supply closet. There's a mop and bucket propped up against one wall, and six packages of toilet paper beside them, visible through the window in the door. Gallagher twists his head over his shoulder, trying to get a look at Murphy's face to see how he's doing. The scene would be funny if they weren't so scared, he thinks. "Gallagher – you're with me," Abernathy barks. He jerks his head to direct him as he leads him into his tiny, shabby office and closes the door behind him.

"I want to make sure there's no conferring," the old man says, sitting down behind his desk.

"Do I need a lawyer?" Gallagher asks, although he's not sure he wants to know the answer.

"No," Abernathy says, calmly. "You're not under arrest – not yet, anyway. It really all depends on what you tell me." Gallagher shifts uncomfortably in the rickety old chair opposite Abernathy's desk, feeling like it could collapse under him at any second.

"Wull...what d'you wanna know?" he asks.

"Just the truth, Paul." It's only the second time Abernathy has ever called him by his first name – the last time was right after he came to tell him they'd found Billy's body – and it unnerves him.

"All right," he says, carefully. "We were headin' out to the woods yesterday t'see if we could get some shootin' in and...that's when we saw 'er...jus'...lyin' there, in the snow..." He trails off as the memory resurfaces, her empty-eyed face hovering at the periphery of his vision.

"And did you know who she was?"

"No. Not at first," Gallagher hedges, torn between wanting to tell the truth and keeping his friend out of trouble. Abernathy looks at him fixedly, scrutinizing his face until he feels like an ant under a magnifying glass. He's starting to sweat again and he's afraid he might burst into flames under the sheer intensity of Abernathy's gaze.

"What do you mean, not at first?"

"Jimmy, um...he knew 'er," he says, swallowing.

"Why didn't you tell anyone?" Abernathy asks again, though more gently this time. Gallagher colors and drops his eyes.

"We were scared," he whispers, hating having to admit it. The old man breathes out through his nose.

"Is there anything – anything else at all – that you've been keeping from me?"

"Jimmy...Jimmy said he...talked to 'er...said she came into Mawhinney's a couple nights ago. But that's all, I swear. He didn' hurt 'er, I know it," Gallagher says, earnestly.

"All right," Abernathy says, a little more gently. "All right. But you just better hope your buddy's singing the same tune." He gets out of his chair and opens the door, cocking his head towards it. "You can go. For now."

Meekly, Gallagher gets up and makes for the door, keeping his eyes on the grimy, cracked tiles, but something makes him hesitate.

"Hey, Chief?" Gallagher says, stopping in the doorway for a moment, forcing himself to look back to see if he can glean anything from Abernathy's expression. "How did you know...I mean...who called you?" The idea that it was Daniel who raised the alarm is eating away at him, bringing back that familiar burning anger.

"Anonymous tip. Why?" Abernathy asks, keeping his gaze steadily on Gallagher as he sits back down at his desk. He looks Gallagher right in the eye and it makes him nervous all over again. He can feel the old man's gaze working its way under his skin, like he can see right inside his head. He shivers.

"No reason," he says, as evenly as he can.

The old man holds his eye for another moment, but he doesn't say anything else, and as soon as he looks back at the paperwork on his desk, Gallagher bolts. He's out the door and in his truck in a matter of seconds. He doesn't even stop to think about Murphy.

Sally Murphy, nee Weiler, is not beautiful. She's not even pretty: she knows this. She's small and skinny, with long, coarse red hair, and close-set brown eyes in a round, freckled face. Her teeth are too large for her mouth, and her waist is thick and square. She has short legs and big feet for her height, and her hands, no matter what she does, are always red and chapped. She looks like her father – a broad, ruddy-faced man, who's always seemed to feel little, and says less – where Katie, her tall, lithe, winsome younger sister, looks like her mother.

Her mother told her not to hope for much from men: she'd better be smart, she said, and resign herself to a loveless, passionless life. She'd better give up, live out her days on the family farm, such as it is – a creaky, leaky house and a rickety barn housing half a dozen cows on a small plot at the edge of town, where she could keep books for her father. Use what God gave you, her mother said. Katie got the beauty, Sally got the brains, and that was the end of it. Passion was for Katie, who, from the age of fourteen, attracted the attention of every man that ever laid eyes on her. The big, wide world was at her feet, and her life was for living – and in turn, for her mother, who settled for being a farmer's wife, to live vicariously through her. She'd go to Hollywood. She'd be a star. That's what beautiful people did: her mother truly believed this. They didn't have to settle for less. They didn't even have to entertain the idea of having to keep books for their fathers. Sally's world, on the other hand, would always be small, enclosed. Through sheer force of will, she did finally manage to move away from the farm when she took a job at the high school – but she'd never been able to shake off this town, however hard she tried.

Be smart. Her whole life, those words have stayed with her. She's always known what it means. Her mother never urged her to try and excel at anything or to make something of herself, or even to move away from home. For Sally, being smart began with killing off any fairy tale notions she might have had as a girl before they even have a chance to form fully. Katie, on the other hand, rode off into the sunset at the age of seventeen, on the back of a Vincent Black Shadow belonging to an itinerant musician ten years her senior, headed for Chicago and never looked back. Sally remembers the musician quite clearly, and she can only hope he never knew how old Katie really was at the time. She never knew his name but she'll never forget the look on his face the day they rode off together: he looked like a man getting away with murder.

Whether by design or by chance, some months later, Katie apparently did fetch up in California, the land of fame and fortune. Someone must have spotted that remarkable face of hers and recognized its saleable quality, too. She quickly found herself working as a small-time model, mostly in picture ads for cars and stereos, at least according to the postcards she occasionally sent back home in the first couple of years she was out there. She'd never been very communicative – the one trait she shared with her father – and the cards didn't give away a lot. They were full of sunny, meaningless platitudes – vague expressions of pride when Sally told her she'd gotten into grad school to study library science, effusive descriptions of how warm it was in California – but nothing real. As much as anything else, once she got word that she'd made it out west, Sally was relieved she'd managed to get out of Chicago alive. There were sporadic, terse calls to her parents from phone booths, but they were often weeks apart, and in the intervening days, Sally would lie awake, imagining all the evil things that might have befallen her sister. There was one particularly elaborate and pervasive scenario that kept coming back to her, which began with the musician cutting a drug deal with a sleazy foreigner of non-specific ethnicity, and ended with Katie being sold into sexual slavery in the Far East.

Eventually, the cards from California became less frequent. At first, she'd send one every two or three weeks, but then weeks turned into months, and then finally they dried up altogether. The very last one came a full year after its predecessor. But even after that, at least for a while, Sally had kept up the habit of calling her sister, once she actually got a cell phone, to check in on her and to hear her voice. They'd been relatively close as kids – before high school, anyway, and even during Katie's freshman year – and Sally still held on to that for a long time. She'd call and Katie would give her a few minutes of chitchat and she could pretend they were seven and ten again, sharing everything. She'd feel like they were still family. Inevitably, she'd hang up the phone and realize Katie hadn't really said much at all – that she'd propped up the conversation herself for ten or fifteen minutes – and it would break her heart a little more each time. But they were sisters, she'd tell herself. They couldn't just fade out of each other's lives. That would be wrong. *Wrong.* She'd repeat the word to herself, and it would remind her of her own rightness in keeping up the calls.

Even though Katie never really hit the big time, in the bits and pieces Sally managed to stitch together over the years, her life still seems a thousand times brighter, better, happier than Sally's could ever be. It's not like she's a movie star or a supermodel or even one of those big-haired, big-busted assistants on some cheesy game show – but at least she's free. Sometimes, Sally imagines herself living that warm, brilliant life. She tries to conjure up an image of Katie's beachfront condo with its multi-colored furniture (of which she's only seen pictures, sent by email once Katie got together enough cash to buy a computer), of her cherry red convertible (used, slightly rusty, but a convertible nonetheless), of the swimming pools, the ocean, the parties, the cocktails. She tries to slot herself into that life, to pluck herself out of her narrow, greyish existence, but even in fantasy, she can't make herself fit.

She's never had any illusions about what her lot would be. There would be no romance, no Prince Charming for her. By sixteen, when, three years her junior, Katie was already blossoming, Sally had become the "practice girl" for half the boys in her class – a pliant, willing crash test dummy for them to fumble around with clumsily, before they moved on to the real thing. Word spread quickly and before long, she found she'd accidentally won herself a reputation that she couldn't really shrug off. Even after she left the school at the end of the day, her mistakes remained. The mothers of the other girls in her class would stare at her when their daughters pointed her out. They'd whisper and snigger and she knew exactly why. Words like "ugly" and "slutty" would catch in her ear, like poisoned arrows. This is the way it's always been for Sally, one way or another. There's always been a pool of shadow all around her, making everything seem a little bit dimmer to her.

There was refuge in books, she found, and refuge in the library, which would eventually become not just a hiding place, but a vocation. She got used to the shadows after a while, and then she got to like them, the way prisoners get to like their cells. No one could see her there. No one could hurt her. She made it her hiding place late in her sophomore year, when the other kids first began to tease and taunt her, after the rumors got out about her exploits with the varsity football team. They'd hurl abuse at her – usually verbal, sometimes physical – and she'd sneak in there to sit among the dusty tomes and cry. Young and beautiful and self-involved, Katie, of course, had been completely oblivious to it all – or worse, she just didn't care, although even now, Sally doesn't like to admit that might be a possibility – even when her own friends joined in the gossip about her sister. Right through four years of high school and four years of college, miles away in Madison – which she attended as much out of sheer pig-headedness as anything else, despite her mother's protests that there was no point because she couldn't hope to meet a man – this has been her life. The slutty sister image faded eventually but the pool of darkness never did.

She'd come back to her cage in the end, of course, but back then, there was still a part of her that longed for light. College had been a small taste of that, but Madison just wasn't far enough, she decided. It could have been worse, of course – she could have ended up at

Northland, the way her parents wanted her to – but there was so much she wanted to see and do. She had to go further to try to get free. Even before she graduated, she'd begun to think about where she could go and what she could do to make that happen, until finally, she lit on the idea of getting her master's in New York. New York. Even its name conjured up all sorts of fantastic visions. People there were all creative and bright and beautiful, and for a little while, she thought maybe she could be one of them, or at least pretend to be. She never told anyone what she was planning, never let anyone know that a little fire was starting to burn inside her. New York seemed big and gaudy and wonderful, and if no one else knew, her disappointment if she failed would be hers alone. There would be no one to crow over it, or worse, not care at all.

It wasn't until she got her acceptance letter that she began to allow herself to hope. By then, the Californian cards from Katie had been coming for a while. Every time they did, her parents pored over them, desperate to glean as much information as they could about what had become of Katie. Any other mail didn't much interest them. When she showed them her welcome packet, her father harrumphed a little and her mother put up a half-hearted show of not wanting her to go, but neither of them really said much about it when she did. They didn't have to pay for it – she had enough in savings and a small inheritance from her grandmother – so they let her go.

Even during her two blissful years living in a shoebox apartment in Manhattan, she never truly let go of the idea that nobody would ever want her, and even if they did, only until something better came along. When she got there, she found everybody was trendy and bohemian and, to her sheltered mind, taking every drug known to man. They were above her, more worldly than her, better than her. While she was there, though, she worked hard to cultivate a new reputation. She took a job at a coffee shop in the East Village to learn how the cool kids acted. She listened to them talk and bitch and gossip, about each other, about people they knew, about bands she'd never heard of. To her own surprise, when they'd shoot the odd sarcastic barb her way, she found she could fire back. There was a wit there she'd never even realized she possessed, much less had the chance to use. That was it, she decided: she'd become the "funny one". It would keep people interested in her and she could keep herself away from her old habits. As long as they laughed, she could convince herself they liked her and she wouldn't have to give herself physically to anyone to keep them around. No one needed to know. She was careful always to keep herself at a slight remove where boys were concerned, too. She led an almost virginal existence while she was there, never alone with a guy, hardly even within arm's reach of one. She even taught herself to speak differently – to drop the Wisconsin, and mimic Katie's affected accentless speech. It would help her to pretend to be someone else, she told herself. The old, sad, slutty Sally would be gone. She could start again. She spent a lot of time in church, too, praying for strength and forgiveness, praying for salvation from herself. She was trying to erase some of the many blots from her copybook, and after her two years were up, she was pretty well convinced she'd succeeded.

She couldn't stay there, though. It couldn't last forever. Candles must burn out. Fireworks must fade. Small and plain and colorless, she could never belong in New York. When she landed in Madison, she felt a little like Dorothy, leaving the beauty and brightness of Oz behind for the dusty brown uniformity of Kansas. But she was back where she belonged.

At twenty-three, when she started working at the library and Jimmy Murphy started showing a genuine interest in her, it came as such a surprise that she fell for him in about half an hour – deeply and irretrievably. He was the first man – for that matter, the first person – to tell her she was beautiful, and when he said it, she knew he believed it, even if she could never believe it herself. More than that, he told her she was sweet and smart and sexy. She didn't have to keep up the routine to keep him around and it caught her off-guard. By then, she'd resigned herself to solitude and before she had time to think, he'd become her whole world. He never told her to be quiet, or lost interest in her the minute a pretty girl walked by. He made her feel comfortable, loved – and she couldn't believe her luck when he asked her to marry him. He was hardly the handsomest man she'd ever met –

that title belonged to Jimmy's buddy Paul, although she knew she didn't stand a chance with him – or the most well-educated or the most ambitious. But none of that mattered. He wanted her like no one had ever really wanted her, wanted her for more than just her willingness to sleep with him or her ability to crack a joke, and that was all she cared about. They were married at St Joseph's in the most lavish ceremony her muted imagination could muster, and for once, she was able to shut out her mother's voice. She wore a simple white dress and a long, lace veil, and for the first and last time in her life, she felt pretty. This quiet, gentle man has always been so loving, so kind, so sweet. But for all her gratitude that he chose her, there's always been a tiny part of her waiting for the rug to be pulled out – for someone to tell her it was all some colossal prank.

Your mother was right. You're nothing special. Shut yourself away. Go back where you belong. Stay in the shadows.

Get real.

Be smart.

The words float to the surface every now and then, and although she's mostly been able to suppress them, lately they cling to the edges of her mind, quietly permeating her thoughts and it's much harder to shake them. Now, she's sitting here in her dark, empty living room on her ugly, lumpy couch, sick with dread, and they drift to the front of her mind again. It's finally happening. Here it is – the horrible payoff to the joke the universe was playing at her expense. She smokes cigarette after cigarette, trying to calm herself down – a habit she picked up in New York, her one little self-indulgence – waiting for him to come back from the police station.

If she's really honest with herself, he's been acting strangely for a long time now. At first, she didn't really think anything of it, and then when she couldn't ignore it any longer, she put it down to stress. Things have been incredibly tough for him since he lost his job – having to drive for hours out to Madison or Kenosha or Milwaukee when he can't find work closer by – but she's always tried hard not to put any more pressure on him. She never complains about the odd hours he keeps even when he's home, or asks him why he's been so distant. She never nags or blames or accuses. She's so afraid to lose him that she almost thinks she'd turn a blind eye if he turned up at the door with a whole harem in tow. Now, though, she's starting to wonder if she's ignored too much, let too many things slip by. She's starting to wonder how much she's managed to make herself forget.

Finally, the front door creaks open, the screen door clacking shut behind it. She jumps to her feet, knocking over the overflowing ashtray as she runs over to her husband, stretching her arms out to him, hardly knowing what she's doing. Through the gloom, he looks tired, wrung out, eyes vacant and unfocused. Sally is torn. She desperately wants to know what's going on, but she doesn't want to know what his involvement is. She holds him silently for a moment and then drops her arms to her sides when his body doesn't soften into her the way it usually does.

"I waited for you after the meeting at the church," she whispers, hoarsely, trying to find the words to ask him what happened. "What did Chief Abernathy… I mean, did…did you go to the police station? You've been gone a long time." He nods. There are tears in his eyes, she notices.

"The chief, he, um…wanted to…talk," he fumbles. She stares at him, finding herself suddenly unable to process what's happening.

"I'm so sorry," he murmurs. Sally can feel her jaw tighten, a swell of nausea threatening to overwhelm her.

"For what?" she asks, at last. It's all she can do to keep herself from passing out now and she finds herself wishing he'd just get it over with.

"I…I kissed her," he stammers, at last. She stares at him, her mouth dropping open.

"You kissed who?" He takes a deep breath, clenching and unclenching his fists.

"Sarah. I kissed Sarah." Sally is silent for a long moment, mind churning, not sure whether to be relieved or heartbroken.

"Say something," Jimmy whispers, determinedly meeting her eye.

"Did...did you do anything else with her?" and then barely aloud, "...to her?" Her lower lip is shaking and she can feel the tears overflowing before she even knows she's crying.

"No," he says, firmly. "I swear. I was just drunk and...and I don' know, I guess I was flattered or somethin'. Sally, you have to believe me. I love you. I'd never hurt you on purpose." She nods silently, swallowing hard.

"I believe you," she says.

He smiles, weakly, and pulls her close, kissing the top of her head.

"I love you," he says again, holding her so tight it almost hurts. As she stands there, hardly able to breathe, a jarring realization runs through her. She doesn't believe him. She doesn't believe him, but she can't bear to find out the truth. She wants to ask him whether he knows anything about the circumstances of Sarah's death – about where she went or what she wanted – but she's too afraid. It's not the truth she's afraid of, she realizes. Even now, more than anything else in the world, she's terrified of accidentally pushing him away. A drunken kiss, she can forgive. Anything else, she decides, she doesn't want him to tell her.

When Katie Weiler got on the back of that motorcycle, she thought she was setting herself free. Donovan Belleville, the itinerant musician and owner of the bike, had travelled all the way from Manitoba and he just happened to light on their tiny town on his way to Chicago: it was fate. It was her way out. Not even eighteen, barely more than a little girl, she was already sick to death of her life – of her mother constantly telling her she was the family's great white hope, that all her dreams rested on her daughter's shoulders, while Sally, at least to Katie's mind, was left alone to live her own life. She hated her own beautiful face and all the things it seemed to mean to so many people. To her mother, she was destined to be a movie star. To her father, she was a precious commodity, a treasure to be kept under lock and key. To her sister, she was a source of resentment and jealousy, however much she tried to hide it. And beyond that, to every man who ever looked at her, even when she was barely a teenager, she was an object of predatory lust.

Donovan wasn't handsome per se – he had a craggy, rough-hewn look about him, with big, calloused hands and long, dark hair – but he had deep, expressive eyes that seemed to speak of a sensitive soul, and there was just something about his whole person that promised freedom and excitement. She met him while he was busking on a street corner one Saturday afternoon and it didn't take her long to see her chance. She'd never even seen a busker before, but when she saw him, a little light came on inside her head. In her desperation to get out, it was easy to convince herself he was different from other men – that he really would be the one to save her, that he wanted more from her than just to possess her, to make her a trophy. He said everything she wanted him to say, promised everything she wanted him to promise. So, with a fearlessness she didn't know she was capable of, she agreed to leave with him before he'd even finished offering to take her.

Sally begged her not to. Her parents stopped speaking to her altogether not long after she told them what she was planning, figuring she'd see sense and give up before they really had to worry. But Sally – home on break from college, Sally sat on her bed for hours the night before she was supposed to leave, pleading with her, trying to persuade her it wasn't safe, that there was better out there for her. Stubbornly, determined not to let anyone take her chance away from her, Katie convinced herself it was nothing more than jealousy, and silently continued to pack her bags. Sally had always been jealous, she told herself, always wished she could have what her sister had. She didn't know what it was really like, didn't know how desperately she wanted to escape. Sally couldn't see past the end of her own ugly nose.

Every now and then, when they were in high school, Katie had felt a little pang at not protecting Sally from the monstrous girls in her class who were consistently cruel to her, to her face and otherwise. She knew she could have done more, and it must have hurt her sister terribly, but high school was a goddamn jungle, and she had her own skin to look out for. Besides, she'd remind herself, Sally didn't have to act like that. She could have been doing more to help herself. For that matter, she could have made her own escape plan. She didn't have to go to the University of Wisconsin, didn't have to keep coming back to this godawful place. It wasn't Katie's fault if she couldn't see that.

It wasn't until the next morning, when Donovan showed up and she was about to get on that bike, that her parents finally realized she wasn't backing down and started to try and do something about it. They were screaming, threatening, cursing, waking up everyone within a five-mile radius. Donovan, for his part, didn't offer anything in his own defense. He was probably wondering what he'd gotten himself into, she realized, and at the time, she'd even given him credit for not just driving off without her. But Sally – Sally didn't say a word. She just stood there, crying. That had cut her deeply, seeing for a split second the reality of the pain she was causing. But in another second, she'd pushed the feeling aside, and she was on her way.

They made it to Chicago a couple of weeks after leaving the miserable shoebox of a town, zigzagging across state lines. They stopped occasionally so that Donovan could make a few bucks playing gigs in dive bars and crappy restaurants – one of which, she remembers, was called Tequila Mockingbird, the memory of which has always made her cringe. After a few of these shows – if they could even be called that, since the audience was never more than about a dozen people, most of whom were semi-comatose, dribbling into their drinks – Katie started to understand why he'd never hit the big time: he was terrible. His voice was thin and tremulous, and his guitar playing was average at best. He mostly played less-than-faithful covers of '80s alt-rock songs, and when he did venture an original composition, it was so hammy and derivative that she couldn't bear to listen. But she didn't – couldn't, wouldn't – give up. Instead, she threw herself headlong into his world, deciding it was better to be oblivious than to go home.

They lasted a few more weeks after they got to the city, sleeping, when they stopped partying long enough, in crummy motels and on the floors of friends of friends. At first, it really did feel just as thrilling as it had promised to be, despite Donovan's lack of talent – the rebellion, the freedom, the license to do anything at all. But it wasn't long before the nagging doubt started to creep into her mind, in a voice that sounded a lot like her sister's. She could hear her telling her she'd told her this would happen, that she never should have trusted someone she barely knew, that she was wasting herself. So when Donovan started saying he wanted to head west, maybe for Oregon or California, she jumped at the chance. She didn't even wait for him to ask her to come along. She just announced it one night after another one of his awful gigs, and then they were on the road again.

When she heard California, a switch seemed to go off in her mind. This was it: her golden ticket. This was her shot at stardom and fortune and fame, just like her mother always said. Seeing what might be her one and only opportunity, she climbed on the back of that bike again, even though she could tell he was getting sick of her. They always did: Donovan wasn't the first and he was by no means the last. These men would become obsessed with her, like she was some siren or nymph or other-worldly thing, and they'd decide they had to have her. They wouldn't be able to think about anything else until they did, but eventually, they'd realize she really was still a little girl, despite her womanly looks, and the spell would be broken. For a little while, she'd miss home then. She'd miss her tiny bedroom and the clean, safe streets, and she'd miss Sally, who, for all her resentment, always did her best to be kind to her. She'd even miss her stifling, overbearing parents. But she couldn't turn back – not when she was so close. So she kept the veil from lifting, ignoring reality for just a bit longer, and followed Donovan one more time.

Jimmy is in bed, sleeping off the awful day, but Sally can't bring herself to follow him. There's a nasty, cold feeling in her gut every time she thinks about lying down next to him that refuses to fade, however hard she tries. For a while, she tried to push it down, to swallow it up with good memories of Jimmy, of times they were happy and carefree, but none are forthcoming. Everything seems tainted now. Finally, she stops trying. Instead, she sits in the dark living room, an unlit cigarette in her hand, staring at the phone. Not for the first time in the last ten years or so, she finds herself not just wanting, but truly needing to call her sister. Since she'd been out west, Katie has never once called her – there were the picture postcards, and the occasional email, with a few photos attached – but she's never picked up the phone to speak to her. At first, Sally had called her pretty regularly. But it never took long for her to start to sound distracted, like she couldn't wait to get off the phone, and for all her self-righteousness about it, gradually, Sally let her calls become less and less frequent. Once in a while, though, Sally still gives in. Every now and then, something big will happen and she'll suddenly remember there's a part of her that needs her sister.

Katie doesn't show any sign of needing Sally, of course. She never has, even when they were kids. Still, there's always been a part of Sally that simply won't let her go. She's forgiven her a lot: for leaving, for never calling, even for failing to come to her wedding. To give her the little credit she deserves, whenever she called, Katie always at least feigned some small interest in Sally's life in those first few minutes, and Sally had been able to convince herself there was still something of a sister in her somewhere. But the last time she called her, when their mother died, four years ago, something was different. Katie had sounded distant, cool – as though she had somewhere else to be, as though she was in some big hurry. She barely said a word after Sally delivered the news, except to say she probably wouldn't be able to come to the funeral. She hung up a few seconds later.

At the time, Sally had persuaded herself not to be angry. It was probably just shock, she told herself. Just Katie being Katie, handling things badly. Probably regret at the way things had ended up between them – fear of how her father would react if he saw her again, shame for not coming back when she found out their mother was sick. She'd call back, talk to her, offer to pay for her plane ticket even. It would be ok. Only she never did. The postcards of the unnamed beaches and the anonymous landmarks – Katie had never said much about where she was, and later, Sally had realized it was just another way of keeping her out of her life – were all she had left after that. They were stowed away in a box under her bed next to Jimmy's handgun, the ones addressed to her closet of an apartment in New York on top to remind her that she, too, had been free once, or close to it at least. More and more time passed, and the longer she left it, the harder it became. Sally let it get as far as the day of the funeral, secretly hoping her sister might show up unexpectedly. But she didn't. Of course she didn't. After that, Sally started to see her differently – to see her the way she maybe always should have, she thought. Katie was selfish. There was no sense of duty or of family in her. She was no sister.

It was the first time Sally had felt really, deeply livid with her. She'd been disappointed time and again – she'd felt sad, rejected, even unloved, but the fire of anger was always missing. There was just a dull, empty ache in her stomach. She'd harden herself to it after a while, the way she always did, and then it would fade. Then she'd remember Katie's beauty, her bright, exciting warmth, and the thrill she got from living vicariously through her, and all would be forgotten. This was the first time she found she couldn't make herself forgive her, no matter what she did or how much she prayed for God to make her strong enough. There was something cold in Katie. Something cruel. For a fleeting moment at the time, Sally remembers, she wondered what must have happened to her to plant that seed in her, and she almost relented. There must be real pain there. There must be something that hurt her, scarred her inside to make her that callous. But there were some things you just didn't do, she thought, no matter what terrible fate had befallen you. You didn't turn your back on your family.

After the funeral, Sally didn't speak to her at all. She focused on her father, throwing all of her energy into trying to help him get over her mother's death. It was like a little piece of him had died along with his wife. Her mother, her beautiful, suffocating, infuriating, wonderful mother, had been everything to him. It was hard on her to see him like that, so different, so…broken. The last time she remembered seeing him this way was right after Katie left. He'd doted on her, she knew that. He'd always done his best not to play favorites when they were kids, at least outwardly, but she knew deep down that Katie was the real golden girl, the one who held first place in his heart. He appreciated how smart Sally was and she knew he was proud of her when she got into a four-year college. It was one of a handful of times she'd ever seen him really, fully smile. But Katie was so much like her mother, not just in her looks but her personality, too – passionate, fierce, headstrong, naïve, brilliant, stubborn, careless. He couldn't help loving her more. After she left, he hardly said a word for weeks. He was stuck with plain, bookish, boring Sally and as much as she tried to fight it, she couldn't help feeling like something of a booby prize.

As time passed, though, he'd started to come back from it, to seem more like his old, tough, Austrian self. He even started to warm up to her, in a way he never had before. He started talking to her, appreciating her developing sense of humor, calling her while she was away at college, inviting her to sit with him after dinner when she was home, while he smoked outside on the porch. But then her mother got sick. The illness took over her quickly, and it was only a matter of months before she died. Everything changed after that. When Sally told him Katie wouldn't be coming to the funeral, it was as if he just shut down. He stopped talking again, stopped smiling. It didn't take long for the truth to emerge, though: he could barely take care of himself without his wife, and the job would fall to Sally. Her entire life, she worked as hard as she could not to resent Katie, to be the bigger person, but when her father showed absolutely no sign of gratitude for what she was doing for him, for her strength in the face of so much pain, for her willingness to throw herself head long into her responsibilities, she couldn't do it anymore. Every bad feeling, every suppressed scream of frustration and injustice became compressed into a stony little ball of rage until she realized she'd started to hate her sister.

She still feels guilty for it, of course. A leopard doesn't change its spots, she thinks, with a sad smile. In a way, it's a blessing, though. The guilt is the only thing that keeps her going back to her father's house to have lunch with him every Sunday, keeps her checking in on him once or twice a week to make sure he has enough to eat and that he hasn't burned the place down. He sold the family farm when her mother got sick – quickly, and at a considerable loss – partly so he could pay for her treatment and partly because the work was getting to be too much for him. He couldn't afford much help and there was only so much he could do by himself, so he sold up the first chance he got, and bought a tiny mobile home on a plot in the middle of town. It's not so bad, really – almost pretty, its wooden exterior painted brilliant white and blue – but it has an electric oven and Sally is pretty sure he'll leave the damn thing on one night and the whole thing will go up in smoke. She's the only one left who can keep him safe, however ungrateful he is. She has to atone for her selfishness, for her own inability to forgive, and she can't think of another way to do it.

Now, alone, afraid, feeling tiny and vulnerable, she realizes she doesn't have anywhere else to turn. She doesn't have a lot of friends in town and the last thing she wants is to stir up gossip. She knows other people must have seen her husband talking to Abernathy after the meeting, knows they must already be jumping to conclusions, and she's decided the safest thing is to keep quiet. But she can't deal with it by herself. She needs someone and her sister might as well be it. There's still a part that hopes she's capable of change, that maybe she's grown up in the last few years. It's the fear that she hasn't that keeps her from dialing as much as anything else, but finally, she cracks and begins to punch in the number. She's not even sure if Katie's still using the same the cell number, she realizes. But now, with the weight of everything that's happened in the last couple of days bearing down on her, she finds all she can think about is hearing her sister's voice.

As she finishes dialing, she squeezes her eyes shut with a little silent prayer that Katie will pick up, not knowing what she'll do if she doesn't.

"Hello?" a woman's voice says. For a moment, Sally's heart stops: the voice sounds strange, unfamiliar. It's deeper than it should be, she thinks. In her head, she realizes, Katie still sounds like the little girl she was when she left home, almost a decade ago. "Hello?" the voice repeats.

"K-Katie?" she stammers. There's a long, heavy silence at the other end, devoid even of breathing, and for a moment, she thinks whoever is on the line must have hung up.

"Sally?" the voice says at last.

"Katie, I…I think…I need you to come home," Sally whispers, her voice cracking. She hears Katie take a deep breath.

"All right."

Donovan – if that was even his real name, and Katie was never convinced it was – finally ditched her somewhere around Coos Bay. They'd taken a meandering, fairly incoherent route west, and they got as far as the coast before he decided to head south for California. It took weeks, and once or twice, she was pretty sure she'd only narrowly avoided being left behind. She couldn't swear to it, but it certainly seemed as though he was trying to lose her, without actually going to the trouble of dumping her. Fucking coward, she thought. But she'd be damned if she gave up after coming so far. She laid off the partying after that, figuring it was better to stay alert so she could always be a step or two ahead of him. The booze and the drugs had made her fuzzy, only half awake most of the time: she couldn't have that. So with the same stubbornness and impulsiveness as she did everything, she abruptly switched the vodka to orange juice, quit the pills and the joints – and started to plan.

Practice makes perfect, she thought. Lacking as he was in the IQ department, Donovan never even noticed when she got sober. So when he was busy sleeping off whatever he'd consumed – she lost track of all the things he was putting into his bloodstream, narcotic and otherwise – she'd work on packing her few belongings as quickly as she could. Pretty soon, she found she could be up and ready to go in a matter of minutes if she had to. Sometimes, she waited for him at the Black Shadow for hours while he emerged from his post-hangover fug or disappeared into a bar to meet a "booker". She'd sit there, in the hot afternoon sun, sticking close to the bike, sometimes stretching out across the seat if he took long enough and she got drowsy. But there were other times when he'd suddenly inform her they had to get out of wherever they were as fast as they could – squats, usually, or sometimes motels when he couldn't scrape together the bill. She needed to be able to get up and go before he had a chance to leave her behind. She needed to be ready.

He'd always be vague about plans, but she found if she listened carefully enough to his conversations and kept an eye on the calls he made, she could figure out what was coming next. Donovan's main virtue, if it could be called that, was that he was stupid. He regularly left his phone unattended and if she was quick enough, she could go through his texts, too. Some of them were clearly from other girls – a lot of the content was eye-wateringly explicit – but she didn't care. It was just until she could get to California, she told herself. Then she could figure something else out. In the meantime, he was easy to read, easy to play. If she could keep him sweet, she could stay far enough ahead of him to keep herself safe. It was still hard work, though. She half-thought of finding some other way to do it – of somehow scraping together the cash to travel cross-country alone, or even putting herself in the hands of some other guy – but there was no way of knowing when or if that would ever work. So she held on.

When they got close to the west coast, he told her he wanted to stop to get cigarettes and coffee, and since she could feel her own watchfulness starting to slip, she agreed. They pulled up at a truck stop diner on Highway 101 and drank their coffee in what might have been mistaken for companionable silence, although she never took her eyes off the Black Shadow, and he never took his eyes off the pretty blonde on the other side of the counter. Weighing her options when they were done, she decided a bathroom break would be smart, since Donovan sometimes liked to ride through the night. So she took the risk – and when she came back from the bathroom, he was gone.

Even years later, the thought of it made her so mad, she could spit. The worst part of it was that she hadn't seen it coming: for all the warning signs, for all her careful planning, she'd never really believed he'd just leave her there, on the side of the road, without even a second thought for what would happen to her. For a good twenty minutes, she just stood there, in total disbelief, half-convinced he might reappear and tell her it was all a mistake or a joke or…something. Then, when the shock wore off, she sat down on the curb outside the diner and cried. She cried and cried and cried. In her wretchedness, she cried harder then than she ever had before, even as a little kid – so much so that her stomach hurt and her eyes stung and her whole body trembled by the end of it. Then, when she was through crying, blotchy and hiccupping, she went inside, ordered a cup of coffee and tried to work up the courage to call home and ask for help.

"You all right, kiddo?" the woman behind the counter in the diner asked, seeing her puffy, tear-stained face. She had a sweet, friendly voice, and a high, beehive hairstyle in an unnatural shade of red, with smudged lipstick in a shade to match. Paired with her green polyester uniform, it put Katie in mind of a Christmas tree. She shrugged.

"Not really," she murmured, not looking up from her half empty cup of coffee. It was stone cold, but since the only money she had to her name was a fifty-dollar bill and the change she had in her pocket, it was all she thought she could afford to buy.

"What's a matter, sweetie?" Beehive asked.

"I, uh…I got…left behind…" Katie said, hating how the words sounded out loud, and hating herself for not coming up with a lie. She was doing her best not to start crying again and she wasn't sure how long she could hold on. Beehive sighed, sadly.

"By a fella, right?" Surprised, Katie nodded, looking up at last into the woman's kind, wrinkled face. "Oldest story in the book. Seen it a million times. But you're doin' better than most – you got a friend now."

"I do?" Katie asked, confused. Beehive laughed, a rasping, smoke-ravaged sound.

"Sure. Me," she said, gesturing at her chest with her thumb. "So whyn't you tell me about it?"

Before she could stop herself, Katie found the whole sorry tale spilling out of her, right back as far as the day she met Donovan. It was strange: the more Beehive listened, the more she wanted to tell her. She just sat there, head cocked to one side, eyes full of sympathy and understanding, looking for all the world like the mother she was starting to wish she'd never left behind.

"Listen – I got a job goin' waitin' tables. It's yours if you want it. Won't pay much, but you don't need no training or nothing, and it'll tide you over for a while. Besides, it ain't like you got a lot of choice," Beehive said, when Katie was done. Katie looked at her, suspiciously. She was smiling benignly enough, but the day she was having, she wouldn't have been surprised to find this was somehow part of the elaborate prank the universe seemed to be playing on her.

"Well? What d'you say?" Beehive pressed her.

"I-I guess I have to say yes," Katie said, more timidly than she meant to. "But...where'll I sleep?"

"There's a Motel 6 about a half an hour away. I'll drive you up there at the end of the day and we'll get you set up 'til you find something else. That'll do you for now. You can look in the classifieds tomorrow. You got a little money, don't you?" Beehive said. Katie swallowed and nodded, knowing the little money she did have would buy her a night, maybe two at the most, in a bed, and after that, she was out of options. She thought sadly of the small, reassuring rectangle of plastic she'd once had in her pocket, which she'd managed to keep hidden from Donovan, but hadn't trusted herself not to use, and, in a fit of pique, had cut up weeks ago. She'd told herself afterwards that it was the right thing to do: she couldn't let Donovan get his hands on it. He'd burned through most of her cash pretty quickly, but the credit card, which was linked to her parents' bank account, was just too much of a risk. Her father had given it to her for emergencies long before she'd ever met Donovan and she couldn't bear the idea of him thinking the lousy bastard had gotten hold of it. The exhausted, resigned look he wore the day she left, when he finally gave up on begging her to stay, was still too painfully fresh in her memory.

"Why are you doing this?" she asked, before she could stop herself, her distrust getting the better of her. "You don't even know me."

Beehive sighed again and didn't say anything for so long that Katie started to shift uncomfortably her seat. She was pretty sure saw tears in the old woman's eyes.

"I had a daughter. Roberta. Robbie, we used to call her," Alma said at last, her face suddenly clouding. "She was about your age when she went off with some good-for-nothin' fella. He took her away from me and next thing I know, she…well, she never came home anyhow. And I wished like hell someone had been around to look out for her when I couldn't." For less than a second, Katie thought she'd caught sight of some terrible tragedy in the old woman's past. But in another moment, her expression cleared and she wondered if maybe she'd imagined it.

"I'm Alma, by the way. Alma Ginsey." She smiled, and Katie almost laughed then, suddenly amused they hadn't even managed to introduce themselves yet, despite everything that had already passed between them. Alma extended a weathered, orangish hand and Katie shook it, mustering up enough energy, exhausted as she was, to smile back.

"Katie. Katie…Callaghan." It was the first surname that popped into her head. It belonged to a girl she'd been at school with, a little younger than her, who'd lived out west for a while. She couldn't be sure, but it seemed to provoke a reaction from Alma. She gave a tiny gasp, like she'd touched something hot, and Katie swallowed a nervous laugh.

"Pleased to meet you, Katie Callaghan," Alma said, her voice suddenly a little shaky. "Say – how old are you anyway?"

"Um…twenty-one," Katie lied. It was the second lie she'd told in as many minutes and the residual Catholic part of her protested a little, making the color flood her cheeks. Alma narrowed her eyes, scrutinizing her face, but if she didn't believe her, she didn't say it.

"All right," she said. "Well, come on in back and we'll find you a uniform. The last girl that worked here was about your size – I think I still got hers."

Alma spent the rest of the day showing her how to take orders and work the cash register, while Katie did her best to focus and keep from scratching under the itchy green polyester dress. The whole thing seemed like one long, strange dream and she kept waiting to wake up and find herself back in some filthy motel with Donovan.

"So tell me, Katie Callaghan. Which hick town did you come from?" Alma asked, as she helped Katie load her meagre possessions into the back of her beat up old Buick that night. Katie looked at her, startled.

"How do you know I come from a –?" she began, a little indignantly, but Alma interrupted her.

"I been doin' this a long time, sugar. I know a hick when I see one," she laughed. Katie blushed, thinking of her family: her sister was the only one of the entire clan to go to college and her mother said things like "irregardless" and "a whole 'nother".

"I'm from Wisconsin," she said, too embarrassed to be more specific.

"Anywhere in particular?" Alma pressed, eyeing her in the rear view mirror as she got into the car. Katie relented and told her the name of the town then, figuring there was no way she'd ever have heard of it – but it provoked the same reaction as when she'd said her name was Callaghan.

"You know it?" she asked. A strange feeling had nestled underneath her skin – the same uncomfortable tingly feeling she used to get when she'd been away someplace and she was approaching home, or what used to be home. She'd always dreaded that feeling. She'd hoped she'd never feel it again.

"Not, uh…not exactly," Alma said, hesitantly. "I…know somebody who lives there."

"Who?" Katie was starting to feel sick to her stomach. Typical, she thought. Goddamn typical. No matter how far away you got, that rotten town followed you. If she'd fetched up in Poughkeepsie or Pittsburgh or Panama City, she was sure she would have run across somebody who knew somebody who knew somebody who knew the town. It was like a curse.

"John Callaghan." There was something in Alma's tone that suggested she expected a reaction from Katie. She eyed her again, clearly waiting for some realization to dawn on her, but Katie, forgetting she'd lied, didn't know what to say. "You related?"

"To who?" Katie asked. She felt hot and dizzy. She couldn't remember the last time she'd had anything but coffee to drink. Alma narrowed her eyes in the rearview mirror.

"To John Callaghan. It ain't a big town, I figured maybe..."

"Oh," she murmured, finally understanding. Taking a deep breath, she tried to clear her mind. She needed to come clean. "No...um...that's...not my real name." She stole a sheepish glance at Alma and she was sure she looked disappointed.

"I see," Alma said, tightly. "Then what is your real name?"

"It's Weiler," Katie said, biting her lip. "I know a John Callaghan though. He came back to town a little while ago. He got rich doing something with computers in California, I think." Katie hoped the imparting of this knowledge might help her get back into Alma's good graces, fearing losing her only hope of an ally. She smiled, sadly, but she didn't say anything else the rest of the drive.

Murphy can't sleep. He knows Sally is in the next room, rethinking everything she ever thought she knew about him, and he's doing more or less the same thing. He loves her: he's sure of that at least. But he doesn't know how to be her husband anymore. There are so many things he's done to let her down, and even if she can forgive him, he doesn't know if he can forgive himself. She deserves more – more than him, more than this. He's always tried to tell her that, to tell her she's worth so much more than she thinks she is, but it always comes out clumsy, ham-fisted. The words tangle in his mouth and tumble out meaningless. Then she'll look at him, with those sad, tired, loving eyes, kiss him and tell him it's ok. He wishes she could do that now. He knows he's weak. He knows Gallagher sees it in him and he can't help but see it in himself. He stopped trying to fight it a little while after he lost his job. He'll never be good enough, so he doesn't try to be. Now he gives in to whatever temptation comes his way, gives in to the darkness inside him. He doesn't look for it, but somehow, it always finds him. He stopped going to church, too. That was it – the final straw. After that, he let go of the last little part of him that thought he could be saved. Sally still goes though, faithfully every Sunday, and he hopes she prays for him, for all the good it'll do.

When he married her, he was so full of hope. He thought maybe he could be a good man for her, that maybe being a husband would stir up some sense of duty in him. And for a while, it did. Making her happy was the best thing he'd ever done. He was rescuing her, he told himself. No one had ever really loved her, or wanted her, or even been especially nice to her: they had that in common. She fell for him quickly and easily, and it gratified him. It gave him a real thrill to think anyone could be so in awe of him and he quietly promised himself he'd try to be what she wanted and needed him to be. He loved it when she laughed at his jokes, loved seeing her smile when he brought her flowers or fixed the washing machine or just told her she was pretty. But there was only so long he could keep it up. They'd hardly been married a year when the cracks started to show. No one ever really changes, he realized. And he was no exception. It was part of why he'd wanted a child. If he could be a father, he'd have an inescapable reason to work on being a better man. He'd have someone to set an example for, someone to provide for. But now, here he is, almost thirty, childless, and afraid he might have killed someone. It almost sounds like a joke, except there's no punchline. It's just one more thing he's done to let Sally down. She desperately wants to be a mother, he knows that. And she'll probably never get the chance, even with somebody else. They've had the tests done: the doctors don't have much hope.

Even he never thought he'd end up here, though. For all the crappy things he's done in his life, he's never physically hurt anybody and he never even thought he was capable of it. It was the one thing his weakness was good for: he didn't have it in him to be violent. But now, with the image of Sarah McIntyre's cold, dead eyes swirling around inside his head, he's starting to wonder. He just can't *remember*. And because he can't remember, he can't be sure. He wants to believe there's some part of him that would keep him from doing something like that, that there is at least enough good in him to keep him from sinking that low. But he's been drinking so much lately, feeling so angry, so destructive. Only a week or so ago, while Sally was at her father's place, he'd downed half a dozen beers, and then he'd taken his hunting rifle out to the dark, grey woods, taking pot shots into the trees. He didn't even know why he was doing it, or not really anyway. But there was a little voice inside him that told him to keep shooting. You want to hit something, it whispered. You want something to die at your hand. Then you can finally be powerful. Then you can finally be a man.

He realizes now it was what he'd been hoping for when he and Gallagher went out hunting that day. He wanted some strong, beautiful animal to fall in front of his gun so that he could feel the thrill of taking its life. He'd never been much of a hunter before, but that day, he needed it. And if he needed it then, maybe he'd needed it that night at the bar with Sarah. He wonders what his parents would think of him now – his mother, a mild, sweet-natured teacher, his father, who'd worked at the machine plant with Gallagher, stern and sober. Not for the first time, he finds he's glad they're not around to see him now. They'd be so disappointed.

There's a big blank space in his head between kissing Sarah and getting home. Anything could have happened. Gallagher was busy kicking the shit out of the Mitchells, after one of them had tripped Murphy on his way back from the bathroom, knocking him on his ass, he remembers that much. He could see them through the window, shifting in and out of focus, a mass of foggy breath, fists and feet. He's pretty sure Gallagher didn't come back inside – he doesn't remember the fresh bruises or the streaks blood that must have crisscrossed his face in the immediate aftermath of the brawl – and he knows he didn't see him with Sarah. She must have been in the bar when they arrived but Gallagher didn't pay her any attention. Hell, he probably thought she was Mary Callaghan, down from Ashland visiting her father – bleary-eyed, half drunk, it had been his own first thought. But then she started talking to him, and he got a good look at her face. She was older than Mary, or she certainly looked it. She was pretty, but there were little lines around her eyes, and thick, rope veins on her hands. Gallagher had disappeared outside. He'd gone home to nurse his bloody fists and Murphy didn't see him again until the next day. He and Sarah must have been alone for a good while, then. He would have had plenty of time. He could have taken her outside, hit her over the head and then dragged her out to the woods without anyone noticing. No one ever paid him much attention. It would have been easy. The last thing he remembers with any clarity at all is awkwardly pressing his mouth against hers. If she'd rejected him – and he's pretty sure she would have – maybe he got angry. Maybe he wanted to teach her a lesson.

But all that stuff about posing her like she was a virgin sacrifice, taking off her clothes and putting her in that dress, leaving her out in the snow. Could he really have done that? More to the point, *why* would he have done that? The questions rattle around inside his head, crashing into each other. A year ago, the answer would have been straightforward. He could have said with conviction that he'd never hurt a woman. Not like that. He could have said he might be a worthless piece of shit, but he's not a goddamn killer. But so much has happened since then – and if he could have killed her, he could have ditched her and posed her, too. If he's honest with himself, he knows exactly when things started to go wrong, and it wasn't when he lost his job, or even when he started drinking too much. He can pinpoint it down to the minute. It was when the doctor told them they could probably never conceive naturally – that Sally could probably never bear his child. It wasn't impossible, the doctor said – but their chances were very, very slim. That was when it all finally fell apart. After that, something in him felt like it had died. He felt so helpless – so hopeless. There was nothing left to keep him from becoming what he was afraid he'd always been and he needed an escape, whatever it might be.

Alone with his thoughts when he's driving all over the state looking for work, that fear takes him over. It washes over him, working its way inside him, to the point that he can't be sure he could stop himself if the impulse to twist the wheel and swing his truck off the road came over him. It's like a poisonous cloud, and he can't help breathing it in. When he stops and gets out, it always fades, but it's never really gone. There's only one place it ever seems to go away completely and that's not here. It's not in this house, it's not in this town. Now, in his own bed, it fills up his mind, his heart, his whole body. Recently, it's even started to show in his face. The lines are deeper now, the dark circles around his eyes a permanent feature. The last year has changed him so much that he hardly even recognizes himself now. He even stopped shaving so that he wouldn't have to look at himself in the mirror. He's done a lot of things he never thought he'd do, changed in ways he never thought he would, to the point that he can't now definitely say that he wouldn't kill a woman and lay her out to look like someone else did it.

Alice Fahey agreed to marry Seth McIntyre not long after she found out she was pregnant. He was eight years older than her, a friend of her brother's, and she'd never thought of him as anything else, much less the man she'd end up marrying. He was dull. He was bland. He could fade into the background like no one else. But he could take care of her. Tall and square-jawed, he was built like a lumberjack, where she was small and fragile and completely friendless. He was a quiet, sensible man, and had studied law at the University of Wisconsin before setting up his practice a few blocks down from the house he grew up in. People trusted him. They put their lives in his hands. Seth McIntyre wasn't made for great things, and nor, it seemed, was he destined to stray far from his home town. But what he lacked in personality, he made up for in strength. What Seth McIntyre had, what she really needed from him was his dependability. He was unswervingly reliable. And he was deeply in love with her – had been as soon as she hit her mid-teens, even if he didn't know or couldn't say what that meant. She knew that for a fact, long before he ever got up the nerve to tell her, and above all else, she also knew she didn't have a lot of choice.

They kept the whole thing as quiet as they could. Both reactionary Catholics, old-fashioned in the extreme, neither her father nor her brother had spoken to her since she told them she was going to have a baby. They looked on her as the worst of sinners, as the lowest of the low. She had fallen and there was no raising her up again. She'd given up her virtue and the evidence was growing inside her. In the end, only her mother and Seth's mother attended the ceremony up at the courthouse in Ashland. Their disapproval was almost palpable. They wouldn't even let her have her hair done, much less wear white. Instead, she wore a plain blue smock dress, hiding her expanding belly, her thick, dark hair hanging loose over her shoulders, and no one looked her in the eye – not even Seth.

Alice never did tell anyone who the baby's real father was. She suspected the man himself knew the truth, although he never said anything if he did. He was the first and last man she ever loved, and she could never bring herself to lay the burden on him. He was meant for more, she told herself – handsome, athletic, brilliant. He was going out west to go to college and then he was going get himself set up in some place called Silicon Valley to make his millions. This was better. Only just eighteen, with nothing but her looks to recommend her, she couldn't bear the thought of raising the child alone, or worse, having to give it up. So she agreed to marry Seth. Sober, silent Seth. He seemed never to have been young or frivolous, unable really to understand someone like Alice – beautiful, flighty, careless – but to his credit, he loved the child just as if she were his own, even as she grew up and began to look more and more like her real father. Seth had never met the man – he was closer to her own age and ran in a very different crowd – and she counted herself lucky for that. Otherwise, he'd have figured it out right away. Alice could see it in her as clear as anything, and it both scared and thrilled her. She had her mother's lovely dark hair, and small, dainty features, but she had her father's big, expressive blue eyes. It was strange to see those eyes again, and in such a pretty, doll-like face. It wasn't just her looks, though. Sarah was smart – far smarter than Alice ever had been – and she could see she was meant for great things, too.

After the little girl was born, her family did start to come around at last, although it took some time. Her mother, the only one who hadn't shunned her completely, had died not long before she gave birth – swallowed up by the same cancer that would eventually swallow Alice – while her brother, a teacher, had decided to take a job in Des Moines and that it would be better to take their father out of state with him shortly after that. Their mother had always taken care of him: he couldn't be left alone, and he certainly couldn't be left to Alice's care.

Her family might learn to live with her indiscretion in time, but they'd never forget. But little by little, as Sarah grew up, they started to visit more and more, spending as much time with her as they could, in awe of the child. They'd drive for hours up from Iowa every weekend, just to be in her presence. She was beautiful and willful and wonderful, and they all fell in love with her. Alice and Seth never had another child, although they talked about it often. A little brother would be nice, Alice said. Someone for Sarah to watch out for, and to watch out for her. But it never happened. And because of that, it fell to Sarah to shoulder all of the family's hopes and dreams.

Alice always wondered if maybe she put too much pressure on the girl – forever telling her she was going to Harvard, that she was going to rule the world – but then her uncle and her grandfather were just as bad, if not worse. They wanted more for her. They wanted to keep her from turning out like her mother at all costs, and they cajoled and coaxed and coached her into believing it would be the end of the world if she didn't live up to their expectations. It was a lot for anyone to take, let alone a teenage girl. It wasn't until it was too late, though, that Alice realized she should have done more to support her, to protect her, and she immediately blamed herself when Sarah told her she was pregnant. She'd tried so hard to keep her away from parties, away from boys – away from anything that might lead her to make the same mistakes she had – and it broke her heart to know she'd failed. Not for the first time then, she wondered what her life would have been like if she'd let Sarah's father into her daughter's life – whether his guidance, his confident pragmatism might somehow have saved her from this. Sarah had never even mentioned she was dating, let alone having sex, and it felt like someone had sucked all the air out of her when she told her.

Alice's first thought was to have her get rid of it before her family found out – she couldn't bear having her father and brother look at her daughter with the same awful disappointment as when she'd told them about Sarah's existence – but when she told Seth what had happened, he wouldn't hear of it. He had always been a deeply religious man – a staunch, unyielding Catholic, more so even than her father and brother – and even worse than the idea that Sarah had managed to get pregnant was that of an abortion. She begged and pleaded with him, desperate for him to let Sarah have the life she was supposed to have, but he was intransigent. Instead, Sarah was to have the baby, and give it up, despite all her pleading, and her mother's. In the same stoical, forbearing way as he did everything, Seth decided no one could ever know about the shame that had befallen his family. So he shut down his practice and moved the whole family out to Chicago, without even the most cursory of discussions. He took a job with the first firm that would take him and that was that. He didn't say anything to his own family, who'd moved over to Madison, let alone to Alice's, hundreds of miles away in Iowa. He didn't even call them until long after the fact, and he wouldn't give them an exact address until after Sarah had given birth and the baby, a little boy, was already gone, adopted by a Lutheran family from McHenry.

Sarah herself began to shut down after that. She'd gone from being the angel child, adored by all those around her, to persona non grata in her own home, and her mother could see it was killing her. Like her own mother, she never talked about the father of her baby either, but Alice knew something wasn't right about the whole thing. She longed for Sarah to open up to her, the way she used to as a child, but she barely spoke at all throughout her pregnancy and worst of all, she stopped studying. Seth had insisted she be home schooled at least until the baby was born, and had hired a weak-willed young woman to be her teacher, whom Sarah found she could easily manipulate. She'd ditch her by noon and disappear to God knew where, sometimes not coming back until late into the night. By the time the child arrived – healthy, by some miracle – her grade point average had dropped from a 4.0 to a 2.8 and she was starting to hang around with the most unpleasant people she could find. Her uncle and grandfather had come to visit a few times immediately after the birth, once Seth finally told them where they were, but the visits quickly dried up when it became clear that there was no reasoning with her, no pleading with her to step back and see what she was doing to herself. She was out of control, beyond hope. She was becoming everything her mother was afraid of.

At seventeen, she'd started drinking heavily, and at eighteen, after the umpteenth time the police brought her home drunk or high, Seth ordered her out of the family home, despite Alice's frantic begging for him to relent.

Alice never saw her daughter again, and she never forgave Seth. Sarah's disappearance consumed her, and she combed the city looking for her, but she was either lost completely, or she simply didn't want to be found. Hating Seth for what he'd done, hating herself for letting him do it, slowly but surely, she began to give up – on her marriage, on her life. She lost more and more weight, became more and more frail, and by the time the doctors realized it was a tumor, it was too late. Alice McIntyre died at forty-two, and Seth took her back home to be buried at the little Catholic church, where one of the local boys had just become the priest. It was the last anyone ever saw of him.

When Katie clambered out of the Buick that first night, her mind drifted back to the events of the day and how she'd ended up where she was. She thought about home and coincidences and fate. Fate, in general, she thought, was an asshole. Fate had brought her Donovan and Donovan had dumped her here. It was too hard to stop thinking about it, and she knew she wasn't going to fall asleep. A part of her wondered if it was all some kind of punishment for daring to think she could escape – as if the universe was saying, "This is it. This is where you end up. This far and no further." She lay there, in the hot, airless little motel room, with a towel between her and the sheets, and giving in at last, she started to cry again.

She must have fallen asleep at some point, though she couldn't remember closing her eyes. She remembered waking up, some time in the wee hours. As her eyes adjusted to the gloom, she realized what had woken her. He was just standing there, a shadowy figure leaning over her bed, one hand outstretched. Immediately, instinctively, she started to scream at the top of her lungs and grabbed the first thing that came to hand, which happened to be the Gideon bible, swinging it wildly at the figure's head. Whoever it was obviously hadn't banked on her putting up much of a fight: as soon as she started shrieking and flailing, he turned and bolted through the open door.

If anyone heard her screaming, they didn't do anything about it. It must be normal, she realized. Either they figured she was having some kind of a good time or they knew there was nothing to be done for her. No one came to find out what the problem was – no one even banged on the wall to tell her to shut up – and she spent the rest of the night wide awake, with a chair pushed against the door, crouching on the floor with the bible poised and ready in her hand.

"Jesus, you look awful," Alma said, startled at her white, frightened face the next morning when she came to pick her up. "What's with you?"

"Someone…someone came into my room last night," Katie whispered. She didn't have the energy to come with a lie, keeping her eyes firmly fixed on her lap, where she still clutched the bible. Alma blanched.

"All right. You're stayin' with me. You can sleep on my couch till you find some place in town." Katie stared at her, disbelieving. She still couldn't understand why a stranger would be so nice to her, without a hidden agenda of some kind.

"Really? Are-are you sure? I mean, I could be, like, a delinquent or something," she stammered. Alma smiled.

"I'm sure," she said. "Get your stuff. We're outta here."

"Shouldn't-shouldn't we call the cops or something?" Katie asked, timidly. Alma looked at her with sad, knowing eyes.

"Wouldn't help."

John Callaghan is not a bad man. These are the words he repeats to himself every morning when he gets out of bed, trying to convince himself that they're true. He thinks about Mary and how sweet and kind she is – some of that must be to do with him, he thinks, although he knows most of it is from her mother, who, in the face of everything she went through, had the purest of hearts. It still sends a stab of guilt through his gut to think of her for too long – of how things ended up – so he thinks about the things he's done. He thinks of the way he's provided for Mary, of how she and her child will never have to want for anything. He thinks of the money he's given to charity, about the programs for disadvantaged youth he's helped to set up, teaching them valuable skills, back in California and closer to home, too. He's done some good, there's no denying it – changed lives, even. He can't be a bad man, then. Not really.

Home. It's a strange word. It doesn't seem to apply to anywhere he's been, although this town is as close as it gets. He came back with Mary after her mother died, figuring it might be better for her – better for both of them. It's small and quiet and unassuming. There's no crime, no hustle or bustle. You could leave your front door unlocked at night and sleep easy. He'd heard from Luke Gallagher that Alice was gone – that she and her family had left for Chicago – so there was no one left from his past there, no ghosts to haunt him. He'd already been back a few years when he found out that she'd died. She'd been buried at St Joseph's but he's never been to visit her grave – could never bear to. It hurt to know he could never really make things right with her – as long as he'd thought she was out there somewhere, alive and walking around, he could hold onto the idea that one day, he'd find her and tell her how sorry he was – but he took some comfort in knowing at least that hers was not a death he could have prevented.

It seemed…right, somehow, to be back. For all the pain and regret, there are good things associated with this place, too. This is where his life began. It's where his parents met and fell in love. It's where he learned to ride a bike. It's where he learned he couldn't throw a football to save his life. It's where he made some of the best friends he's ever had. It's where he was when he found out he got into Stanford. It's where he figured out what he wanted to do and where he wanted to go. It's where he fell in love for the first time – and he had loved Alice, however badly things might have ended between them. It's where he became who he is now, where those seeds were first planted. This is where he and Mary belong.

It's been so peaceful for such a long time. He was almost starting to think maybe he'd been forgiven – that someone out there had granted him clemency for his sins. Maybe he'd done enough. Maybe he'd finally atoned. Mary, mercifully, has shown no signs of having inherited her mother's illness. Her death came almost as a blessing to the girl. Every now and then, her mother would burst back into her life with promises of excitement and adventure, but more than that, of making their family whole again. She'd swear she could be better, that she could be a real mother. When she was very young, Mary had believed her – had enjoyed being swept along with this beautiful whirlwind. But after a while, the promises, always unfulfilled, started to wear thin. She loved her – of course she did – but her mother was more a child than she was herself, and all too often, when she couldn't be who she promised to be, Mary would find herself having to try and calm her down. She'd be the one to hold her and soothe her when she was screaming on the bathroom floor, or to talk her out of it when she was being rousted out of her bed at two o'clock in the morning to come and watch the waves from the Golden Gate Bridge. Mary's always been quiet, studious, but it took a toll on her, he's sure of that. A few times during her childhood, he'd tried to broach the subject of her mother, to explain why she was the way she was, why he still loved her more than anything. But she'd always shut him down. She didn't want to understand her. She didn't want to forgive her for the chaos she wrought in her life. As far as she was concerned, there was nothing motherly about her and there was no way there ever could be.

When he broke the news to Mary that her mother had died, he remembers, she didn't say a word. As soon as the police had let him, he'd driven almost four hundred miles out to San Fernando, where she was at summer camp, so that he could tell her face-to-face. It was what she deserved, he'd thought at the time. He couldn't tell her over the phone. When he finally got there and took her to one side to do what he knew he had to, she just nodded, and silently started to cry. She seemed more angry than sad, he remembers, although she never really told him what she was feeling. At the time, it had seemed strange, but after a while, it had started to make sense. Although she never talked about it, even a long time after that, he knew the way it must have seemed to her: it was just one more thing her mother had done to let her down, one final and absolute way she'd abandoned her.

They left California a few weeks after the funeral. He remembers Mary's grandmother, her mother's mother, calling the night before they left, begging him to change his mind, begging him not to take the girl so far away. But he knew he couldn't stay. His life there was over, after Robbie died. They needed to start again – to go right back to the beginning. Mary would be safe. She could go to the same sleepy, unremarkable high school he did. She could grow up, fall in love, settle down. What he hadn't banked on was who she would fall in love with. There are two big reasons for hating the man his daughter has chosen, despite the fact she hasn't introduced him yet: he doesn't have a job, according to Mary, and he knocked her up. But John was determined not to push her away. When she told him she was pregnant, he was adamant that he would be the one to take care of her – to keep her from getting married for the sake of getting married. He didn't want that for her. He knew what the consequences would be. There was something joyous in the news of the pregnancy, too, despite the circumstances. The idea that he could become a grandfather filled him with a sense of unrestrained hope. He could make good. He could atone at last, once and for all.

There are always ghosts, though, always little shreds of your history that cling to you. There's a terrible inevitability to that. There are always shadows, always parts of the past waiting to creep up and poison everything. He should have known, he thinks – should have realized no one is ever truly forgiven, least of all someone who's sinned as deeply as he has. No one ever gets to start again. He lies awake the night after the meeting at the church, thinking about Mary's pretty, innocent face, about how much she looks like the dead woman – how much she looks like Sarah. The two converge inside his head, swimming sickeningly behind his eyes.

"How did it end up like this?" he says aloud. "What happened?"

Abernathy is at the station long before dawn on Tuesday. He can already feel the pressure mounting. People want answers. They want him to have found whoever is responsible for killing Sarah McIntyre, and barely a day has passed. The trouble is, he doesn't even know where to start. He can't help wondering what would have happened if that call hadn't come in, telling him not just where she was, but who she was, too. They checked, of course, but it was her all right. She had a criminal record of her own that made his eyes water when he saw it.

He'd tried to have the call traced after it came in, but it had been made from a payphone, and Shelly, who took the call, had been adamant she didn't recognize the voice. It sounded disguised, she said – intentionally muffled. He sighs, thinking about his own complacency – his own inadequacy. The most serious crime to take place in the town during his entire tenure was vandalism: that time Paul Gallagher set fire to a dumpster, and then a little more recently, a couple of dumb kids spray painted some obscenities on the wall of the high school library. They were swiftly caught and punished, and that was that. The little shits hadn't even thought to get rid of the evidence. That was almost ten years ago, now that he thinks of it. It's the quietest of quiet towns, without a population big enough or interesting enough to cook up anything really awful. For more than thirty years, he's been grateful for this. As a kid, he watched his father preside over everything that went on in the town, learning from him how to deal with this petty squabble or that. As he grew up, he came to realize it was always ordinary in the extreme – and he liked it that way. When his turn came around, he threw himself with aplomb into the town's minutiae, taking great delight in the annual flower show and the endless bake sales and rummage sales and silly bickering over whose turn it was to organize the bake sales and the rummage sales. When he became a cop, it was to protect that: to preserve that very ordinariness that he'd come to cherish. It became his duty to act as custodian of all that was inane and trivial and wonderful about his town.

Now, though, that ordinariness is gone. He feels like he's failed in that most sacred duty. Everything he thought he knew has changed. A pall hangs over the town, and it's darkest right over his head. Silently, he stares at the photo of Sarah's body, alongside the one of her as a happy, healthy teenager, dredged up from a high school year book, pinned to a dry erase board in front of his desk. When the county medical examiner looked her over, he found faded track marks on her arms, but other than that, and the blow to the back of the head that killed her, she was in good health, he said. It looked like maybe she'd had a habit, but she was getting past it. There were no traces of drugs in her system – not even alcohol. All signs said she was clean. Sad, Abernathy thinks. Sad that she should have ended up with a habit in the first place, sad that she had her chance at starting over taken away from her. He sighs.

"What were you doing, Sarah?" he whispers. "How'd you end up out there?"

He cups his hands around his coffee mug for warmth and wonders whatever happened to her father. He knows her mother, Alice, died some years back – her husband had brought her back here to her home town to be buried at St Joseph's and he remembers going to the funeral – but the family had been living in Chicago for a long time before that, and there were no other ties to the town. Any family they had was gone – out of town, even out of state. A few of them had come back to say goodbye to Alice, but none of them stayed long. Seth McIntyre himself spent less than forty-eight hours there. He arrived, alone, to make the final arrangements with the priest – Father Dennehy, Father Carmichael's predecessor, Abernathy remembers, who must have been way past seventy years old at the time, and all but retired – and he was gone before anyone even had a chance to condole with him. In fact, it was one of the first services Father Carmichael had been allowed to perform as a newly ordained priest. Sad for him too, Abernathy thinks, to be handed such an office when he was still so young. He must have known Alice – probably knew the girl when he was at school, too, even though he's sure they would have run in different crowds. Daniel Carmichael was always such a pious, quiet young man, he remembers, and Sarah…what was it that happened to her? She got herself into some kind of trouble – probably the reason her father packed her off to Chicago – but he's not sure he ever knew what it was. It's going on fifteen years ago now and his memory of kids at the high school back then is patchy at best. He remembers breaking up the odd rowdy party, slapping the odd kid on the wrist for shoplifting – all that run-of-the-mill stuff – but nothing about Sarah. His own kids would have been out of school by then and he wasn't part of that world anymore.

The McIntyre house sits empty now. He doesn't know whether it was ever sold, but even he has to admit the place makes him uneasy. No one would want to live there if they didn't have to. Even without knowing anything about it, it gives a person a cold, sinister feeling. There are skeletons in those closets, he thinks. If he were a gambling man, he'd put money on it. You know it the minute you see it. It's haunted. You can just tell.

What he needs to do is talk to Seth McIntyre directly. He has Hausmann trying to track him down, but so far, there are no leads. There are no leads of any kind at all, in fact. The only thing he can say for sure is that the clothes she was found in weren't the clothes she was killed in – the absence of bloodstains confirms that. The gash on her head would have made quite a mess of whatever she was wearing when it happened. The dress she was found in must be significant, he thinks, but he hasn't figured out why yet. All he knows is that someone must have hated her enough, or at least been angry enough to do this to her – and that Jimmy Murphy was probably the last person to see her alive. Exactly what his connection her death was, he still doesn't know, but he has a horrible feeling he's not getting the whole picture from him.

Because of the cold, it's hard to say exactly when Sarah died, but the medical examiner's best guess is about seventy-two hours before they found her, which would mean her time of death was pretty damn close to when Murphy claimed he was with her. And then, of course, there's Paul Gallagher. He has a reputation for getting physical when he gets angry, not to mention a fiercely protective nature, especially when it comes to Murphy. If he thought Sarah was doing something that might hurt his friend, he could easily have lost his temper. Maybe he didn't mean to do it. Maybe he wanted to cover his tracks and that's why he posed her like that. Maybe he's a lot smarter and more manipulative than Abernathy ever knew. Maybe…

At this point, of course, he knows he's just speculating, letting his imagination run away with him. Paul Gallagher, for all his overreliance on his fists to make his point, has never given any indication of being anything remotely close to a cold-blooded killer. The fact is, almost anybody could have done it. He needs *evidence*: something, anything tangible to point him in the right direction. This is the first time he's ever found himself wishing he'd aimed higher. They don't have a lab of their own, let alone any crime scene investigators, like on all those dumb TV shows. All they have is a few computers, two of which are so ancient that they barely manage word processing, and only one of which is capable of accessing the internet. Any evidence they do find will have to be sent up to Ashland for analysis, and that could take days. Now, after decades of sitting behind a desk, of dealing with nothing much more taxing than asinine neighbor disputes, he finds himself questioning his own existence, questioning everything about himself – questioning whether he's ever really done a day's police work in his life. Even now, he's very much aware that he won't be the one doing most of the real work. While Hausmann's running down Seth McIntyre, he's tasked Legler with questioning Sam Mawhinney about what he saw the night Murphy claims he was with her. Sam, a tough, taciturn old bird, has owned the bar for thirty years and he loves it like the wife he never had, making a point of knowing all its goings on. Showalter, on the other hand, is out questioning all the Mitchell brothers – they're rarely apart and as a result, Abernathy is never really sure which one is which – and anyone else who might have been around that night. Little Shelly Eriksen, meanwhile, is at her post behind the front desk, fielding call after call. There've been hundreds in the last day alone, mostly from cranks and busybodies, but he quietly realizes this might just be their best shot, and he desperately hopes she might somehow pick up a lead.

Tommy Hausmann is twenty-three years old, and hardly more than a boy. His first day at the station six months ago, fresh from training, he remembers Abernathy asking him whether he was lost. He hadn't put on his uniform yet, or been issued his gun, and he must have looked like a scared teenager. It still rankles now, but if anything, it makes him more determined to prove himself. He comes from a big German family, the youngest of six brothers, all of whom are bigger, tougher, harder than him. He's the runt of the litter. He's tall like they are, but stringy, skinny, with none of their bulk to bolster him. His oldest brother, Hank, would make two of him. Of all them, though, he's the one with the biggest dreams. He harbors visions of becoming a real detective one day, in a real city with real crimes to solve. Then they'll have to respect him. Then they'll have to treat him like a man. It's all he's ever wanted: to feel like their equal. This is the first time he's ever been confronted with something as truly horrible as a murder, and he finds himself starting to wonder if he's up to it after all. He hasn't seen the body – not in the flesh, anyway – only a photograph of the dead woman's icy face. It's not even as if she was shot or stabbed or mutilated. In fact, in the photograph, she looks serene, peaceful even, but that was enough to turn his stomach. It made him feel small, pathetic – unequipped.

If that's true, he might as well quit now, he thinks. If one murder is all it takes, then he might as well go along to his brothers this second and tell them they were right the whole time – that he really is a little pussy, who can't even stand the sight of blood, never mind a dead body. But he knows he's not willing to do that. He's not ready to admit it to himself yet, let alone anybody in his family. The day he told them he'd been accepted for police training was the one day he can remember throughout his entire life when his family actually seemed proud of him. It's a powerful feeling. It spurred him on when he thought he couldn't handle the physical side of the job, kept him from giving up on his training, kept him pushing himself as hard as he could. This case is his chance, then. This is his time to prove himself, to prove he really can do what he set out to do. So he keeps pushing forward, forcing himself to stare at Sarah McIntyre's lifeless face, to trawl through the sad, sordid details of her life, hoping to find some clue.

This is grunt work: he knows that. Tiny as the town is, Showalter and Legler are the only two experienced cops on the force besides Abernathy and of course, they have the bigger tasks – questioning potential witnesses, gathering evidence – but he quietly believes he might just find something before they do. Maybe he'll find Seth McIntyre. Maybe he'll even find something to give them reason enough to get a warrant and search Jimmy Murphy's place. Then they can prove it was him and everyone can rest easy again. They'll make the arrest, of course. They'll cuff him and take him into custody and get on the front page of the local newspaper, but he'll know. He'll know he was the one who cracked the case. The only problem is he's not sure Murphy is the one who killed her. He knows what Showalter and Legler think – he's heard them talking about it between themselves – and he's pretty sure even Abernathy has his suspicions. But something doesn't sit right about the whole thing. Something doesn't quite add up. There's a key piece of this puzzle missing, and he's determined to figure out what it is.

He vaguely remembers the McIntyres. Seth, the father he's trying so hard to find now, was a big, silent man, with a law practice in town. Funny, he thinks. He probably knew more secrets than anyone – knew who was getting cut out of whose will, knew who was divorcing who, knew who was in trouble with the law, or about to be. He could have held almost anyone in the town to ransom, and he wasn't under any obligation to any of them – not like, say, a priest. He could have spilled the beans any time he wanted, and then he upped and left. That must have made a lot of people very nervous. All those dirty little secrets in all those backyards, and he took them all with him. Not even Abernathy has that kind of power.

"Where did you go, Seth McIntyre?" Hausmann whispers. He stares at the computer screen, scanning through all the little details that make up the life Sarah was leading in Chicago. She has a rap sheet a mile long and he lets out a long, low whistle, reading through it: there are at least twenty arrests for solicitation, a dozen for disorderly conduct, five or six for possession, and one for indecent exposure. It seems a lot of the time the charges didn't stick, though, and it looks like the longest she's ever spent in jail is a few days. She'd abscond or there wouldn't be enough evidence or she'd pass out while she was in custody so she'd have to be taken to the hospital, and one way or another, she'd slip through the cracks. It's a sad story but he can't help being surprised it ended this way. As far as he can see from the picture he's managed to piece together, right before she died, she was getting back on track. She had a job, a permanent address – a life.

Frustratingly, after Sarah turned eighteen, there are no references anywhere to Seth, nor to any family at all. Her mother died a few years back, and if there's anyone left on her side, they weren't in Sarah's life. It looks like she completely cut ties with all of them right around the time she started getting into trouble with the cops on a regular basis. Once she hit her twenties, there's a long stretch where it seems like she didn't have any known associates at all. Pimps and dealers drifted across her path from time to time, but it's not until near the end of her life that a name sticks out. Several references emerge to a Jacob Christie, whom she apparently met at a rehab clinic – there are records of both of them at the same treatment facility in downtown Chicago at the same time. It's clear there was some kind of relationship between them: in her other records, too, his name pops up again and again. Christie is the cosignatory on a loan application, a character witness at a court appearance, a reference to a landlord. He's even the second name on a joint checking account.

More than that, Christie has a pretty impressive criminal record of his own. He's in a different league to Sarah, of course – rich, privileged, able to pay fancy lawyers to help him escape punishment on technicality after technicality. His record makes for interesting reading, though. There are at least ten counts of disorderly conduct, one for criminal trespassing, a few for affray, and one for assault, but almost no consequences, it seems. The heaviest punishment he's ever been saddled with is community service. Most of his arrests seem to have happened while he was under the influence of one substance or another, too, leading up to the court-ordered rehab that put him in Sarah's path. His rap sheet stops around the time he crops up at the same rehab center as her, but it looks like he has a nasty temper, based on the arrest reports. Suddenly a little light comes on in Hausmann's head.

"Him..." he says out loud.

He saw those two motherfuckers outside the church, clear as day – saw them talking to Chief Abernathy, all quiet and serious. One of them has to be involved. He knows it.

Brian Kowalski is not a smart man, nor a particularly good man: he's made his peace with this. A lion doesn't change his roar, he thinks, and he doesn't see any special reason to try. He's hot-tempered, rash, always quick to turn to his fists when he can't think of a better solution to a problem, which is most of the time. He's not funny or especially friendly – in fact, most people are at least a little afraid of him. His idea of a joke is to fart in someone's face. He's thick-necked and abrasive, a trait common among his friends, most of whom he's known all his life, and he's good for very little other than menial jobs and getting into brawls at Mawhinney's after a few too many beers. But he knows right from wrong and if one of those two losers had something to do with killing that girl, something has to be done about it. He doesn't have much faith in the cops – one skinny little girl, one skinny little boy, two know-nothing city types and the old man – and if they can't get it done, he damn well will.

Part of him wants it to be Paul Gallagher, wants to see that fucking cissy destroyed once and for all. He feels cheated by the fact he wouldn't get to see him fry, but he might at least rot in jail for the rest of his sorry life, and that's almost as pleasing a prospect. Kowalski hates him deeply, inexorably, with a conviction he usually reserves for the few people who've ever beaten him in a fight and for Democrats. Gallagher is a special case, though. Whenever he thinks of him or sees him in the street, a powerful, wretched rage boils under his skin. It fills up every sense, every sinew and he can't get away from it. Gallagher wronged him in a way he can't fully articulate and in a way he knows he can't forgive. So if he ever gets a chance to exact a little revenge, and be justified on top of that – well, wouldn't that be sweet.

It wasn't always like this. He didn't used to be this angry, this full of hate. He's always had a temper but he got by ok. He never really let it get the better of him, never really got out of control the way he does now. Other than the people he used to pick on in school, no one was really afraid of him. They knew better than to piss him off, but they used to say hi to him in the street, used to smile back if he smiled at them. A few of them even used to like him. There's not much to smile about anymore. He's been in fights – more than he can count – but he'd stop himself before he did any real damage. Now, he finds he'll keep swinging long after the fight should have been over. It's more than just getting payback. He wants to inflict pain, to try to quiet the screaming rage inside him.

He can't remember exactly when the last good part of him died. It was gradual – so much so, he hardly even knew it was happening. One day, he just woke up and it was gone. He didn't even feel it go. The last little piece of his innocence – the last part of him with the capacity to let go of resentment and reproach – just faded away. Now, he stores all of it up until he can't stand it anymore and he blows his top. There aren't many men in town who haven't landed in the hospital at his hand, and he thinks of that fact with a weird mixture of pride and guilt. He does know it started right around the time he and Gallagher parted ways. They were friends as teenagers – good friends, best friends even, so much so he was willing, more or less, to overlook Gallagher's friendship with Murphy – but he can't go back to that. Not now. Not ever.

If he thinks about it, of course, he can see it's pretty unlikely that Gallagher had anything to do with it, other than maybe covering for Murphy. Gallagher doesn't go near girls, of that he's sure, and the way they found her, the way she was dressed, it had to do with sex. He's watched enough cop shows that even he can see that. It has to be Murphy, he thinks. He can't prove it – he doesn't have the smarts – but the whole thing stinks. Even if he didn't actually do the deed, the scrawny sack of shit must have had some hand in it: he did something to put her in the way of getting killed. And if he did, then Gallagher knows what it is. It all swirls together inside his head and he can't make much sense of it, but the idea that the two of them – and Murphy especially – are to blame is slowly crystallizing.

It's not just that the cops can't do anything. The cops won't do anything about it, Kowalski decides. Stupid, liberal-leaning fuckers, he thinks. They'll take weeks just to get off their sorry asses and try and figure it out. So somebody else has to, and it might as well be him. He looks over at the woman in his bed, making sure she won't wake up when he picks up the phone. She's out cold – she must weigh all of ninety-eight pounds and she downed a pitcher and a half of beer earlier that night. He'd been mildly impressed until she puked all over the dash in his truck. He needed to get his kicks, though, and she still seemed willing enough as they stumbled into his tiny apartment. Rolling her over, he reaches for his cell phone, deciding which of his buddies he should trust with this. There are plenty of guys in town who share his loathing of both Murphy and Gallagher – guys he grew up with, who haven't really grown out of their high school personas, who hate Murphy just for being Murphy, small, skinny, twitchy. They hate Gallagher for reasons less amorphous than his own, but he lets them think his motives are the same as theirs.

Andrew Mitchell is a good bet, he concludes. It's not long since Gallagher pounded seven shades of shit out of him, on Murphy's account no less. He owes him, too – it was Kowalski who fought Gallagher off. It felt good to do it – Gallagher is one of the few people who can match him physically, even he can admit that. He landed a solid right-hook to his jaw, knocking him down into the filthy snow outside Mawhinney's. Right after it happened, something shifted inside him. The memory drifts back to the surface: he remembers standing over his former friend, remembers how strong the urge was to stretch out his hand and help him up. He physically shakes himself to get it out his head before he makes the call.

"Hey, Mitchell?" he says. "Got a job for ya. Need you to keep an eye on that skinny little fucker."

It's not long before the whispers start – less than twenty-four hours, maybe. In the days that follow, Sally can feel their eyes on her when she goes to the grocery store, hear them muttering to each other in the pews behind her when she goes to church. She's been going to mass daily, but it's becoming unbearable. Everywhere she goes, it's there – that judgment, that revulsion – and nowhere more so than in the church. She hasn't felt it this strongly since she was a teenager. The judgement there is worst of all, heightened by the presence of the priest. She knows what they think. They think her husband is guilty. They think he killed that girl, and that means, by extension, she's just as bad for carrying on living with him. Even at the school, in the silent, empty library, there's no solace. As soon as that damn meeting was over, the kids there will have heard from their parents about that monster Jimmy Murphy. They saw him with the chief and they made up their minds then and there. They've tried and convicted him before he's even been arrested. She knows it. Now, their children, so young, so receptive to their parents' bile, will be storing up their hatred, too.

In some ways, that's worse. Whenever things were hard with Jimmy, she'd always had her job to turn to for sanctuary: she could work extra hours, or even just use her master key when the school was closed to sit between the darkened stacks when she couldn't face going home. Since she started working at the school, she's always been blissfully anonymous – the faceless custodian of the books the students barely use. Now, they seem to be coming in just to whisper and point, and it's like being sixteen all over again. She wants to tell them all to mind their own damn business, to let the police do the detective work, but she doesn't have it in her to fight on his behalf. Besides, she tells herself, it's probably all in her imagination. She's just being paranoid. Surely they have better things to do, better things to gossip about.

With the best will in the world, she can't keep the doubt at bay. It scares her how fast it takes her over. Something's changed in her and all of a sudden, she just knows. Deep down, in her heart of hearts, she's stopped believing in him – maybe never did. When she doubted him before, she'd only have to think of the day he proposed to her. He told her she was the best thing that had ever happened to him, told her he wanted her for the rest of his life. She'd conjure up those words and any niggling little worry about him would fade away. Now, it's as if a door has been opened in her mind. All too quickly, it crept up on her, took her by surprise: a crack at first, and then at last, flung wide, as though someone had kicked it down. The whispers, the pointing, the blaming – it all slithered into her mind, leaving nasty, poisonous seeds and now it's taken root. She'd thought at first that her love for him would be enough – that she could never think such a thing of him, that trusting him was a matter of course. For years, she'd kept that door closed, kept her shoulder pressed against it to keep them out. Jimmy's never been a well-liked man – in fact, Paul Gallagher's his only real friend – but she never cared what anyone said or thought about him. She ignored his flaws, ignored what was right in front of her. All that mattered was that they were together, and she wouldn't let anyone take that away from her. But now, more strangely than anything else, it's as though all the talk among her neighbors is letting her see him as they see him – to see him as he really is, for the first time.

She's having a hard time trusting Jimmy even to come home when he says he will and she's spending more and more time sitting in their tiny living room with the lights out, staring into the gloom, with nothing but her ever darkening thoughts for company. Katie, despite what she'd said, has yet to show up, and Sally has never felt more alone. Bit by bit, she's coming to believe that the man she married isn't who she thought he was anymore – probably never was – and the fear of what he might be capable of is only getting worse. She doesn't say it to his face – doesn't even force him to sleep on the couch, since she's barely slept herself in the last few days – but without meaning to, she's pretty much lost all her faith in him. She doesn't want to think it, doesn't want to believe her whole life with him has been a lie, but all sorts of horrible scenarios dance inside her head like little red demons. Maybe he tried to force himself on her. Maybe she said no and he got mad. Or maybe it was an accident. Maybe he panicked and thought he could make it look like some sick serial killer did it. Maybe he burned the clothes she was wearing in their own backyard.

She's tried desperately to come up with another answer, but she can't make one appear. Everything she comes up with seems weak, implausible. The fact is, he *could* have killed her. She can see that now, and if he could have, then maybe he did. She can't make herself believe he doesn't have it in him anymore. On purpose or otherwise, he could have been the one who did this to her. *He killed her.* She lets the words form, and they begin to rattle around in her head like a distant train, always approaching, never passing.

Once the thought has taken hold, it's as if she's walking around in a lurid waking nightmare. All of a sudden, everything seems bright, hard, painful. She can't even look Jimmy in the eye anymore and she finds herself coming up with excuses to spend less and less time in his company. Even grocery shopping is an escape and they now have more boxes of eggs and cartons of milk than she knows what to do with, or even has room for in the fridge. All too quickly, it becomes almost a compulsion: any time she wants to get out, sometimes two or three times in a day, she'll come up with something else they've run out of that needs to be replenished immediately. "It's almost Christmas," she tells him. "We need to stock up."

Of course, the gallons and gallons of milk spoil, the dozens of eggs rot, and the dozen loaves of bread grow fuzzy white mold. They have far more than they could ever hope to consume and when she runs out of room in the fridge, the food sits in their damp, overheated kitchen – Jimmy never did fix that damn boiler. She finds herself taking at least a dozen trips to the garbage cans outside their house to get rid of the sulfurous stink. That, of course, only makes things worse. "What must be going on in that house?" she hears them whisper. "There must be something rotten in there." And she believes it. The house feels evil.

She lies down beside the man she thought she loved and trusted more than anyone else in the world, and it hangs over her in a sick fug, heavy, suffocating.

It's not until a few days later that she finally hears something to make her think maybe there's a different explanation for what happened to Sarah McIntyre. She's in the bathroom at the supermarket, during one of her twice-daily trips there, when they come in. She's already in the stall, but she can hear them: two women, deep in conversation, coming in only a few seconds behind her. It's one of those strange serendipitous moments that she might at one time have called fate. That she should be safely hidden inside a stall when they come in, that it should be these two, that she should be able to hear every word: it's a beautiful coincidence, despite the circumstances.

It's Kathy Rafferty and Lorelei Lefferts – she recognizes their voices from her church group, and the two are notorious. She well knows their taste for anything the least bit salacious, not to mention their uncanny ability to dig up dirt before anyone else. Very little gets past them, and that which does probably isn't worth knowing. The two are middle-aged housewives – Kathy, a little mannish, thickset, platinum haired, is a few years older than Lorelei, who's small and birdlike, with beady, suspicious eyes – and more than once, Sally has found herself admiring them for their capacity to find joy, however shameful, in their small, limited lives. Their thirst for knowledge doesn't stray beyond the bounds of the town; that's enough for them, and Sally envies them that.

Keeping completely still, she grits her teeth while she waits for them to finish their conversation. She hasn't even sat down yet and she takes the opportunity to perch on the closed lid, tucking her feet up underneath herself as quietly and as quickly as she can. She doesn't dare come out of her stall and let them know she's been listening, but more than anything else she wants to find out what they've heard. The tastiest piece of gossip in years – maybe even in their lifetime – has landed right in their laps: they're bound to be ahead of the curve. Sally holds her breath and waits.

"You know Seth McIntyre's back in town," Kathy says, more than a hint of triumph in her voice at the possession of this piece of information. There's an audible gasp from Lorelei, apparently disappointed her friend beat her to the punch on this one, and Sally feels herself twitch as she tries not to make a sound.

"No!" Lorelei says, in a hammy stage whisper. She's always been such a drama queen. Sally pictures her jaw dropping theatrically and she can't help rolling her eyes. "How d'you know?"

"Saw him with my own eyes. He was in the cemetery, by Alice's grave, when I was shovellin' the snow at the church," Kathy says. Sally can almost see her nodding for emphasis, waiting for her friend to react, both to the news and to the not-so-subtle self-congratulation. Silently, she pictures Kathy, with her broad, masculine shoulders, industriously shoveling the walkway near the cemetery, thick woolen hat on her head, men's gardening gloves on her hands, stopping and staring without a moment's thought for subtlety when she saw Seth McIntyre. The image is so comical, she almost laughs.

"No kiddin'!" Lorelei exclaims. "You think he knows...you know, about what happened to Sarah?" Everything is quiet for a second, and then Sally hears the two of them head into adjoining stalls. She suspects Kathy is also trying to build a little more suspense.

"Knows? O' course he does! Heck, I think he did it!" she hisses through the partition. At this point, Sally very nearly gives herself away, only just stopping herself from breathing in audibly.

"But I thought Jimmy Murphy...?" Lorelei ventures, evidently not ready to concede to her friend's greater knowledge just yet.

"Well, there's still a chance he had somethin' to do with it, o' course, but you've seen that little bag o' bones. You really think he could even hardly knock anybody over, let alone kill 'em?" There's another pause in which Lorelei seems to think about this. Sally pictures her small mouth twisting, as she considers the question. This is probably as pensive as she ever gets.

"Listen, I'm tellin' you, it's Seth. You know they left town 'cause she got knocked up, right?" Another gasp from Lorelei. "Well, I heard she started gettin' in all kinds o' trouble after that. Parties, booze, the whole bit. Think about it. That'd be enough to make any father crazy, plus you know how religious he was. He musta followed her back here, banged her over the head and then left her in those weird clothes. Looked like she was wearin' a baptismal gown, don't you think? You know, like he was cleansin' her or something?"

"I bet you're right!" Lorelei says. "Gee, I wonder if the chief knows?" There are two flushes in quick succession, and then silence for a good thirty seconds after this as they two of them step outside again. Sally imagines Kathy shrugging at her friend, shooting her a knowing look, then the sound of the faucet running and the women's footsteps as they head for the door. She gives it another full minute before she emerges from the stall, wide-eyed and shaking, wishing she could find out if there's any truth to what she's just heard.

Mary Callaghan nearly jumps out of her skin when the phone rings. Following their latest fight, her boyfriend has been gone more than a week now, and the house has been deadly quiet ever since. It was about the pregnancy – he'd called her, all indignant that he'd had to hear about it from someone else, demanding to know why she hadn't said anything to him, and she'd told him, as much out of spite as anything else, that she wasn't even sure she was going to keep it. Her father has been particularly fond of referring to him as a lowlife despite never having met him, and this will only add fuel to the fire, she thinks. Part of her is disappointed, then, when it's her father's voice at the other end of the line.

"Hi Daddy," she says, trying to hide it.

"Hi sweetie. You by yourself tonight?" His sounds somewhere between worried and hopeful, and she immediately knows what he must be thinking.

"Yeah. Look, I know people are saying that woman looked like me, but I'm fine, I swear." Word had got to her pretty quickly – a friend in town had called right after the meeting to tell her the cops had found the dead woman and that the dead woman could have been her twin – and since then, she's been trying to convince herself it's just a coincidence. "Besides, I'm way out here in Ashland – it's totally safe." She hears herself say it, but even she doesn't quite believe it. When Abernathy held up that picture at the town meeting, her friend had said, he might as well have been holding up a picture of her. Now, it's impossible to shake the feeling that her own face might somehow land her in the same position as her dead doppelganger.

She's alone now – completely alone, since her nearest neighbor is an eighty-four-year-old woman with five cats and a barely functional hearing aid – and it's the first time that fact has made her feel really unsafe. The thought that a woman who looked so much like her had been out there somewhere, and that someone had hated her enough to do that to her, fills her with a hard, cold fear – much worse than anything she ever felt living in San Francisco. There, there was always a sense of being one step removed from any real violence, even if it happened right on her doorstep. That'll never happen to me, she'd tell herself. I'm too careful, too smart. This, though – this feels far too close to home. This feels personal.

Beyond all that, it's nights like this – cold, blustery, the wind whistling through the clapboard of her grandmother's old condo – that she always misses the bright, garish warmth of California, despite everything that happened there. She misses the roar of the ocean, the sound of the traffic rushing by her bedroom window. She misses the good coffee and the good bookstores. She never thought she'd end up here, living in the home of her father's mother, whom she never even met, away from everything that made her feel safe and happy. California was her own mother's domain – of course it was – but it was the only real tie she had with her, and for all her anger and resentment, it made her feel close to her in a way nothing else could. The life, the vitality of the city reminded her of her mother when she was at her best: full of fun, full of love and adventure. Here, though, it's so quiet, sometimes all she can hear is her own breathing. Some nights, she lies awake until dawn, just waiting for a sound to remind her there's something alive out there. It's worst of all when it snows and the heavy white blanket deadens the world around her even more. When the child comes along, of course, all that will change. She'll be alone with this tiny, defenseless little creature, with no one to protect them. There's a pause and her father sighs.

"Listen, Mary, there's something I need to tell you. I should have told you a long time ago, but…well, it all happened so many years ago, way before I ever met your mother, and I just… I never…"

"Daddy? What is it?"

"Frank? You're awful quiet. You still thinkin' about that poor girl?" Elizabeth says, as they sit down to dinner. A couple of days have passed and nothing has really changed, other than Hausmann's hunch on the boyfriend, and even that has yet to come to anything. The kid managed to turn up a phone number, but when he tried to call, there was no reply. All he can hope for is some hard evidence, but Showalter and Legler's efforts have so far been fruitless, too. It's as if she was a ghost before she even ended up out there in the snow.

Abernathy sighs, fearing a dead end is looming and with no other leads to speak of other than the fact that Jimmy Murphy happened to kiss her the night she died, he's starting to feel like he's beating his head against a brick wall. They haven't found the clothes she was wearing when she was killed, or any of her belongings at all, despite combing a two-mile radius around where her body was found, and they don't have enough yet to go poking around Murphy's place. What's worse, they can't seem to figure out what she was doing in town, or what her movements were before she came to the bar that night. She wasn't staying at the hotel and she didn't go into the diner or the grocery store or anywhere in town. She didn't spend any money or even make any phone calls. He has this sense that if he could just figure out *why* she was there, that would make everything somehow fall into place. He has Showalter and Legler talking to pretty much everyone who could conceivably have seen her, has Hausmann combing over every scrap of CCTV, but nothing is turning up. No one remembers seeing her, and she doesn't seem to have been caught on camera either. Now, he feels like he's failing Sarah, failing the town – failing himself. There are no answers, and without answers, there can be no justice. Besides that, or maybe because of it, he's been seeing ghosts of Seth McIntyre's face everywhere he goes, just as live and large as if he were really there – but he can't tell a ghost that his daughter is dead. He looks over at his wife, her kind, sympathetic eyes searching his face.

"Not just that," he says. "I think...I don't know, maybe I'm goin' crazy, but I swear I've been seein' Seth McIntyre all over town lately." She cocks her head to the side, urging him wordlessly to go on. It's one of the things he loves most about her: her ability to get him to talk. In thirty-five years of marriage, you could count the number of disagreements they've had on one hand and he credits a good portion of that to her. She'll quietly reach for his hand or kiss him lightly on the cheek and suddenly everything will seem clear. Right from when they were first dating, it's been like that. He remembers the day he saw her for the first time, as clear as if it were yesterday. She was standing outside St Joseph's on a sunny Sunday morning, talking to a girlfriend, and when he first laid eyes on her, he found her so beautiful, he thought he might cry. It was strange. They'd gone to high school together – he remembered her name when she introduced herself later – but he'd never noticed her before. He didn't admit it to her until years down the line, but it took him weeks to pluck up the nerve even to speak to her, let alone ask her out. Abernathy has always found it hard to express himself. He's the oldest of four boys and stoicism was a family trait. But Elizabeth, with her mild blue eyes and sweet, heart-shaped face, has an uncanny knack for encouraging him to open up. And that smile. God, that smile.

"The other day, for example – my hand to God, I saw him in the cemetery. And then today, I thought I saw him in the parking lot at the station," he says, turning away from her as the filmy image of his face flickers in front of his eyes. "Honestly, Lizzie, I think this case is getting to me already." She touches his arm, giving it a gentle squeeze.

"Hon, did you ever think maybe you're not goin' crazy – that maybe...he really did come back here?" she ventures. He shrugs and quirks his eyebrows. The thought had naturally crossed his mind, but it had seemed too odd that the man wouldn't say anything. He thinks about the way he'd react if he ever got news like that, and it just doesn't add up. It made more sense to think he was seeing things.

"Maybe," he says. "But why wouldn't he say anything?"

"Maybe he's scared, or in shock or something," Elizabeth says. "I'd be willing to bet you'll see him again. Maybe next time you should try talking to him." Abernathy sighs again, hoping she's right, but he's not sure he believes it yet.

"I think I better call another meeting, see what I can shake out," he says.

Sarah shot up for the first time when she was eighteen, right after Seth kicked her out. She only had a few dollars to her name and no place to go. She'd found herself in some kind of halfway house, surrounded by people already deep in the abyss. Broken, hopeless, angry she closed her eyes, shrugged her shoulders and cast her lot with theirs. That was her road. That was where it started. She could pinpoint it to the minute, and she immediately blamed him for it. A hard little seed of resentment was already putting down roots inside her and it was as much a way to get back at him as anything else. She was committed to it. See, Seth. See what you made me do.

By twenty, she wasn't Sarah anymore, or not really. One by one, everyone who'd ever cared about her or thought she could be something else had drifted out of her world, and then that world, the one where there was love and safety and hope, fell away beneath her feet – and she let it. She let herself disappear. She might as well, she thought.

For a while, still just below the rim of the abyss, she could see it – a bright circle of light above her, just out of reach. But the further she slipped, the smaller the light became, until it was just a pinprick at the periphery of her vision. Already addicted, she gave up. All she wanted was oblivion. In those early days, it felt like the only way. This was her path and she had to follow it. She'd started stripping to support her heroin habit, and at twenty-one, she found herself on a street corner without even thinking about it. It was almost like a compulsion – like someone terrible and powerful was making sure she stayed on the road to hell. Pimps came and went, wringing her out and then casting her aside, but mostly, she was alone. She existed at the edges of life, always clinging to the outside of the wheel. To normal people, she was all but invisible, a flicker of movement, half-seen and then forgotten. They ignored her, or pretended to, for fear of the weight of comprehending her.

Sometimes, it almost made her laugh, in a sick, deathly way, to think about what her life had become: she was a cliché. She'd turned into every parent's worst nightmare, a living checklist of wrong turns. It had been so easy, too, to drift out of the world. To disappear. She imagined some greater power – God, whoever – clipping her out, like a picture from a magazine, shutting her away in a drawer somewhere. There was the world, she thought, and then there was the abyss. It was imperceptible to anyone but those who lived in it, a shadow encircling everything, full of the people who didn't belong – criminals, addicts, whores. People who'd never be *normal*. People you didn't want to see – so you didn't. Ghosts.

For the most part, she could numb herself to it, detach herself from the reality she'd slipped into. She could close her eyes and she was in the oblivion of space, bodiless, blank, a wisp of cosmic dust. In her lowest moments, she found she could still weep. She'd float up out of herself, see her shrunken, frail body, see what she'd done, and she'd weep for herself, for her lot. She'd think about what was and what could have been, what was planned for her and ruined, and feel crushed by the weight of it. Choking. Dying.

At first, some of the men were kind to her. They'd smile at her when she got into their cars. They'd put a hand on her back, tenderly, like a lover. Like a friend. They'd offer to take her away from it all, save her. But when they saw what they'd done, when they looked at her in the hard, unforgiving morning light, they wouldn't come back. Little by little, the ones with any semblance of decency would retreat. They'd see where they'd ended up and they'd cut and run. It was almost like she was a wake-up call for these men – the ones who'd made their own bad choices and needed to be reminded of how low they'd sunk. Of course, the ones who were less chivalrously inclined stuck around. There were the ones who wouldn't pay, or worse, the ones who'd turn violent. At twenty-three, she'd lost count of the number of times she'd been slapped or kicked or beaten. Her nose had been broken, her ribs cracked, her arms fractured. There were times when she'd wake up without any memory of the night before except the pounding around her eyes where some twisted son-of-a-bitch had punched her in the face just to feel the thrill of it.

At twenty-four, Seth found her downtown, holed up in a rotting SRO in Roseland. He'd come there to tell her that her mother had died, and almost turned back without even going inside when he saw the place.

"How did you find me?" she asked, once he'd got up the nerve to go inside the decaying, reeking building and talk to her. There was a powerful smell of marijuana smoke in the hallway, and in her tiny, squalid room, too. He perched on the edge of her one lumpy, sagging chair, and it was almost funny to see such a big man acting so gingerly. But he looked at her with a mixture of horror and sadness, sitting there on her filthy mattress in an old black bra and a torn mini skirt, ribs jutting out painfully, hardly any flesh on her at all, and she couldn't laugh. There they were, those same big, doleful eyes she remembered from her childhood. She knew how she must have looked to him, sallow and sunken-eyed, every trace of her mother's beauty gone, and she almost felt sorry for him, seeing her so ruined.

"I hired a PI." She laughed, humorlessly, and lit a cigarette.

"You know, I thought someone had been following me," she said, inhaling the smoke through her crumbling teeth. Without even flinching, she watched his eyes land on the spent syringe on the floor.

"Are you coming home?" he whispered, forcing himself to look at her again.

"Home? What home?" she snorted, angrily. "You took me away from my home and when I wasn't the perfect fucking daughter, you kicked me out of yours. There is no goddamn home anymore – not for me." In a way, the anger made her feel better for a second. It was a sign she still had some shred of humanity left inside her – some fight. But he must have known it was too late for her. He nodded silently, tears in his eyes as he got up.

"Sarah, please – let me help you. Let me make it right," he begged. He kept his eyes on her, and she had to give him credit for that.

"You can't."

He stared at her, gaze agonizingly steady, until finally, she got up, slowly, slowly, rising carefully on her bruised, spindly legs. She was moving to usher him out, but he stayed put, still staring at her.

"Look, Seth, you shouldn't be here, ok?" she said, as gently as she could. "You don't...you don't belong here. It's...not safe."

"I'm sorry," he murmured. Then at last, he dropped his gaze away from her to the filthy floor, and he turned to leave.

"Seth, wait," she called after him. "You got any money?" He snapped his eyes back up to stare at her again for a moment, disbelieving. But he took a couple of hundred dollars out of his wallet all the same, and she saw his hand was trembling as he gave it to her. Hearing her call him by his name must have hurt him badly – maybe more than anything else. Neither he nor Alice had ever told her the truth about her real father, although of course she knew, and he must have known she knew. There'd been slip-ups along the way – certain things her mother had said or done, photos Sarah had stumbled on in old albums that she couldn't explain – but it had never been said. As far as anyone had ever been concerned, he was her father. Calling him Seth, then, she'd finally made it clear to him just how badly he'd failed her. Even then, even after everything that had happened, she knew he was willing her to call him "Dad".

"Thanks, I guess," she said, flatly, taking the money. She'd expected him to go then but he carried on standing there for another minute, staring at the wall behind her, and finally, it got under her skin.

"Look, I'm sorry, ok? I'm just...I'm not ever gonna be what you want me to be. I never was. You don't want me at the funeral." He smiled, sadly.

"Yes, I do," he said. "Take care of yourself, Sarah – for her sake."

And then he was gone.

She never saw him again after that. Even the PI stopped following her. Eventually, she did regret it, but by then, the light was gone altogether. She'd gotten herself into a tailspin she couldn't get out of, at least not on her own. She'd slipped so far into the abyss that it seemed like there was no clawing her way out, like maybe there never was. Before Seth had come to see her, she'd always been able to convince herself she could stop, she could pull herself back – that there was still some hope left for her, still some little part of her old self that she could hold on to. Some way to get started. Something to salvage. She'd get around to it one day. She'd get back on the right track. She'd be ok. But after her mother died, she slid so far that finally, she was sure there was no way she could ever go back. She was sinking deeper and deeper into the sickness of it, giving the last of herself to it, her body wasted and frail, and at twenty-five, she had her first overdose. At twenty-six, she'd had her second, and she was no longer a person as far as the authorities were concerned: she was just another addict, another irredeemable junkie whore.

At twenty-seven, on the edge of oblivion, something finally snapped inside her. After being found naked and high, in the middle of the day, in a public fountain, she'd been put in court-ordered rehab for the third time. This was it, the judge said – her last chance – and for some reason, it finally stuck. She still wasn't sure she wouldn't waste it, that this wasn't just the end of the road, but the more time passed, the more it took root: she started to think maybe she could do it. She was in her second week there when something finally happened, something to give form to this feeling of hope. Something *good*.

His name was Jacob Christie. He came and sat with her at lunch, without asking permission, without saying anything at all. He just sat there, silently, and she was so surprised, she let him. Then when she couldn't take it anymore and got up to go, he'd grabbed her hand, probably a little more roughly than he meant to, and introduced himself. Caught off guard, she wrenched her hand free and ran away from him, suddenly scared. But the following day, he sat with her again, and the day after that, they started to talk. He felt drawn to her, he said. He couldn't help himself. It was fate, or something like it. It had sounded so kooky at first that she'd almost laughed at him, but she stopped herself. It was…nice.

After that, it became a routine: he'd find her at lunchtime, and they'd keep talking, keep getting to know each other. Then it was dinner and lunch, then cigarette breaks, then watching TV together, then suddenly they were spending all their time with each other. The staff must have noticed, but they never said anything. They must have seen it before, this kind of intense, immediate bond between patients. It was unavoidable. It still felt odd to her, this almost-coupledom, especially with someone like him. But the longer it went on, the more she liked it – the more she liked him.

Jacob was a commodities trader and a recovering cocaine addict. He told her those two things straight up, and then he told her about how he'd ended up there. There was no point in keeping secrets, he said – not in here. She'd nodded, but she still held back a little, at least at first. He was the only man ever to show her any understanding and it felt…wrong, somehow. He was also the first man in a long time to tell her she was beautiful, and, importantly, mean it. He could see her, he said. He could see what she was, what she could be. He brought her smile back, brought her humor, her spark of life back, and it was strange and terrifying and wonderful all at the same time. But she didn't quite trust him – not right away. It took time, and a lot of patience from him, to get there, and when she did, she realized he'd completely changed her.

It was extremely painful when he left the facility at the end of his treatment – too painful. She'd gotten so attached to him, it was like losing a limb. Like losing her mind all over again. For the first few days on her own, she was right back on the edge of the abyss, and she was starting to regret letting him get so close. But even after he got out, he'd come back and see her, reassure her, support her – not just emotionally, but financially, too. Like him, she was only supposed to be there for a month, but he covered the cost of another two. She'd tried to say no, tried to tell him it was too much, that they barely knew each other, but he wouldn't hear it. He wanted her, *needed* her to be well, he said – whatever it took. He loved her, he said, and for all it terrified her, she accepted it.

She began to believe, after three months clean, that there might be some hope for her after all – that maybe she could be a real person again. The ground underneath her was starting to feel solid again. She could stand on her own two feet without fearing it would all fall away, without fearing the abyss – and gently, quietly, she found she was in love, too. For so many years, heroin had been the love of her life. She cocooned herself in its beautiful deadening embrace. The idea of giving that love to another human being had become utterly alien to her. It almost felt like cheating. But it was too powerful to dismiss, too deep to ignore, and too good to give up.

Against all the rules, he let her stay with him after she got out of rehab. It was too dangerous, too co-dependent, her doctor said. But she ignored him. Jacob gave her what she needed, what she'd never had. He gave her stability. He helped her stay in control, helped her with her medication. He let her talk to him, vent her frustrations and her fears, all without judgment. It was weird at first, being there with him, back in that bright sphere of existence she'd been so far removed from for so long. Back in the real world.

She still wasn't used to such kindness and she felt uncomfortably out of place in his big, plush apartment. The space seemed almost scary at first. She could hardly remember the last time she'd been in a room where she could stretch out her arms and not be able to touch opposite walls. But he never made her feel unwelcome, never made her feel like she didn't belong. He even helped her get a job as a waitress at a pizza place down the block from his apartment, acting as a fake reference, conveniently neglecting to mention her criminal record. He encouraged her to quit smoking, to eat right, to start taking care of herself at last. He made promises to her that he actually kept, and she realized no one had done that for her in a very long time. More than that, he made it clear that he wasn't going to let her get away with taking any backward steps. He wasn't going to give up on her. She was his damsel in distress, he said, and he was going to do everything he could to be her knight in shining armor. She couldn't help laughing when he said that – it sounded so corny – but she knew he meant it. He knew what she'd been through better than anybody else because he'd seen it first-hand. He wouldn't judge her. Instead, he'd work as hard as he could to overcome his own shortcomings, his own weaknesses, so that he could be what she needed him to be. She'd given his life meaning, he said. Purpose. She'd given him a reason to be a better man. That was the key, he said. They'd always work to be better for each other's sake.

As the months went by, she started to put on weight again and she was finally able to look in the mirror, for the first time in years, starting to see her old self looking back. The urge to use was still there – probably always would be, she realized. It flared up occasionally if she struggled at work, or Jacob wasn't home to hold her and console her, but it faded day by day. She could live with it. Her treatment as an outpatient was going well – better than she or her doctors had ever hoped – and the more time passed, the more she began to believe she might just be all right. There were lines around her eyes and mouth, and scars on her arms, but she was starting to look healthy – to *be* healthy. She felt strong. She felt *good*. The one thing she hadn't done, though, was fix her crummy teeth: they were yellow and cracked after the abuse she'd put her body through, and every time she opened her mouth, they were there to remind her of that. Jacob had offered – more than offered, all but insisted – to pay for the dental work, but she wouldn't let him. It was important to her that she fixed the damage herself, even if it took months to save up to pay for it. Then she could finally start to feel fully human again. She needed to know she could do it on her own.

Beyond everything else, Jacob was also the first man with whom she was finally honest about her past. There was a root, a reason for everything that had happened to her, and she'd kept it buried deep inside. She hadn't even told her therapist about it. With him, she'd only gone back as far as getting kicked out of the house. He didn't know what had come before and didn't have access to any medical records because she'd been uninsured for so long. But Jacob...Jacob needed to know.

"I had a baby," she said. Just like that. Bare. Unadorned. She took a sip of coffee, and waited. It was a Saturday afternoon, a few days after her final dental treatment, and she'd been reveling in baring her newly restored teeth in a hand mirror, seeing, if not a perfect smile, at least one that didn't immediately bely all her mistakes. They were sitting in his living room, in companionable silence while he flipped through the newspaper, and she'd decided, there and then, that it was finally time to tell him the whole truth – the place it all started, the origin of all the evil that had befallen her – the reason they'd met. He stared at her, startled.

"What, just now?" he asked. She shot him a look and threw a pillow at him.

"Come on, I'm trying to be serious." He held up his hands, apologetically.

"Sorry. Uh… when?" She took a deep breath, clenching and unclenching her fists. It had taken her months to steel herself to tell him the story and once she'd come to do it, she found she hardly knew how to start.

"When I was sixteen. I had… he was adopted," she said, keeping her eyes firmly on his. She took a long, slow breath, and sat up a little straighter, closing her eyes for a second. It was the first time she'd laid it all out and she needed to force herself not to flinch.

"I don't know anything about the people that took him in. I couldn't bear to." She was trying to be as matter of fact as she could, but it was the first time she'd even really thought about it in years, and she found it hurt her more than she was expecting. It was a wound that hadn't healed, even then. Jacob's eyes widened and he whistled, quietly.

"Wow. Who was…?" He broke off, suddenly unsure. It was one of the rare occasions she'd seen him doubt himself. She knew he was questioning whether he should be asking her at all.

"The father? My high school boyfriend." She paused for a second, half amused by his timidity, before she went on, preparing herself to tell him what she'd never been able to tell anyone, even her own mother. She felt a little stab of guilt about that, about the things she'd put her mother through before she died. But she pressed on. "It… it wasn't exactly rape, because I didn't say no and he was my boyfriend, but... I didn't say yes, either." Jacob looked at her with eyes that seemed to ache. There was such love and such pain there that she found she couldn't bear it, and she had to look away as she started to cry.

"Come here," he whispered, reaching his arms out to her. "It's ok now. You're ok now."

Hausmann sits up in bed, looking over at Shelly's sleeping form beside him, and sighs. They've only been dating a few weeks, and already, he's pretty sure he's falling for her. She's funny and smart – much smarter than anybody gives her credit for – but it's hard to have fun and goof around and just be in love when there's so much darkness around them. He feels almost resentful about it. It's as though Sarah, without ever knowing it, has robbed him of the best part of his relationship, of the joy of falling in love. It's not as if he's dated a lot of girls, but the beginning has always been his favorite part – the part where every little touch is electric, every joke hilarious, every story fascinating. For Christmas, he'd been planning to take her down to Iowa City, where his parents are living now, but he knows there's almost no chance they'll get much vacation at all, let alone have the time to make the seven-and-a-half hour drive down there. Now, with this pall hanging over the town, Sarah McIntyre is the only thing anyone can think or talk about – not that it does any good. They chatter and they speculate and they gossip, but they don't say anything. They don't know anything. Nobody does. Just her, and whoever killed her.

He's been trying as hard as his body will let him to find answers, working every hour Abernathy will give him, but everything seems to turn into a dead end. Showalter and Legler aren't turning up much either, which at least makes him feel a little less incompetent, but it's no less frustrating. They still treat him like crap. They started calling him Brain Trust for a day or so, mocking him as he sat hunched in front of a computer screen, but Abernathy put a stop to it pretty quickly. They looked at him with eyes full of resentment and he felt his cheeks flush, face burning. But there's another town meeting coming up on Monday morning, and they have nothing. He doesn't have time to give in to his humiliation.

They still don't have much on Jimmy Murphy, and not much hope of finding anything, either. Hausmann knows the chief likes him for killing Sarah, but their best witnesses are a bunch of beer-brained morons who can barely remember to tie their shoes, much less what they were doing after a night of drinking themselves into oblivion. Their next best shot is the boyfriend, but he hasn't been answering his cell phone and no matter how many times he calls, the Chicago PD hasn't been any help either. Jacob Christie's probation is over, they tell him. He's no longer on their radar – they don't need to keep an eye on him anymore and he hasn't been arrested for anything else. There's nothing to suggest he has anything to do with Sarah's death and there's nothing they can or will do. He could hear the scorn in the voice of Christie's one-time probation officer – a jaded-sounding man named Gil Harrison, whom he finally managed to speak to earlier that day, after hours of going through switchboards and secretaries – and it boils his blood. "We have better things to do," he seemed to say, without actually saying it. "Fuck off, kid."

"Look," Harrison had said, his voice ragged with the crackle and rasp of decades of smoking three packs a day. Hausmann knows that rasp. It's the way his dad's voice sounds now. Harrison had stopped to cough a couple of times and Hausmann was pretty sure he heard him spit. "I'd like to be able to help. I really would. But when they're out of the system, that's it. Far as we're concerned, they paid their debt and they ain't our problem anymore. We gotta move on to the next one."

Hausmann had hung up on him after that, hardly able to believe what he was hearing. He'd told Shelly about it, burning with righteous indignation, but she didn't seem as surprised or as angry as he'd thought she would. He just can't understand why no one seems to care as much as he does about the fact that this woman turned up dead, right on all their doorsteps. Thanks to the countless hours he's spent trawling through her record, he knows more about her past than anyone – about the drugs and the arrests and the horrible things she did and had done to her – and yet he's the only one who remotely gives a shit, as far as he can tell. Of course, Abernathy has always been nigh impossible to read – always measured, always calm, always circumspect – but he'd hoped for something, anything to suggest he had some sense of the tragedy, the injustice of it. It feels as though the burden of the whole thing has landed squarely on his shoulders, and he's not sure he can handle it.

Worse than all that, though, a lot of people are starting to say they've seen Seth McIntyre around town, including Abernathy. It had come as something of a shock when the old man confided that to him. He'd stopped by his desk maybe a day or two ago – it's hard to say when exactly, the days just seem to bleed into one another now – and stood there silently for a minute or so, as though wondering whether he should say what he planned to say. Then he'd simply announced it. He'd seen McIntyre around town and he wanted him to find a way to get a hold of him. He had come to them, Abernathy had said. He'd landed right in their laps. It was up to them to reach out to him. But Hausmann can't seem to find any of trace of him. If he was hard to find when he wasn't in town, it seems he's even harder to find now. He has yet to catch sight of the man himself, and all he has to go on for a frame of reference is a grainy, thirteen-year-old black and white photo from the local paper when it reported on the fact he was shutting down the town's last surviving law office.

If he is back, and Hausmann still isn't convinced he is, he's not staying in the town's one and only hotel, and the last known phone number for him seems to be a cell phone that's never switched on. He's heard stories about the old McIntyre house – that the reason it's sitting empty now is because Seth never sold it, and sure enough, when he looked up the deed, his name was still on it – but when he went to check, no one answered the door and all the lights were out. It was as cold and silent as it always was. It was locked up tight.

He sighs heavily again as he lies back down beside Shelly. Maybe he should just act like they do. Maybe he should stop caring as much as he does. But the fact of the matter is, for all his big dreams and his grand ambitions, he loves this town, and it saddens him deeply to know something so awful could happen here. He's the last of his family still there – his brothers all moved away as quickly as they could find work somewhere, anywhere else, and his parents moved out to Iowa the previous winter, to be closer to his mother's sister – and he's fiercely protective of the town. With its faded, shabby storefronts and its tiny, insular population, it's his home – and someone has wounded it.

"Daddy?" Mary repeats. Her father has been silent for more than a minute and she puts a hand to the small bump just beginning to emerge under her shirt, suddenly protective and afraid at the same time. She never had any intention of getting rid of the baby: she knows that now.

"It's…it's about Sarah…about…the dead girl," he says at last, and she can hear him taking a deep breath. She's never heard him sound this nervous before. Everything he's ever done has been with such force, such confidence that she didn't even know he was capable of fragility. Even when she told him she was pregnant, he'd been completely calm, completely controlled, which is more than she can say for her boyfriend. He has yet to redeem himself and she's starting to think he probably never will.

"What about her?" she asks, swallowing hard. She's not sure what she's expecting him to say, but her heart is already thumping in her chest and she knows it can only be something awful.

"She…she was…I mean, I…" he falters and she hears him sit down on his big, squeaky leather couch.

"Dad, come on, you're scaring me." She finds she has to sit down herself suddenly, her legs shaking, threatening to give way under her. Her father sighs again.

"She was…she was your sister. I was…am…her father." Mary almost laughs then; the words sound so ridiculous.

"What are you talking about?" she asks. "Chief Abernathy said her name was McIntyre – she was Seth McIntyre's daughter. You can't be…"

"No. No, Mary," her father says, more firmly this time. "She was my daughter. I was dating her mother – right before I went out west. Right before she…got married…"

"Come on…that doesn't mean…I mean, how do you know? Maybe her husband…?" Mary breaks off, nausea swelling in her stomach.

"Mary, listen to me. Please," her father whispers, his voice shaking again. "It's true. I knew her mother was pregnant. I knew she was pregnant and I never even told her I knew. I just…left anyway. I was selfish and scared and I told myself it wouldn't be right to stay when I knew I didn't love her anymore. Then I heard she married Seth and I…I thought she'd be ok. Her and the baby. I thought…I don't know, maybe they could be a real family." He sounds like he might be about to burst into tears, but the fear that he might have done something unthinkable is overwhelming her sense of compassion for him.

"What did you do?" she asks, quietly, digging her nails into the palm of her hand.

"Nothing!" her father cries, suddenly defensive. "Mary, you don't really think I…?" He trails off and it takes her a long time to decide what to say.

"I don't know what I think," she says at last. Her heart is pounding.

"I didn't hurt her, I swear. I don't even know if she knew…you know, the…the truth." She lets his words sink in. The strangest part of it, she thinks, is that it's never even crossed her mind that her father could be anything less than perfect – that there might be something below his good-natured, unrufflable surface. She loved his sense of duty as a father, his strength, his smooth, even temper. He'd barely ever yelled at her when she was a kid, and all her life, she'd idolized him, without really thinking about it. It seemed natural to her. He'd been the only constant in her often chaotic world when she was growing up. Most of the girls she'd been friends with back then were starting to say they hated their parents in a meaningless sort of way – the way teenagers do when they don't get what they want. But when they'd bitched about not being allowed to stay out past midnight or getting caught with a boy in their rooms, she'd stayed quiet. As far as she was concerned, her father was the best in the world, and that was that. But now...now.

"Why are you telling me this now?" she asks.

"Because I wanted you to hear it from me. I mean, she looked so much like you – I knew somebody'd notice," he says. She hears him take a slow, juddering breath. "Mary, please...please tell me you believe me. I might be a selfish coward, but I'm not a murderer."

"All right. I believe you," she says. "But Dad, if you're keeping anything else from me, you have to tell me. Right now. Otherwise, I can't trust you anymore. Not ever again."

"Ok," he murmurs, almost inaudibly. "There's one more thing."

"What happened to your daughter?" Katie asked, during a rare lull, one afternoon almost a year after Alma had taken her in. Six months before, she'd helped her get set up in a tiny one-bedroom apartment near the beach, and things had finally stopped feeling so completely hopeless after that. It was hardly Hollywood, but it was quiet and cozy and there was something comforting in that, after the way she'd lived when she was with Donovan. Even the itchy green uniform had begun to bother her less.

Alma, she'd come to believe, was some kind of miracle. For whatever reason, she was supposed to find her. It made her think maybe fate wasn't such an asshole after all. For all Alma's kindness, though – for all her easy, open friendliness – it had taken Katie that long to work up the nerve to ask about her mysterious daughter, and in the end, cursing herself for it, she'd accidentally done it almost as tactlessly as possible.

"She died," Alma said, flatly. Katie had been hoping she might be willing to open up to her without any further questions, and it took her a few minutes to steel herself to press the subject.

"How?" she whispered, not even sure Alma had heard her.

"She drowned," Alma replied, keeping the same flat, hard tone, fixing her eyes on the counter, as though she could see her daughter's face there. She was silent for a long moment and Katie thought maybe she wasn't going to say anything else. "The police called it an accident. She was always so damn reckless, they just didn't question it, but...well..."

"How did she drown?"

"She fell into the ocean. She liked to go out to the Golden Gate Bridge in the middle of the night and climb up on the railing so she could pretend she was a tightrope walker, only…only she'd been drinking…" She stopped for a second, glancing at Katie's grave, earnest face. "They found her when the tide was out, a little ways away."

Katie stared at her, open mouthed, for a good few seconds before she regained her composure. She half-wished she hadn't broached the subject at all, but the curiosity was overwhelming.

"What was she doing in San Francisco?" she asked. Alma smiled, sadly.

"She fell in love." Katie let out a long, slow breath. Finally, a picture was starting to form. Finally, the truth of the situation was starting to creep up on her.

"Oh my god," she murmured. "With John Callaghan." Fate strikes again, she thought. Alma nodded.

"You catch on quick," she said, with a mirthless chuckle. "I knew he could never take care of her. Not really. Not the way her family could. Not the way she needed. See, she was…fragile. She could be standing out in front of the diner singing show tunes one day, and the next, she'd be holed up in her room, bawling her eyes out for no reason at all."

"She was…sick?" Katie whispered, only just stopping herself from saying "crazy".

"You could say that. My, but she was beautiful, though. Usually, the boys would give up after a little while, once they realized she was more than they could handle, but John…well, he was a persistent son of a bitch, I'll give him that. He thought he could save her." She shook her head then, almost as though she was trying to shake off the pain of the memory before she went on.

"They ran away together. Got hitched on her twenty-first birthday. Hell of a thing. He was at Stanford and then I guess he did a little drivin' around on the west coast before he settled down. He was in town two weeks before he went back down to San Francisco – that was all it took. God knows how he fetched up here, though. I never even saw it coming, but she seemed so happy. Really happy, not that wild, scary happy like she used to be. I'd never seen her like that. For a while, I thought maybe they'd be ok. She'd been stable for longer than she ever was, but…well, she got herself knocked up and then all hell broke loose. She stopped taking her meds, stopped seeing her doctor. Then she started…saying things…pulling crazy stunts like she did when she was at her worst…tell you the truth, I never thought she'd make it – her or the baby."

"So what happened after that?"

"Miracle of miracles, she had the kid. A little girl."

"Mary…" Katie whispered. Alma nodded, taking a deep, shaky breath.

"Things calmed down a little after that, but…she was never gonna be able to take care of her. Not really. They were never gonna be…normal," she said. She paused for a moment, steadying herself, and it suddenly occurred to Katie that she might never have told this story to a stranger – or even to another human being – before. "She hung on as long as she could – God love her, she was always stubborn. But she was in and out of the hospital for almost fifteen years, in and out of her little girl's life, in and out of reality. John wanted her on as many pills as they'd let him give her – thought it would keep her safe – but she hated it. She hated being so… fogged up was how she put it. She couldn't take it. It was like it pulled the life right out of her. But without 'em, she'd get out of control. She wound up in a secure unit about a month before she died and she was worse than she ever was…God knows how she got hold of the booze, let alone how she got out..."

Katie could have guessed the rest by then, but something in her told her to let Alma finish the story – that she needed it. She needed to get it out.

"He took the girl away after that – back to East Jesus, Nowhere. He never hardly let me see her anyhow, but…oh, I hated him for that. I hated him for taking away the only piece of my little girl that was left. That was…that was why I got all…all wound up when you said your name was C-Callaghan."

Without saying anything else, Katie reached out to the old woman, putting her arms around her bony shoulders, and let her weep. She wept and wept until thick, black rivers of mascara ran down her face and afternoon turned to evening. Then the dinner rush began, and she wiped her face and never said another word about it.

"What is it? Dad? Come on, you're really scaring me now," Mary says, gripping the arm of her chair hard as she tries to keep herself from throwing up.

"It's...it's about your mom. Look, I...I want you to know that I loved her. I loved her more than anything in the whole world and I never meant..." He breaks off and she can hear him swallow, holding back the tears.

"Dad. Please," she whispers. All sorts of horrible thoughts dance around inside her head, merging together into a nightmarish soup, making her dizzy. Her father swallows again and takes a long, deep breath.

"The reason...the reason she got out... you know, the night she...was because...because I let her," he falters.

"What do you mean, you let her?" Mary asks, feeling her whole body begin to shake as the room starts to spin around her.

"I signed the forms. I told the doctors I was taking her home. She was there voluntarily, so they couldn't...they had to let her go."

"Dad, what are you saying?" There's a long pause, as he tries to collect himself, tries to find the words to explain to her the reason her mother is dead.

"I'm saying...I'm saying it's my fault," he whispers. "She died...because of me. I don't know, maybe she would've done it anyway in the end, maybe it was just a matter of when, not if, but...I helped her do it."

"You mean...on purpose?"

"No! No, God, no! Of course not! But she was so desperate to get out of there, begging me, promising me she'd get better, promising me we could be a family again, I... I couldn't take it. I thought...I don't know, I guess I thought maybe somehow, we'd be ok. Maybe she could really do it – really get better."

"So then...how did she get up on the bridge? And why didn't I know about any of this?"

"You were at your music camp. You remember, I...I had to come get you?" He stops again, letting her think back to that summer – the summer her mother had gone from a mad, bad, sad ghost hovering always at the periphery of her world, occasionally crashing into it and then crashing back out again, to something real and hard and broken that she couldn't make sense of. Through her death, she'd become more present to her than she'd ever been. "You know, I hated doing it, even with...everything. I was so out of it after she...I mean, after the police...I remember thinking you'd be mad at me. Isn't that crazy? You were so sure you wanted to be a clarinetist. I still have pictures of you in your band uniform – you were so determined and I was so proud of you. I never had the heart to tell you that you were totally tone deaf."

"Don't," she says, through gritted teeth. "Don't do that. Not now. You can't. You don't have the right. Not anymore." There's another pause and she hears him take a shaky breath.

"I'm sorry. You wanted to know how she got up there. To tell you the truth, even...even I'm not sure. I just...just wanted to feel free – just wanted her to be free. I let her talk me into getting some whiskey and...God, we both got so drunk and...she used to love it so much...I didn't even think..."

"So...you were there...when she...?"

"Yes."

There's silence for a few more seconds, and then she hangs up, without saying another word. She's torn between grief for her mother, compassion for her father – and anger. In amongst all of it, there's raw, visceral anger. She can't understand how he could do that. Worse than that, he *lied* about it for so many years. She wants to believe him, to believe he couldn't have hurt Sarah, but if he lied about so many other things...

She gives it another few minutes before she picks up the phone again. She knows what has to be done – what she has to do.

"Hello, Mrs. Abernathy? It's Mary Callaghan. Is Chief Abernathy home?"

"I think you should go back," Jacob said, out of the blue one day, while they were picking out paint samples for her new apartment. He'd wanted her to stay with him a little longer, but the fiercely independent part of her was making its presence unignorably felt, pushing her to break out on her own. It was reassuring, she thought, to know that it was still there: to know, after everything, that she was still her.

"Back where?" she asked, comparing a little aster blue card with a little aqua card for what seemed like the nine hundredth time.

"Back home – back to the place you grew up," he said. She stared at him, confused. The thought hadn't even occurred to her.

"What? Why?"

"Because I think it would help you. I think you should confront him."

"Confront who?" she asked, although she knew what he was about to say.

"You know. Your old boyfriend." She sighed, and sat down on the couch, pushing a hand through her hair, which was just beginning to be thick and dark and lovely again.

"Jacob, be serious. I don't even know if he still lives there."

"It's easy enough to find out. What do you think the internet is for?"

"Cats pictures and porn," she said, drily. It was her way: to say something flippant and silly when things became more real than she wanted them to be, to wrest control of the situation with a joke. But this time, he didn't laugh. "You're really serious?"

"I am. I think it'll give you closure. I think you need it." Sarah sighed, dropping her gaze. The fact was she'd thought about it – had gotten as far as putting her hand to the keyboard to search for his name – but she'd never let herself do it. She was too afraid of what would happen if she did. But Jacob was always so sure, so convincing, and once a seed had been planted, it was hard to stop it from taking root.

"Ok," she said. "Ok, I'll do it. I'll do it if you really think I should." She turned to face him then, looking him hard in the eye. "And you're sure you'll be ok without me for a few days? I mean, you don't wanna…come with me?"

The request wasn't just for her own sake. It wasn't something they talked about much, but they both knew she'd been as much help to him as he had been to her. The focus she gave him kept him from sliding back into old habits. She was living proof that he could be good for someone else – that he could be selfless. She knew his own problems, his own demons were just as real and frightening as hers, but his way of dealing with them was far removed from hers. Most of the time, he preferred not to talk about them, and she knew better than to try to force him. But every now and then, he'd wake her in the middle of the night and it would all come pouring out of him. His fears, his frustrations, his sadness would overflow and the only thing she could do was hold him while he wept. The morning after nights like that, he'd be calm and in control again, but she knew he needed that release – to know he had that safety net of love and understanding to fall into when he was overwhelmed or depressed or feeling like he couldn't hold on.

He smiled.

"I'll be fine," he said. "Go."

If she remembered seeing him before they met in treatment, she never said it. But he'd been aware of her for quite a while before that. The first time he saw her, in fact, she was nearly naked, swinging from a pole, already thin and damaged-looking under the cruel colored lights, cheap glitter glinting on her protruding ribs. He'd seen her dancing in a club he couldn't even remember the name of, deep in the dark heart of the city. But he remembered her. He remembered her big, haunted eyes. It felt like she was looking right at him – right through him – and suddenly, he felt naked, too. It was as if she could see all his weakness, all his selfishness. It startled him, made a light flicker on somewhere inside him.

The part of him with the capacity for empathy, to think about anyone other than himself, snapped back to life. He'd thought he'd burned that out long ago, if it had ever been there in the first place. It was like a new heartbeat: a different rhythm, making him suddenly aware of where he was and what he was doing. It was the first time he'd ever thought of one of these women as human. Before, they'd always been one more thing for him to possess, albeit temporarily. He could pay them to do and be whatever he wanted, and then cast them aside when he was done. But she changed that. In the blink of an eye, everything started to feel wrong, alien. It was the beginning of something.

It wasn't immediate. He'd managed to push her from his mind for a little while after that. He'd put it down to some sort of momentary lapse, maybe even something to do with the drugs, and then he'd carried on as he always did. He went back to normal. He'd all but blotted her out, in fact, until a ghostly face, with sad, powerful eyes began to creep into his dreams. She'd come to him at night, a terrible, wounded angel, and whisper his sins out loud. At first, it scared him, and then it started to make him angry. He'd worked hard to kill that part of himself – to stop caring. It was part of what made him so good at his job. He couldn't say when exactly he'd come to that turning point, decided to give himself over to excess and indulgence. But someone, somewhere along the way, had told him he could have whatever he wanted, and he'd taken them at their word. The more money he made, the more he spent and the more dissolute his habits became. The people around him only encouraged him, inflated the feeling of godlike invincibility, stopped him from stopping.

But she wouldn't go away. She was bleeding into every aspect of his life, and he saw his kingdom beginning to crumble. Suddenly, he started to see her everywhere. Her face was there, in every shadow and every corner. It was in the decay and the rot all around his glittering tower block. It was starting to change him, to open his eyes. He knew he needed to atone, and eventually, he'd make her his way to do it. She'd be his totem for everything he needed to make right.

He didn't lay eyes on her again in person until a few months later. He had yet to amend his behavior, despite the way she'd been haunting him – was fighting hard against it, in fact, hardly sleeping or eating, hopping from one club or party or woman to the next. Some part of him still wanted to preserve that life. He wasn't ready to give it up, and it took him a long time to believe what was already happening. The more she haunted him, the harder he partied, the more she haunted him, and round and round and round, until he wound up in the zoo on the roof of the lion house in the middle of the night. It was as he was being led out of one courtroom in handcuffs and she was being led into another that he saw her again. She glanced at him briefly as they passed each other, and there they were – those awful, beautiful eyes. He'd been hauled up for the zoo incident and was expecting to get away with a few hours of community service, which, thanks to his obscenely expensive lawyer, yet again, he did. It wouldn't be long before he could dive right back in. But a seed had been planted in him and after that, it started to take root.

This was still long before he ever spoke to her. Once he got a decent look at her face, he could see she'd been beautiful once – could be beautiful again if she could get healthy – and he knew what he needed to do. He hadn't been spinning her a line when he told her he was drawn to her: he was, all too powerfully. Very quickly, it turned almost into an obsession. He became convinced she'd been put in his path for a reason – that he *needed* to help her, or risk offending some amorphous higher power. So he started following her. He made it his business to find out her name, to find out where she lived, to wait for his moment. He kept an eye on her court dates and made sure he could be there, watching, when she was handed the court order to go into rehab. In one of his wilder moments, he'd thought about paying his lawyer to represent her, but even back then, he could see that would have been too much. She didn't even know who he was yet. He needed to stay quiet, to stay in the periphery of her world, at least at first. She couldn't know.

It wasn't a coincidence that they wound up at the same center. He could have had his pick of treatment facilities – had the money to pay for it and wasn't under any legal obligation – but he twisted arms and greased palms until he landed himself there with her. It was perfect. He'd get clean and then he'd swoop in like a superhero and save her. She was only supposed to be there for thirty days – it was as much as the state would pay for – but he could see that wouldn't be enough, so he'd insisted on paying for another two months. She'd said no at first, but by then, having spent almost every minute with her, he'd already formed the bond with her he'd hoped he would. By then, she trusted him.

It was working. He was helping her. It had been a huge gamble – she could so easily have put up walls, kept him out – but it was paying off. He was making her life *better* for his presence in it. More than that, though, something else was happening, something unexpected. He couldn't explain it right away, but eventually it dawned on him: he was falling for her. His desperate desire to be her savior was rapidly becoming entwined with a strange, complicated kind of love. He hadn't been anticipating it. He knew what he wanted to be to her, but he wasn't prepared for what she would become to him. He'd spent so long planning a way into her world that he hadn't stopped to think what might happen once he got there. She had a strength and a pull beyond anything he'd been counting on. She'd opened the floodgates to a deep reservoir of feeling inside him, and once it started to wash over him, he couldn't hold it back. Without her, he knew he couldn't keep it up. He knew he couldn't keep the good part of himself alive. He knew he couldn't let her go.

Murphy knows Kowalski and his buddies have been following him. They're not exactly subtle about it: they stand around in the corners at Mawhinney's when he dares to show his face there one night, circling him like animals, and once or twice in the last day or so, he's pretty sure they've been on his tail as he drives back from the odd jobs he's managed to pick up before Christmas. There were cars he half recognized, half familiar faces obscured by shadows and heavy woolen hats. They're like predators – jackals maybe, all wicked eyes and bared teeth, waiting to tear the flesh from his bones. He can feel them watching him, feel them judging him. What's worse is he's not even sure they're wrong.

In school, they'd spent so much time beating the crap out of him that he more or less got used to it. Once they graduated and it finally stopped, he found it took him years to stop expecting them to be waiting for him at every turn. It was part of why he'd become so twitchy. The daily threat of violence had been with him for so long that he could never completely shake it.

After high school, they'd left him alone for the most part. They grew up, as much as they were ever likely to, and that meant ignoring him, rather than tormenting him. They'd mutter the odd insult if they saw him in the street, but that was as far as it went. He was nothing to them, not even worth the trouble of hassling, and he'd liked it that way. He could get on with the business of living his quiet, inevitably unfulfilled life in peace. But when they turned on Gallagher, they turned on him. He had his chance to be one of them, to choose their side of the fence, but he didn't. He chose the wrong side, and as far as they were concerned, that made him just as bad as Gallagher. It's the one thing in his life he feels remotely proud of. He didn't abandon his friend, the way everyone else did. He was loyal.

There was a cruelty in them he'd never really realized was there. Before, he'd seen them as aggressive, destructive, but there was no particular malice to it. It was what big, brainless animals did. They asserted their dominance by picking on the weak members of the herd, and he was far and away the weakest. It was inevitable. It was their nature. But the minute one of their own – and Gallagher, with his athletic ability, his size and his strength, had been one of their own – broke ranks, that was when he found out what they were really capable of. It wasn't just routine high school stuff anymore. It died down after a year or so, but in that year, Gallagher landed up in the hospital four times, had his car torched and the most disgusting obscenities spray painted on the side of his house. Murphy helped him scrub the walls down and repaint them the best he could, but even now, in the right light, the scars still show.

Now, he's paying for his loyalty as much as anything else. There's no way to know what would have happened if he'd ditched Gallagher – no way to know if they'd be on his ass the way they are now, no way to know if he'd even have had anything to do with Sarah McIntyre. But if he has to watch his life fall apart, he might as well do it knowing there was one thing he did right. It's been harder since he lost his job, of course. Gallagher's been on him night and day to take a job at the machinery plant, and that makes it harder to dodge questions, harder to lie. But if there's one person he truly wants to think well of him, even in the smallest way, it's Gallagher. And if he takes that job, he knows whatever tiny shred of respect his friend might still have for him will disappear. If he takes that job, there's no way he can hide the fact he's been cheating on Sally for the last six months.

Gallagher has so many conflicting feelings when it comes to Billy that he hardly knows how to handle all of them. First and foremost, there's love. It's a deep, abiding, gut-wrenching love – a love that won't ever fade, no matter how much time goes by. It's in his blood, in his bones. He remembers when they first met, how quickly it overwhelmed him. He's never really believed in love at first sight – still doesn't – but this was pretty damn close. He was in awe of Billy: so free, so sure of who he was, so unafraid. In those first weeks, he did everything in his power just to be near him, and when he wasn't, he physically ached for missing him. He's never known a feeling as intense as this, good or bad, before or since.

Then there's anger: anger at Billy for destroying what they had together, for leaving him alone to face the hatred and the bigotry of his former friends, for showing him he wasn't enough of a reason to stick around. He knew from the beginning that Billy struggled sometimes – that there was a sad, broken side to him that he never fully explained – but Gallagher had always had faith in his own ability to soothe him, to let him know how loved and needed he was. In the end, he couldn't get past the walls Billy put up. He failed, or as he saw it, Billy wouldn't let him succeed. Abernathy told him they'd found his body, already partly decomposed, hanging from a tree in the potter's field a couple of miles outside town. It was July, almost six years ago, hot, humid, fractious, and the old man told him he really oughtn't to come and see the body. They'd had to identify him from his dental records. It wouldn't be right to see him like that, to remember him like that, Abernathy told him.

Gallagher was grateful to him later. Old-fashioned as he was, the old man understood love, understood how important it would be for Gallagher to remember Billy as he was when he was alive. More than that, he was one of the few people who'd never treated him any differently, although it was hard not to direct a certain amount of anger at him. The problem, of course, was that it had taken so long to find him: Billy had a tendency to disappear for days at a time. Gallagher had learned to accept it as part of his self-proclaimed "artistic temperament", but it also meant he didn't start to worry until he'd been gone more than a week.

Then of course there's the anger – the real rage, in fact – that he still holds for Daniel. Billy's death was ruled a suicide more or less immediately, and Gallagher had wanted to have his funeral as quickly as he could. He wanted to be able to mourn for him properly, had wanted to get in touch with his friends out of state so that his life could be celebrated. He didn't have much in the way of family of his own – there was a rift with his parents, something else he never fully explained, and he had no siblings – but he had people who loved him, Gallagher's family included. Even his stoic, staunchly conservative father had eventually warmed to him, something he still finds amazing when he thinks about it now.

It was tough going, he remembers. He'd taken a lot longer to come around than his mother, and he never quite reconciled himself to the idea that the two of them could be as much in love as he was with his wife. It was an idea as completely alien to him as Sunday without church or Thanksgiving without turkey. But Jenny had talked to him – to this day, she won't tell him exactly what she said – and slowly, slowly, he began to soften. Finally, he'd been as friendly and open to Billy as he was to anyone, in his own gruff, blundering way. But Daniel had encouraged him not to do it – had all but forbidden him from having the service at the church in point of fact, implying people wouldn't take kindly to it, for reasons he didn't need to articulate. In a small, reactionary town, populated mainly by unyielding, right-leaning Christians, he didn't need to explain what he meant. Gallagher knew all too well. The scorch marks on his drive way and the spray paint on his walls had already told him. But the idea that Daniel had robbed him of a real funeral was too much to bear, and the last of his faith dried up not long after that.

For all Abernathy's careful protection, it didn't stop the nightmares. Billy's face, as he imagined it must have looked when he was found, would come to him in his dreams, blackened and shrivelled, lips curled back around his teeth, eyes bulging from shrunken sockets. He'd stare at him, demonic, almost unrecognizable, silently reproaching him for not missing him sooner. For months after his death, Gallagher would wake up almost every night, sweating, shaking, crying. It was slowly breaking him, but he hardly ever let it show. Instead, he hid at work, putting in more overtime hours than he had in his life. It was how he learned how to numb himself to it all. There, no one really knew anything about him. There, he could pretend.

Underneath all that, and most painfully of all, there's a lingering sense of resentment. Gallagher has always known he was different, but before Billy, he didn't really understand it. Had it not been for him, he probably never would have. He would have lived his life alone, muted, never knowing who he really was. But Billy – he brought it out in him, brilliantly, fiercely, inescapably. He thinks of that line in the Simon and Garfunkel song, from a record that belonged to his parents, played often in his childhood and etched into his memory along with so many other useless things – if I never loved, I never would have cried. He could have gone his whole life without this. He need never have known what it was to love someone like Billy, much less have him taken away. He would have been alone, but he never would have felt pain like this. He wishes he could squash this feeling the way he's been able to squash the others, to push them down so that he can function day by day, but it won't go away, and that, on its own, is worst of all.

They met ten years ago, when Gallagher was barely twenty, and Billy, a few years older, had found early success as a writer. A native Chicagoan, he'd been living in New York after going to college there, and had written two novels, both of which had won critical acclaim. Comparisons were even being drawn – he didn't like to brag, he said – with Faulkner and Fitzgerald. His star was on the rise and he was on his way to writing a third novel when he abruptly decided he needed to leave the city. He wanted somewhere quiet, somewhere anonymous, where he could focus on his work, he said. He'd pitched up there in a little old Figaro, pea-green in color, and immediately stood out. Gallagher remembers clearly seeing the car before he saw the man and feeling an unfamiliar kind of thrill. Somehow, he knew that someone new, different, exciting had landed in their little backwater. He'd been living a strange kind of half-life up to that point, pretending to be as interested in girls as his friends were, yet unable to explain, even to himself, why he wasn't. He never could fully quantify why the pea-green Figaro had filled him with so much hope, but everything changed after that.

    He first spoke to Billy in Mawhinney's, where he was doing his best to drink a bottle of Pabst and not look like he was hating every sip. Gallagher had seen him go in and had determined, with surprising decisiveness, to go inside and find him. He was alone, sitting at a table in the darkest corner of the bar, clearly trying to look inconspicuous and failing utterly. He stuck out a mile against the thickset, empty-eyed men, most of whom wouldn't know Faulkner or Fitzgerald if they rose from the dead to spit in their eye. Tall, slender, with big, expressive, almost feminine brown eyes, and unkempt, chestnut-colored hair, Gallagher remembers even now how struck he was by Billy's beauty. He was like a colt, sleek, lustrous, wild. He certainly didn't measure up to the masculine ideal instilled in him by his father, but there was something inexorably attractive about him. Without really knowing what he was doing, without even asking permission, he sat down opposite him – buoyed by the fact he hadn't been carded on the way in – and stuck out his hand.

    "I'm Paul. Paul Gallagher," he said, gruffly. Billy looked up, startled. To his credit, though, he had a ready smile and a kind look in his eye for this big, blond, ungainly youth, and shook his hand warmly.

    "Billy," he said. "Billy Peterson. So, Paul Gallagher. What brings you to this godforsaken corner of the world tonight?" Gallagher stopped himself just short of saying "you" and instead, smiled and shrugged, hoping it wasn't too obvious that he was blushing.

"A man of few words, eh? All right, Paul Gallagher, let's see if we can't loosen you up a bit." He had an odd, slightly stiff way of talking – almost British, Gallagher thought – and he liked it. It was so different, so other-worldly: all he wanted was for him to keep talking. Billy spent the rest of the night calling him by his full name, buying him drink after drink, until he decided he'd "loosened up" enough. Bold with liquor, Gallagher found himself telling Billy everything he'd never told anyone before. He told him how he'd never had a girlfriend – had never even kissed a girl, for that matter – how he was afraid there something wrong with him, how he didn't know how to say any of this to his supposed friends. Billy had smiled sadly, knowingly then, realizing what Gallagher hadn't yet. For his part, he told story after story about the people he'd met in New York – some less true than others, Gallagher suspected – imitating their voices, their facial expressions, even pushing his hands through his hair to effect a particular look, and gesticulating so much, he looked like he was having some kind of attack. There was one character in particular, Gallagher remembered – Lady Ruby, Billy had called her, a British aristocrat forced to live in poverty after her ne'er-do-well American husband cleaned out all her bank accounts – who required so much physical contortion to portray that he crashed headlong into Brian Kowalski's father, very nearly spilling his drink. As luck would have it, though, the old man was so drunk himself, he could hardly have swung a punch, and let Billy off with a threatening grunt. Gallagher stared in amazement, never having known Mike Kowalski not to resort to violence at the slightest provocation, and decided then and there that there was something truly magical about Billy.

"C'mon," Billy said, turning back to his companion with a high, nervous laugh, once he was sure he wasn't about to be beaten to a pulp. "Let's go someplace else." Gallagher snorted.

"'S no place else *to* go," he slurred. "This's a one-horse town. A less than one-horse town. A…a half horse town." Billy laughed again – loudly and uproariously this time, probably as much to make Gallagher feel good about himself as anything else – and got up.

"Then we'll have to make up a place to go," he said, with surprising force, given he was swaying slightly. Gallagher stared at him, uncomprehending.

"What're you talkin' about?" But Billy just grinned and strode towards the door, steadying himself on a table as he went, pausing to gesture him to follow. As soon as they were outside, though, he took off, sprinting through the humid summer night, without even looking back. Still an athlete – his days on the varsity football team were barely behind him – Gallagher quickly caught up, but half wished he hadn't, feeling his stomach churning uncomfortably, the booze roiling around inside him. He was pretty sure it was only a matter of time before he threw up and he didn't want to do it in front of Billy.

"Where you goin'?" he yelled, breathlessly, as he came alongside Billy, already starting to sweat.

"I told you. Someplace else!" Billy said, throwing his head back and letting out an almighty whoop.

"Ok, but why do we hafta run?" Gallagher asked. He was beginning to doubt very much he'd make it wherever Billy was taking him before he keeled over, but the adrenalin was pounding in his veins, and he knew he couldn't stop.

"Fastest way to get where you're going!" Billy howled, picking up pace. "Didn't anybody ever tell you that?"

Before he had time to think, they'd run clear across town, and he realized they were heading in the direction of the river. They'd gone past the Weilers' farm as the last of the summer sun faded and he could see the water in the distance, glinting in the nascent twilight. Still Billy didn't stop. He carried on going, hardly even slowing down, and when he hit the river bank, he leapt straight into the water, fully clothed.

"What the fuck are you doin'?" Gallagher yelled. "Are you crazy?"

"Probably! Come on, join me!" Billy hooted.

"You know there's prob'ly eels in there," Gallagher said, but if Billy heard him, he didn't care. He was splashing around in the chilly water like a child, clothes clinging to his wet skin, and for all his reservations,

Gallagher found himself tugging his t-shirt over his head and plunging in after him, not wanting the night to end.

"*Fuck!*" he shrieked, as he hit the water. "You are crazy!" Billy grinned inanely, and made a lunge at him with unexpected force, knocking him backwards. Gallagher came up coughing and spluttering with a lungful of river water, and he was starting to wonder if he shouldn't make a run for it, but before he had time to scramble for the bank, Billy grabbed him again and pressed his mouth firmly against his. Startled, Gallagher almost pulled away, but when Billy kissed him that first time, it was like a light had come on: suddenly, everything made sense.

For five years, Billy Peterson was his whole world. For the first few months, they managed to keep it a secret, meeting in the little apartment Billy had bought on the east side of town, away from the prying eyes of his family. Then, one by one, as Gallagher began to break the news, with the exception of Murphy, his friends left him. But with Billy to stand with him, he didn't care. He learned to tolerate his unexplained disappearances – accepted them as part of his wild, enigmatic charm – because when he was there, everything else faded away. He fizzed and sparked like a firework and Gallagher was besotted, blinded, at least for a while, to his selfishness, his sadness.

Gradually, though, he started to learn how to deal with it, to help Billy come through the dark periods. They bought the house together after one such episode – a particularly prolonged one, he remembers – about a year before he died, and he'd thought maybe they'd be ok. He seemed to be getting better. He was more even, more tranquil, letting Gallagher take care of him in a way he never had before. The problem was, of course, that the third novel never came. He'd go through fits of creativity, staying up for days at a time, writing pages and pages and pages on his ancient typewriter, and then suddenly decide it was all garbage and toss it into the fire. Then he'd descend into despair and he'd disappear for a few days.

Right before he died, he hadn't done it in months. He'd call Gallagher at work and tell him if he was going out to Chicago or New York, with exact details of his flights and his arrival times, and more importantly, when he was coming back. He'd come home when he said he would, do the things he said he would. It felt good, he remembers. It felt normal, in the way his parents would have used the word. He was even writing, and more than that, he was keeping what he'd written. He still insisted on using the rickety, clickety typewriter, but the pages were gradually stacking up, and his calls with his publisher were less fevered, less fraught. But then he vanished again – no note, no call, just like he used to do at his worst, and Gallagher saw it all crumbling away in front of him. Eight days later, Abernathy turned up at his door to deliver the news.

Jacob sat by the phone for less than a day before he decided he couldn't take it anymore. Sarah had promised to call as soon as she got there, but the last time he heard anything from her was when she sent him a text to say her train was delayed because of the snow. It wasn't long before he started to get antsy by himself, worrying about her, but also worrying about the ugly specter of temptation. Since he'd been with her, effectively taking charge of her recovery after she left the rehab clinic, he'd been able to forget, to keep the bugs from bursting out of his skin. Without her, he felt itchy, restless.

Alone in his big, empty apartment, he'd begun to realize at last just how much he needed her there to keep his mind occupied. There were the times when he'd wake up in the wee hours, feeling like he was coming apart at the seams, but with her there to put her arms around him, stroke his hair, soothe him, that would fade. Without her, he'd start to think about things again – about his excesses, his sins. So many of his belongings still remind him of that time – the thousands of dollars he spent on useless trinkets, the overt displays of his wealth. Before Sarah, it gave him a sense of pride to be able to see what he'd accomplished, there in front of him in tangible form. In some ways, it was like that with the pills and the coke, too. He'd made himself a king among men and he could get away with anything. He could be as self-indulgent as he wanted and people would clap him on the back and congratulate him for it. Part of him is horrified now that that was ever his life – but another part realizes how easy, how *right* it would be go to back.

The last time he was arrested – because of the zoo incident, and in so many ways, because of her – he'd been awake for three days straight. The cops picked him up at midnight some time around the middle of January in Lincoln Park. He'd already broken into the zoo, high as a kite, hardly able to remember what he'd taken, and naked as the day he was born, despite the sub-zero temperatures. He doesn't remember much of it directly, but he does remember the police asking him later whether he recalled being absolutely insistent that he was in fact secretly an African lion and that he needed to be with his own kind. One of them even said he'd had half a mind to throw him in there with the big cats to see if that would straighten him out. He'd managed to climb up on top of the Kovler Lion House when they found him and it took three officers to tackle him once they got him down. It makes him cringe to think of it, the memory still relatively fresh in his mind. But it also makes him remember the euphoria of feeling like he was invincible, like he could jump off the Sears Tower and land on his feet.

He hid it from her most of the time – the angry, greedy, egotistical man still inside him, the one who'd cared for nothing and no one, the one who'd loved nothing more than chasing the next thrill. He needed to convince her he was a good man, and so in her presence, he became one. Eventually, the charade and the reality started to blend into one another. If he could convince her, he could convince himself. He wanted *truly* to be the good man, to make that who he was once and for all. He wanted to erase the broken, selfish, ugly part and replace it with selflessness, purity. He was just never quite sure he could.

When she was there, he could see in her the living proof that he was finally doing something worth doing. By cleansing her, he was cleansing himself. He'd cast himself in the role of her redeemer, and after a while, he really did start to believe it. Without her, though, it was just a matter of time before his faith in his ability to hold onto the man he'd try to make himself began to crack. There was no one to be good for. He had to do something, to pull himself back before it was too late. Hating himself for his own weakness, without stopping to think about it, he hastily threw a few things into a bag, got in his car, and before he knew what he was doing, he was heading for Wisconsin.

He was lucky not to get arrested, the way he was driving. He knew he must be drawing attention to himself, careening along the interstate in his cherry red Ferrari. But he didn't trust himself to be alone anymore and it was the only thing he could think to do. He wasn't sure how far ahead of him she was, but he knew he needed to find her, to see her, to talk to her. She could make it ok again, make him good again. He hated it, of course. The thought of admitting just how much he needed her, given how much store he'd put into being the strong one, scared him more than he was prepared for, and he was half out of his mind before he hit Milwaukee.

As it happened, he arrived in town about twelve hours after Sarah. He fetched up in the ramshackle little hotel on the outskirts the evening of the same day. The place was empty when he got there, save for the tiny, elderly front desk clerk and the blank-eyed stag's head, stuffed and mounted on the wall above him. It gave him the creeps but he had nowhere else to go, and he needed some rest. So he stayed. He needed a little time to collect himself before he went looking for her, he decided, so he set up camp in his room, hardly venturing out at all, other than on the day he arrived. As much as anything else, it was bitterly cold outside and he liked the warmth. Bad things happened when it got cold, he remembered. His father died in the winter. When he was a kid, he lost his favorite bike – cream and red and shiny and beautiful – to a nasty crash during a snowstorm. Most of his arrests had happened when it was freezing, only of course he'd been too wasted to care at the time. Better to stay indoors, probably. He'd get some sleep, he told himself, and give her as much space as could. He'd read and eat the heavy, rich breakfasts and let the world pass him by for a while. He'd find some way to distract himself. Then he'd call her and everything would be ok.

Only of course it wasn't. It couldn't be. There were only temporary fixes for his problems – that much was clear at last – and he was finally out of luck. The front desk clerk was full of the news when he went downstairs one morning a few days after he arrived. He'd ignored most of the idle chatter the old man had been spouting, but this was different. He looked genuinely shaken, bug-eyed and jittery, and it made Jacob stop and pay attention in a way that surprised him. There was a meeting in town, the clerk said. Some girl had been killed. Sarah something. Dead three days before they found her. "Funny," he said. "Nothing ever happens in this damn town and now we got a murder. Hey, buddy? Buddy? You ok?"

He thought he might throw up or pass out when he heard it. All the blood drained out of his face and his hands and feet suddenly turned numb. He felt himself sway violently and he had to grab the edge of the desk to keep himself upright. He didn't say anything to the clerk, though. Instead, he turned on his heel and went straight back up to the tiny, poky hotel room.

He's barely moved since then. He's sitting on the bed now, staring at the broken television, with his phone switched off, trying to figure out what to do. The sickly yellow paint on the walls is giving him a headache and his mind is racing. The local police have been trying to call him and now he knows exactly what they must be thinking. But he doesn't have the strength to deal with them. All he can think about is Sarah. Sarah, and the gram of coke in his bag. How easy it would be to take it and forget just for a little while. He'd bought it during a momentary lapse a few weeks back, hardly even thinking about what he was doing, but, coming back to himself shortly thereafter, he'd been able to make himself forget about it. But he hadn't been able to make himself get rid of it. There it is, tucked away in a little plastic bag in the inside pocket. He doesn't even remember picking it up, but he knows it's there, taunting him. Until now, it's been ok. He's been able to keep himself steady, one way or another. As fortune had it, a woman checked in at the hotel a little while after he did – cute, young, exactly what he needed – and he did what he did best. He turned on the charm and he used her to distract himself. He even managed to convince himself he was doing it for Sarah – that by cheating on her, he was committing the lesser of two evils. But that was before he knew. Now he can't take his mind off it anymore.

Strange, he thinks. If he'd never met Sarah, he wouldn't be here, in this room. Hell, he might well be back where he was before he ever knew she existed – he might never have gotten help, might never have tried to change. He might still be living his extravagant, empty life, the one without consequences, without remorse. She changed him. She made him realize just how hollow that life was. She was weak too, of course, but she had so much more reason to be. She was wounded in a way he never had been – but she was getting stronger all the time. She was starting to flourish on her own. He'd wanted to help her get there, to help her heal – he *did* help her, he told himself over and over – and in turn, maybe he could find some healing for himself. Now it's all over. He couldn't save her in the end – maybe she just couldn't be saved – and now he probably can't save himself. She managed a day and part of a night without him and now she's dead. He should have been there, should have done something. She's fucking dead, and if she hadn't come here, she wouldn't be. It's all his fault.

Before he knows what he's doing, the little plastic bag is in his hand and he's emptying its contents onto the little nightstand. Hands shaking, he finds a credit card and divides the pure white powder up into neat little lines. How easily it comes back to him, he thinks. Still trembling, he takes a dollar bill from his wallet, rolls it up and inhales a line, letting the chemicals hit him hard. He closes his eyes as the familiar feeling takes him over. Soon, it'll work its magic. Soon, he'll lose control. Soon, he won't care.

"Fuck," he breathes, falling back onto the bed. "Fuck."

Staying in the crappy little hotel was an uncomfortable reminder of her first night out west for Katie. The place had always been a little creepy. She'd pass it with her friends on her way to school and they'd delight in giving each other the willies, coming up with stories about all the gruesome things that might have happened there. It was all just for fun. She knew that really. But there was this one story that she'd never been able to forget, about how a guest back in the forties had killed his wife, cut her up into little pieces and packed her in his suitcase. Her friend Penny had told it. She had a gift for the dramatic, which she usually applied to thinking up practical jokes to play on her friends, but this was…different. There were so many details, so many little things that just didn't seem like they were made up. She knew the guy's name, his wife's name, his room number. She knew every aspect of the crime scene, and described it in florid, gruesome depth. Katie remembers asking her where she was getting all this, but Penny had just smiled and tapped the side of her nose. At the time, she'd shrugged it off, assuming Penny must have gotten it from a cop show or a horror movie or something, but it had haunted her ever since.

The story was on her mind when she arrived in town. More than once in the intervening years, she'd thought of looking it up, of trying to see whether there was some true crime book or website devoted to it, but she'd always come to the conclusion she was better off not knowing. When the front desk clerk handed her the key to her room, she wished more than ever that she'd taken the plunge. If she'd been brave enough to find out for sure, even if it were true, at least maybe she'd be over it by now. The heavy bronze key chain bore the number nine. The very one from Penny's story.

There was only one other guest when she got there – a man in his thirties, travelling alone, who arrived earlier the same day she did. She knew exactly what lone men in their thirties had a tendency to do and at first, she was duly wary of him. When she caught sight of him, the man himself didn't exactly look threatening. He was tall and fit-looking, though not especially muscular, and more pretty than handsome, she thought. In fact, he put her in mind of a Ken doll, all expensive clothes, perfectly coiffed sandy hair, and big, long-lashed blue eyes. She could spot his type a mile off: pampered, privileged, and probably able to charm his way out of or into any situation. She was intrigued by him. There was something in those big blue eyes that appealed to her. There was a little glimmer of something there, a little whisper of mischief, belied by his clothes and his smooth hands and his Gucci loafers. Nobody like him had ever showed up in town without a good reason, and as she climbed the stairs to her room, she decided she'd like to know what his was.

Sleep was pressing in on her when she got there. She was exhausted and all she wanted to do was collapse. But lying there, on her lumpy, rickety bed that first day, Penny's story and her own unpleasant memory of almost falling victim to God knows what became intertwined with one another inside her head. She stared fixedly at the ceiling, willing herself not to look for the shadowy figure in the doorway. But she couldn't help it. She couldn't stop herself from waiting for the door to creak open, for the familiar presence to loom over her. Of course it never did, but sleep still eluded her, until finally, she couldn't take it anymore. She had to get out.

She'd thought about going to Sally's place right away, but when she arrived in town, suddenly, somehow it seemed wrong. Her first impulse had been to lock herself in her room, but she couldn't do that, either. She needed some other way to occupy her time that first night, and once she'd convinced herself the handsome man in the next room wasn't going to kill her in her sleep, she'd hit on another idea. She needed a distraction – he might as well be it. As much as anything else, she desperately wanted to know what his deal was, and she thought maybe she could kill two birds with one stone. So she stayed put at the hotel, and set to work. She knew she'd already caught his eye – that much was obvious. It might take a little time, but it would be easy enough. All she had to do was wait around for a while, and eventually, she could casually bump into him in the lobby. The rest would follow, as it always did.

In the meantime, she needed to pull herself together – prepare herself for seeing Sally. She hadn't called first. No one, other than Phil at the front desk and then the not-so-mysterious man, knew she was there. When Sally finally called her, saying she needed her to come home, she couldn't quite bring herself to tell her she was already there – had been for nearly three days already. In fact, she'd been working up the nerve to leave the hotel finally and go into town, when her cell phone rang.

She couldn't say what exactly had compelled her to come home in the first place – only that the idea of going back had suddenly occurred to her and it wouldn't leave her alone until she'd booked the plane ticket to Madison. It was getting close to Christmas, when all those godawful ads, full of ghoulishly grinning, overly happy families and exhortations to spend time with those most closely related to you, would pile in on her. She'd always ignored them in the past, even after her mother died, but something in them must have gotten through to her this time. It had seemed like as good a reason as any to try to make amends, with Sally and with her father, whom she'd barely spoken to in almost ten years. Suddenly, it just seemed like time. But when she got there, and took out her phone to call her sister, she froze.

Aside from anything else, she never did tell her she hadn't made it to California – that she'd gotten stuck in Oregon and that's where she'd stayed. The postcards were all fudged – pictures that could have been taken anywhere, landmarks that didn't give away a location. At first, she felt guilty, lying to her sister, but after a while it got easier, and then it became second nature. It wasn't hard to stage the photos to make it look like she was living the high life – cocktail in hand, one friend or other on her arm to pose as a handsome, anonymous paramour, or an as-yet-undiscovered actress – and she really had bought a little red convertible a few years after she'd moved out there. But it was all just fantasy – a cheap trick to avoid telling her sister the truth. She'd given up on becoming a movie star pretty quickly, and resigned herself to life with Alma at the diner. It wasn't so bad, of course. She liked the customers and they liked her. More than that, she liked the feeling of belonging it gave her. It was something she'd never really had before and there was comfort in that. She even took over running the diner from Alma after she'd retired a couple of years back. But there's a part of her, she realizes now, that still feels ashamed – of the lie and of the fact her life never did become what it was supposed to be.

It was why she hadn't come home when her mother got sick and why she hadn't come back for her funeral. She'd died thinking she'd made it, that her dreams for her daughter really had come true, even if she'd had to run off with Donovan to do it. She couldn't bear to see the looks of resigned disappointment on her family's faces, so she'd stayed away. She regrets it every day, but she'd told herself there was nothing she could do to make it right, and she might as well just get on with living the life she'd ended up with. That had been enough, at least for a while, to keep the memory closed off. But now, for reasons she hasn't been able to understand yet, it's not.

It's better this way, Abernathy decides – better to do it in person, better to do it where the whole town isn't watching. He owes him that at least. He pitches up at John Callaghan's door late on Saturday afternoon and it takes him a good minute to get up the nerve to knock. He looks around three times to make sure none of his neighbors are twitching their curtains. The houses here are bigger, further apart, and it's harder to snoop than it is elsewhere. That's something at least. It's funny, he thinks. In thirty years, the number of times he's knocked on somebody's door to deliver anything other than bad news probably comes in below five. Before now, though, it's never been quite as bad as this. There was the car wreck that killed Jimmy Murphy's parents and the day he found Billy Peterson swinging from a tree, but this – this feels different. Personal. Worse.

The big problem is Callaghan is his friend. He's known him a long time. They'd been passing acquaintances before he went out west, but when he came back, Abernathy found himself crossing paths with him almost daily. He'd bowled up to him after a town meeting, reintroducing himself, saying he wanted to volunteer his services to the town in whatever capacity they might be needed. He'd made his fortune. He didn't need to work. He was at the town's disposal, he said. He'd been so friendly, so helpful, wanting to be a part of everything. He'd thrown himself headlong into town beautification projects, school dances, charity drives. He'd given a lot – his time and his money – and Abernathy had quickly come to like him. He'd thought, as much as he did of anyone, that this was a good man. This was someone almost unimpeachably decent and kind. Other than his wife, Callaghan was pretty much the only person in town he felt he could completely trust. If he ever found any proof that Callaghan was anything other than a model citizen, he thought, he would have felt personally injured.

Finally, his heart heavy in his chest, he taps the little brass knocker against the door. It takes almost another minute for Callaghan to come to the door, and he finds himself hoping maybe he isn't home. Maybe he won't have to do this right now. Maybe he can come back another day, when he's had a little time to get used to the idea that someone like him could have done something like this. Maybe he doesn't have to tell him he's in the frame for murder. But then he answers the door.

"Chief!" he says. He looks genuinely startled. "What brings you by?"

"Can we, uh…can I come in?" Abernathy asks, quietly. "I don't want to do this on the street." Callaghan nods silently, brow furrowing, and steps aside.

"What's…what's this about?" he asks, as they head into the living room. He swallows, thickly. He sounds nervous, agitated, but not quite the way a guilty man would, Abernathy thinks. Now, though, he's not sure he trusts his own judgment. He's not sure of anything anymore. Suddenly everything seems like a lie. Maybe he's been walking around with his eyes shut this whole time. Maybe he could have been fooled.

"Sit down," he says, gesturing at the couch. "I need to talk to you." Obediently, Callaghan perches on the edge of the couch, apparently not daring to sit comfortably. He looks like a child, suddenly small and meek.

"All right. What about? Come on, Chief you're scaring me. Is Mary ok? Did that man…? I mean, he didn't…? She's not…?"

"Mary's fine. Far as I know, she's safe and sound in Ashland and that's where she'll stay. But, uh…she is sort of the reason I'm here." He pauses, waiting for Callaghan react, to flinch or twitch, but he doesn't move. He looks different, though, and Abernathy realizes he's never seen him scared before. He's never been anything less than completely at ease, always affable, always genial. Always composed.

"What do you mean? If she's ok, then…?" he asks.

"She called me. She, uh…she told me…about Sarah."

"Oh," Callaghan says, flatly. Abernathy has a feeling he already knows what Mary must have said to him. There wasn't much to it in point of fact. She told him firstly, that her father had told her he was Sarah McIntyre's real father and secondly, that he might have had reason to want her dead. She was scared. She knew how important his reputation was to him, she said. He could have felt threatened. He could have gotten angry. If he could have hidden Sarah from her all these years, there was no telling what else he could have been hiding. It was speculation, of course – Mary was clearly upset – but she sounded just convinced enough of the possibility her own father could have it in him to have done something like this that he'd decided he couldn't ignore it. He'd promised her he'd go and have a little talk with her father – just to be on the safe side. It was just a precaution, he said. He'd told her he was absolutely positive there was nothing to worry about. Now he knows he was lying to her.

"I'm…I'm afraid I have to ask you where you were the night Sarah died," he whispers. Callaghan sighs, his broad barrel chest visibly rising and falling.

"I figured you might. I was home all night. Alone."

"Ok. Did anybody see you?" Callaghan takes a long, slow breath and scrubs a hand over his face.

"I don't know. Maybe. I think…I think I probably took the trash out at some point. Oh, and I…I watched some pay per view. There must be some way to track that…right?" He drops his voice as he finishes speaking, as though he's afraid someone else might be able to hear him. It's almost funny. Here he is more or less being accused of murder and he's afraid someone can hear him confessing he watched a little porn a few nights ago.

"Ok. Ok. We can run that down with the cable company, and we'll talk to your neighbors, too," Abernathy says, gently. "But John – I need you to tell me the truth. Did you have any idea she was back in town? Did you ever hear anything from her at all?"

"No! As far as I knew, she was still in Chicago. I didn't hear a word from her or her mother after I went out west. I don't even know if Alice knew I came back. Chief, I…I'm not a killer."

"I want to believe you, John. I really do," Abernathy says. He waits, half-expecting Callaghan to give some impassioned speech in his own defense. But Callaghan just looks at him, pleadingly.

"But?" he whispers. Abernathy sighs and folds his hands in his lap, dropping his gaze to floor.

"But your own daughter doubted you. That…that says something." Callaghan breathes in slowly and lets it out through his teeth. He looks wounded.

"I know. I wish I could say I blamed her for it," he says. "I know you need to check my credit card or my cable bill or whatever. But Chief, I swear to you – I didn't want her dead. I wanted her to have the life I never gave her. I want to know what happened to her as much as you do."

"Ok, John," Abernathy says. He stops for a second, and looks around the neat little room, and then back at Callaghan's face, trying to read him. But his expression hasn't changed. His skin is grey, his eyes sunken and bloodshot. He looks drained, broken. "Look, you're not under arrest or anything. But if we find anything out of place, if we find somebody who saw you around Mawhinney's that night, if we find so much as a whisper that you weren't where you said you were…"

"I know." He smiles, grimly.

"All right. I better go. We are gonna figure this out. I can promise you that." Abernathy gets up and heads for the door, but Callaghan catches his arm, grasping it just a little too tight.

"Chief, wait a sec," he says, suddenly sounding urgent. "Do you…do you really have to talk to my neighbors?" Abernathy nods.

"Yes. We do. I'll be in touch."

In church on Sunday, everything feels strange, dreamlike. Everyone sits apart from her now: there's a two-pew exclusion zone all around her. Sally finds she wishes they'd sit closer, so that she could listen in on the whispers she'd so hated before. She wants desperately to find out whether there's any truth to what Kathy had said in the grocery store. Instead, she has a whole pew to herself and no access to the gossip she now craves. She tries to listen to what the priest is saying, but she finds he isn't as comforting or even as coherent as he usually is, and she can't stop herself from straining to hear the whispers around her. A couple of times, she even cranes her neck to see who's closest to her and whether she might be able to scoot a little nearer to them without drawing too much attention to herself.

The third time she turns, she sees him, right at the back, clear as day. It's Seth McIntyre. She'd know him anywhere. There was a big to do when he left town and his picture had been in the paper. She'd had enough to deal with in high school and had never crossed paths with Sarah, who was a year younger, but her father's face stuck in her memory. She must have been in Jimmy's class, she realizes, and she allows herself a second or two to wonder how much they'd had to do with each other back then. Her mind quickly snaps back to Seth, though, live and large and right in her line of sight. She remembers seeing him at a couple of school-related things way back when and he'd always given her the creeps in a way she couldn't fully explain. He was one of those people, she remembers, who'd stand there, looking at someone, waiting for them to respond to his presence instead of announcing it, and then when they realized he was there, he'd scare the living daylights out of them. His face was always so expressionless, so unreadable. It was like he was a robot. It looks the same now, albeit a little more lined and a little less firm in the jaw.

He must know she's staring at him but she can't help it. It's like looking at a car wreck. There's death in that face. Everything is lining up inside her head, finally shifting into place. This is it. This really is the explanation she's been waiting for. He is here, and that means Kathy must have been right, however much she hates to admit it. He must have followed his daughter here and decided to mete out her punishment, give her what he thought she deserved for her sins. She shivers but she still doesn't look away. She's transfixed.

As she stares at him, there's a little stab of something in her gut that she can't quite quantify. At first, she thinks it must be guilt for her lack of faith in her husband, but that isn't quite it. If she lets herself think about it, she'll figure it out. She'll know. It's doubt. She'll realize she doesn't quite believe the story she's telling herself, and she can't have that. So she squashes it down and hides it away with everything else she's been trying not to feel.

More than anything else, there's a feeling of cold, pure terror. A few times in New York, she'd see a man in the street and she'd wonder. He'd have a look about him. She'd catch his eye and in that instant, a whole world of horror would flash up inside her head. Then her imagination would kick in and she'd think about the things that might be behind that look, the horrible acts he might have committed. Now she *knows*, though. She knows what it is to look at the face of a killer, and that face, she's decided, is Seth's. Finally, she forces herself to look ahead again, but she can feel his eyes on her, burning the back of her neck. He knows she knows. Her imagination is running away with her now, setting out the whole story in her mind. She feels wild, manic. This is it. This is her chance. This is what will prove Jimmy's innocence, once and for all, to her, to everyone. This is it, this is it, this is it. She repeats the words inside her head like a prayer, and then she lets her imagination really go to work. Maybe that's why Sarah was back – maybe she was running away from Chicago, running away from him. Maybe this is what he's been hiding all this time behind that blank face of his. Maybe he's been waiting for his chance.

It was all so perfect. He remembered seeing the woman in the room next to his check in, and then the plan immediately began to form. She stood out to him because of her beauty – tall and slender, with striking red hair, big hazel eyes, and a pretty pink mouth that he could imagine engaged in all sorts of unseemly activities. The doorway leading into the little dining room looked directly onto the front desk and it afforded Jacob a perfect view as she smiled at the little old man and took her key. She mustn't have realized he was looking at her – if she had, she probably would have told him to stop staring – but something about her made him feel better somehow. It reassured him to know he wasn't totally alone there – that maybe this place wasn't as creepy as it had first seemed. More than that, it was what gave him the idea. It was a bad idea – really bad, almost the worst one he could come up with – but in the long run, he'd decided it was the best of the options at hand. Later that day – the day Sarah died, as he later found out – he set himself up on the little couch in the reception area with a newspaper, and waited.

A few hours passed before she came downstairs. It was already dark outside, and the desk clerk – Phil, his name was, as Jacob had learned when he'd allowed the old man some small talk earlier in the afternoon – had dozed off a while before that. She looked a little rumpled and tired, but if anything, it made her even more beautiful. There was something inexplicably sweet about her – something of the spark he'd seen in Sarah back when they first got to know each other. He looked up just as she drew up alongside him and smiled. He was still very much aware of the effect his smile could have on women and he was counting on that effect then. It was too late to turn back. He knew what his only other choice would be if he failed. Chemical comfort was a grim prospect still hovering in the periphery of his mind. He couldn't fail, then. She looked at him for a second, sizing him up, and then she smiled back.

"Hi," he said, as casually as he could.

"Hi. I'm Katie." She extended a lily-white hand cordially and he got up to shake it. It was already working.

"Jacob," he said, steadying himself. "So. What brings you to this godforsaken part of the world?" She laughed – a strange laugh that he couldn't quite read at first.

"I grew up here," she said. He flushed, feeling his cool started to slip just a fraction. She was still smiling, though. He hadn't lost yet.

"Oh! Sorry!"

"Don't worry about it," she said, kindly. "It's a pretty common opinion."

"Maybe you can help me out, then," he tried again, swallowing. "What exactly does a person do for fun around here?"

"Well," she said. "There is a bar the other side of town, but I doubt it'd be your scene."

"What makes you say that?" he asked, trying to keep her talking as long as he could, trying to pique her interest in him. She laughed again.

"If you think this town is godforsaken, let me assure you, it's nothing compared to Mawhinney's. That bar belongs in the depths of hell." He smiled. He could tell she was softening, starting to like him even, but she clearly hadn't quite made up her mind yet.

"All right. So what are our other options?"

"*Our* other options?" she asked, raising an eyebrow.

"Yeah. Might as well keep each other company. I don't think Phil over there is up to the job." She appeared to think about it for another second or two, glancing over at the gently snoring old man, and then she sat down beside him on the couch.

"Ok. Well, let's get to know each other a little first. And then if I decide you're not an axe murderer, maybe I'll think about sharing the bottle of wine I brought with me."

"Deal," Jacob said, sitting down beside her. It was like a first date. As they sat there talking – each, no doubt, carefully leaving out as many details of their personal histories as the other – he began to relax, almost to the point that he forgot why he was doing this in the first place. Katie was funny and flirty and he found he really did like her.

"So what's the verdict?" he asked, after an hour or so had passed.

"The verdict?"

"On that bottle of wine," he pressed, trying not to sound too urgent.

"Oh." She was quiet for just a second longer than he would've liked, and he was pretty sure he'd blown it. But she smiled. "Well, it's up in my room. How about we steal a couple of glasses from the dining room?"

"Lead the way." He smiled, as benignly as he could, and took her hand as he got up, helping her out of the sagging old couch.

In the end, they had to settle for coffee cups – Phil hadn't gotten around to putting the glasses for breakfast out yet. Jacob made something of a production out of rinsing the dust out of them in the bathroom, giving himself a second or two to collect himself before he poured the wine. It was a little awkward at first, as they sat down beside each other on her lumpy bed. He felt like a teenager again, out on a date with a girl who was way out of his league. But he pressed ahead.

"Cheers," he said, raising the chipped floral cup. She smiled.

"Cheers." She seemed nervous, he thought, but not unwilling. She had no reason to be. He knew exactly how charming he could be when he wanted. After all, she didn't know anything about him. He was just a handsome stranger, about to give her a good time. It happened the world over. People were attracted to each other. They had sex. Sometimes they'd see each other again, sometimes they wouldn't. There was nothing wrong with that, he told himself. Sarah didn't need to know. When he leaned over to kiss her, too, she didn't recoil. She let him. The residual guilt at the front of his mind faded into the background then. It felt good. It felt...normal. Here was someone who, as far as he knew or cared, had no past, no wounds to heal. She wasn't a call girl or a gold digger, either. She was just a girl who saw a guy she liked and went for it. Here was someone who wasn't broken or damaged. Here was someone whole.

The sex itself was…quiet. He'd undressed her clumsily, hurriedly, and he didn't waste much time on foreplay. In fact, it was all over and done within a matter of minutes. But still, that had felt good, too. It had felt comfortable, like they already knew each other intimately. Like they were already lovers. He'd fallen asleep in her bed in a happy post-coital fug, his mind a million miles away from Sarah. The problem, of course, was that he couldn't keep it that way. He couldn't stay here forever. Soon enough, there'd be no more hiding.

The town gathers again in the church, exactly a week after the first meeting – exactly a week after Sarah's body was found. There are more of them here this time, packed into the pews and between them, too, right up to the door, which barely stays closed behind the last of them. They all look just as scared as they did a week ago, but there's something else there, too – something dangerous. They look frustrated, angry even. They're all muttering amongst themselves and there's an almost threatening hum to their chatter, which is getting louder. Abernathy can't remember the last time he felt nervous in front of them. He feels queasy, unsteady, but he knows he can't show it. He swallows and grips the lectern for support.

However much he didn't want to believe it, he'd thought maybe he was onto something with John Callaghan. Hating himself for it, he'd caught himself almost *hoping* his alibi wouldn't hold up. Then he'd have something to give them – something tangible. But one of Callaghan's neighbors had seen him taking out the garbage around the time Sarah should have been in Mawhinney's, and no one had seen him go anywhere after that. His cable company had confirmed three payments, all during the window when she should have been dead or dying before she was ditched in the snow. He would have had to drive her out there, and there were no tire tracks and no one could recall hearing his car. All the evidence said he couldn't have done it. It just wasn't possible. Beyond that, nothing had come up on Jimmy Murphy that would give him probable cause to search his house. Showalter and Legler had canvassed everyone who'd been in the bar that night and all they could do was place him at the bar with her. All they could do was verify the story he'd told them in the first place. He'd tried to kiss her, she'd rejected him, and then...nothing. No one they talked to could say what happened after that. There's a big hole in the timeline and there's nothing to fill it. Abernathy is right back at square one. All he has to tell them now is that he thinks maybe Seth McIntyre is back in town. If he spins it right, he might be able to make it sound like McIntyre is a suspect without really saying it outright, but he knows it's pretty damn weak – certainly not enough to assuage their anger and fear. He doesn't even know if Seth knows the truth about Sarah's parentage and he doesn't remember enough about him to decide whether he might be violent. He was always so damn silent – never had any buddies, never really talked to anybody other than his wife's brother, and then when he left town, that was it. He basically shut up altogether. Abernathy remembers there was some sort of problem with the girl – some reason why they packed up and left so suddenly – but no one ever found out what it was, despite their best efforts. The rumor mill churned out all sorts of theories – drugs, abuse, affairs – but they upped and left so quickly that there wasn't time to get to the bottom of it.

"All right!" he yells over the din. "I know you're all wondering what's going on and I want to be able to reassure you. But I also want to be honest with you. We don't know a lot right now, but we're working as hard as we can to figure this out." There's silence for a second, before the chatter starts to swell again. Abernathy collects himself, and holds up a hand.

"Listen! I understand you're all scared and I know you're frustrated. These things take time and we can't expect any quick fixes. There's no button to press here. We just have to keep going until we build up a picture of what happened." There's a ripple of noise as he's speaking. He can feel the tension rising and he's starting to sweat. He raises a hand to silence them again and he realizes he's shaking. He clears his throat.

"But I'm not here to tell you we're empty-handed," he says. He pauses again, knowing he's about to make a much bigger deal out of Seth McIntyre's presence than he really should, but it's the only card he has to play. "Sarah McIntyre's father is understood to be in town.

We think he arrived the same day she did. We don't know why he's here, but please, do not approach him. We want you to be vigilant and to tell us if you see him." They're quiet again for a long moment then, obviously expecting him to say something more – to say he thinks Seth could have killed his own daughter.

"Not just Seth," a voice says, from deep within the crowd, buried among those who've managed to find a seat in the pews. He peers out, trying to pick out the source, but suddenly all these faces look the same. They blur together, a sea of pink and white and red. There's nothing to choose between them.

"Who said that?" he says at last.

"I did." A man about his own age gets up. He looks familiar, but Abernathy finds he can't place him. If he ever did know this man, it must have been a long time ago.

"And who are you?" The man gives a dry laugh.

"Chief, I'm hurt." Abernathy squints, scrambling to recognize the voice. "I'm Zachariah Fahey. Sarah's uncle." Everyone turns to look at him at the same time, the chatter rising to a low rumble again as they strain to get a look at him. Abernathy's more than just nervous now. He's about to have a riot on his hands.

"All right! All right!" he yells, trying to keep his voice steady. "Meeting's over!" Without thinking, he all but jumps down from the altar and forces his way down the middle of the church. Without thinking about what he's doing, he physically shoves people out of the way to get to the source of the voice. Finally, he can see Fahey clearly. He's there with an older man, presumably his father. All he knows is that he needs to talk to them and he needs to do it now.

"Come on," he hisses, grabbing the younger man by the arm. "You, too." He jerks his head at the old man, motioning for him to follow. He can feel him grasping his elbow, and there's a sudden stab of sympathy for his frailty as the three of them barge their way out into the snow. He glances back for just a second, watching the confusion growing inside. He has minutes at the most before all hell breaks loose.

"You mind telling me what the hell that stunt was in aid of?" he asks. Fahey, Jr., glares at him.

"*Stunt?*" he growls. "I'm *trying* to find out what happened to Sarah – something you seem to be totally failing at." Abernathy can feel himself color, but he forges ahead.

"Ok. Well, why not come see me? Why give me a goddamn riot? How exactly is that helping Sarah?"

"You needed a kick in the ass," Fahey, Sr., pipes up. His voice is creaky, as though he's hardly used it in years. "All you've got is Seth McIntyre. We've got the goddamn boyfriend." Abernathy stares at him, as much startled by the profanity coming from the mouth of a man who must be well past eighty as he is by the news that they've somehow tracked down Jacob Christie.

"How?" he whispers, before he can stop himself. The old man laughs, mirthlessly, and looks at his son.

"Luck. He's staying at the hotel. So are we. Got there late last night," Fahey, Jr., says. "I saw his name on the register."

"But...how'd you know who he was?" Fahey, Sr., sighs heavily. He has a look Abernathy recognizes from his early days as a beat cop. He's about to unburden himself – about to relate something he maybe never told anybody before.

"We've been lookin' for Sarah for years – almost as long as Seth has. But we were always a step or two behind him. I mean, he had the money and the time – we never did. We did as much as we could, but we couldn't keep goin' back and forth to Chicago, and...well, we never got as close as he did. I don't know, maybe if we'd...maybe she would've..." Abernathy glances back and forth between the two of them, trying to understand. The older man looks like he's trying not to cry. He steadies himself, clenching his wrinkled hands. "We know he had a PI on her for a while – think maybe he even found her once – but he dropped it around the time Alice died. Figure if he did find her, he probably thought she was beyond saving. She didn't come to the funeral, you know."

"But he picked it back up again, didn't he?" Abernathy says, quietly. So many things are starting to fit together now – why Seth was so close behind her, what he's doing in town – but suddenly, there are a thousand more questions, too. Fahey, Jr., nods.

"Yeah. We were out in Chicago in the fall and we got as close as we ever did. We found out he picked it back up a few months before she came here. So we bit the bullet and put a PI on his PI – let him do the legwork. He led us right to her, at an address under Christie's name. We were gonna call her, but she dropped off the radar again when she came out here. Our guy said Seth's PI figured out where she'd gone, but he lost her again after she left Milwaukee – right before she…" He trails off, unable to say it. Abernathy sets his jaw and swallows hard, trying to push down the feeling of total incompetence that threatens to knock him over. He's humiliated and ashamed, but he still has a job to do.

"All right," he says, quietly. "You go down to the station for now – both of you. And for god's sake, try not to attract any more attention."

"Wait!" Fahey, Jr., calls, as he turns to leave. "Where are you going?"

"To get Christie."

Sally's head is spinning when she gets outside. There was uproar when Abernathy told everybody he was basically nowhere with the investigation and she'd dived out before chaos descended. It's snowing again, but she's sweating, feverish. She'd made herself so sure it was Seth McIntyre. She'd made herself believe it was so reasonable, so obvious. But the cops don't think so. She knows that now. If they had some reason to suspect him, Abernathy would have said something – and that means they don't have anything on him. There's no proof. And if they don't have anything on him, then they'll come right back to Jimmy. On top of that, if anything, he's been behaving even more erratically lately. He's hardly been home the last couple of days, and when he is there, he's been drinking more than ever. He doesn't say anything to her – just slouches in front of the TV with a bottle of cheap whiskey. Lately he hasn't even been using a glass, swigging right from the bottle until his eyes turn bleary and red and then he passes out. He's there when she gets back from the meeting, eyes half-lidded, bottle on the floor, almost empty already. She opens her mouth to say something, but stops herself. There's no point.

The TV is on with the sound down. Some asinine gameshow is playing, but she doubts he has any idea what it is, or that it even matters. He half turns to look at her, but his eyes don't focus and he swivels his head back to the garbage on the screen. He's way past halfway to oblivion and he won't move tonight. Sally considers sitting down beside him, maybe even switching the channel over to something she actually wants to watch, but it seems wrong now. It seems like a lie. Everything is different. She doesn't know the man sitting on her couch now – if she ever knew him at all. There's a wall between them and it won't come down. Even if it all goes away, even if the cops do find proof that someone else is to blame – Seth McIntyre, whoever – it won't be the same. Nothing can go back.

She lies down on the bed and stares up at the ceiling. It's still early, but there's nothing else for her to do. If she tries to read, she won't be able to focus; if she tries to make herself something to eat, she won't be able to stomach it. There's only one thing to be grateful for in all this: she doesn't have to lie beside him. The wall is highest between her side of the bed and his. Even lying there alone, she keeps rigidly to her side all the same, but if he were there, she wouldn't sleep at all. She only dozes fitfully now, dreaming of dead women and things she can't get back. She dreams of the days when they were first dating and she was so happy, she thought she could die for sheer joy. She can still just about feel that joy now when she calls on the memory of it, but it lasts only a fraction of a second, a burst of bliss before the wretched darkness comes again. She tries to get it back, tries to cling to the images of sunlight and dancing and camping trips, holding hands, making love, but they're all tainted now. There's something else there – a shadow creeping into the edges of everything, swallowing up all the good in her memories of him. In that shadow, there's a face. It's Sarah's ghost, she realizes, invading her head, keeping her from rest. There's nowhere to hide anymore – not even in her own imagination.

She thinks about all the things she read about love when she was a teenager. Back then, she'd been convinced that was all she'd ever know of it. It had seemed so beautiful, so pure, and for a long time, the fantasy had sustained her. Her ability to retreat into daydreams was the only thing that kept her going, some days. She could retreat into that world inside her head, and live there. She never needed to know that that wasn't how it was in reality. She knows the truth now. I burn, I pine, I perish. Bullshit. Love isn't all-consuming passion, burning desire, unremitting joy. It's a lie, as unrealistic and ridiculous as the fantasies in her books, and the worst thing about it is you don't even see it until it's too late. It tricks you – she can see that at last. It makes you believe in it, makes you think you're invincible, and the more you feel it, the more you want it – the more you need it. When it's get taken away, you shrivel up, made sick and small without it. She feels sorry for the people who still don't know, and at once, she envies them, too. They still have it, still have the fantasy to sustain them. She's without it now, and it's slowly killing her. Bit by bit, she's shrinking, fading. If she'd never known it, never had that fleeting good part, she wouldn't be here now. She'd be alone, but at least she wouldn't be in pain. She couldn't miss what she'd never had.

If Seth McIntyre regrets anything at all, it's letting Sarah's trail go cold after Alice died. He found her in that SRO and he left her there to rot. If he'd just been a little more forceful, if he'd just picked her up, put her over his shoulder and dragged her out of there when he had the chance, maybe she never would have wound up where she did. Maybe he could have stopped it. He knows now at least that she had a short period of sobriety, of health. But she could have had more. She could have been more. In his darker moments, he imagines what her life could have been if he hadn't made her have the baby, or worse still, what would have happened if she'd never gotten pregnant in the first place. If he'd had a closer eye on her, if he'd protected her better, things could have been so different for her. She might be a doctor or a lawyer or a dancer or a singer. She always did love music. Without Alice, he has only his own thoughts for company, and they've often tended down this track. He never quite forgave himself. He still wakes up nights, even now, berating himself for not knowing she had a boyfriend, for not putting a stop to it when he had the chance. It eats away at him that he never even found out who the damn boyfriend was. It was why he'd caved and called the PI again a few months back. The guilt got the better of him.

He came back to town in the dead of night, on a tip from the detective, who found out Sarah was heading out that way – only it was already too late by then. He'd been off the case too long, had lost the scent. He'd let her get off his radar. She was harder to track, it turned out, when she'd settled into a normal life. There were no more run-ins with the cops, no more red flags to help them pinpoint her whereabouts. He followed her as far as Christie's place after she got out of rehab, but when her name was removed from the lease, he lost her. He'd managed to track down a credit card payment – through less than legal means, Seth suspected – for her train ticket from Chicago to Milwaukee, but he'd lost the thread again when she started heading north, alternating between cabs and buses along the way. He was too far behind her by then, and the next news he got was that she was dead.

Seth had sold his practice in town – there was another lawyer in there for a while, although when he drove by to check, the place looked deserted – but he never sold his house. He never told Alice, or anyone else for that matter. He kept the deed the whole time, and he still has it now, just as it was when he left it, furniture and all. He'd told her they needed to start completely fresh, and that meant they couldn't take anything with them but their clothes. She'd been so focused on Sarah, on trying to get her through her pregnancy in one piece, that she'd hardly even questioned it.

The door stuck a little when he unlocked it, but inside, everything was the same. He rented it out for a little while, but the tenants he'd managed to sweet-talk into taking the place didn't stick around long, even though he'd given them a huge discount on the rent. There were three sets of them – a couple first, then a group of friends, then a family. But none of them stayed. They all moved on, the way everyone always did, and after that, he didn't bother to bring in new ones. No hard feelings, they all said, but this house is fucking creepy, or variations thereon. He can see their point. He let it sit there, and the longer it sat there, the more desolate it became. The paint started to peal. The hinges on the doors started to rust. Now, here it is, waiting for him, power, water, heat all still working, but cold and silent as the grave – everything just the way it had been the day the last tenants moved out. He knows Sarah's already dead. His PI, a paunchy, impatient man in his late fifties named Wallace Wick, with skin puckered and pitted by teenage acne, had come up here once he figured out where she was heading, and sneaked into the first town meeting about her. He'd been sitting in his car, getting a feel for the town, he said, and then he'd caught wind of some kind of a commotion, and he'd followed everybody into the church, not even knowing what was going on. It amazes Seth somewhat that no one saw him or spoke to him: people here could smell an outsider a mile off, and they would have been on high alert, too, once they found out what happened. Wick must have been like some kind of fat, middle-aged cat burglar to get in and out undetected. What he needs to do now, though, is find out whether Jacob Christie is the one who killed her.

He knows she was here before she died. She was in the house. He's sure of it. She probably found the spare key on the lintel, where it's been since he bought the place. He thinks about her reaching up to grab it, having to stretch up on tiptoes to get to it, and almost smiles. Before things got bad, when the worst trouble she ever got in was staying out past curfew, he'd caught her once or twice, trying to sneak back into the house without anybody noticing. She'd stand there, hangdog, hiding her face behind her hair, and then he'd reprimand her gently and send her to bed. He misses that little girl more than anything.

It wouldn't have been too hard for her to find out that his name was still on the deed and it would have been easier for her to hide here than at the hotel. She didn't need to pay for anything or give her name to anybody. She'd have had to take a chance that the heat and the electricity were still connected; he imagines how relieved she must have been when she turned the thermostat up and felt the temperature rise. There was a little residual warmth when he got there. It was almost like he could have called out and she'd have answered. She couldn't have stayed long – there was nothing in the fridge, no crumbs or food wrappers anywhere. But she was here. There was – still is – a nightgown hanging over the chair in her old bedroom and a toothbrush on the nightstand, just like when she was a child.

Since all this started, his money isn't, has never been, on the girl's real father. He didn't even know who the man was for a long time, but Wick had figured it out eventually. Seth had given him permission to dig into Alice's past, and he'd dug up John Callaghan. But Callaghan is spineless – always has been. He's a gnat, a fly in his peripheral vision, the cowardly pretty boy who stole Alice's heart, then cut and ran when things looked too much like hard work. He'd run away before he'd do anything that took real balls, and killing somebody would certainly fall into that category. Besides which, he wouldn't want to get those lily-white hands dirty. The boyfriend, though. The boyfriend is more of an unknown quantity – Wick's words. He picked up a little of the lingo as time passed, learned to talk like a detective and to think a little bit like one, too. When he hired Wick for the second time, it took him over. It became the only thing he really knew. Finding her became his sole purpose. All his money, all his time, all his energy went into the search. There was always a strong possibility that there would be a body at the end of the trail. He knew that. He wasn't naïve enough to think a happy ending was guaranteed. But now that he's here, now that he knows for sure there's no saving her, he still can't stop. He can't give up on her.

Christie reminds him a little of Callaghan – good looking, smooth, charming. Slippery. But he's got an edge to him that Callaghan never had. He's got a criminal record and a hot temper, according to Wick. He stopped asking how Wick got his information early on – he's sure at least some of his methods aren't above board. Twice, he met him in his tiny, stinking office, and twice, it was enough to make Seth's blood run cold. But despite his recent lapse – for which Seth blames himself more than the detective – he hasn't led him astray so far. He knows which leads to follow, which ones aren't going anywhere. In the beginning, there were a few ex-pimps and ex-dealers who were good for old addresses, but not much else. Wick had a sort of freelance goon squad to help him "question" these men, but they could only help them to figure where Sarah had been – not where she'd ended up. Computer records, on the other hand, could be gold mines. Seth had just nodded silently when he said that, knowing it was extremely unlikely the police would just let him casually nose through confidential records. So he stopped asking questions and let Wick do what needed to be done.

There's something else, though. Wick's been staying up in Ashland, away from the prying eyes of the town's more ambitious gossips, and something caught his eye. There was a girl, he said – a girl who looked almost exactly like Sarah. It had, in his own words, almost given him a goddamn coronary, the resemblance was so striking. So he'd followed her – all stealthy, don't you worry, McIntyre – and set up camp outside her house, not really sure what he was looking for. He waited almost the whole night and he was about to call it quits when somebody showed up at her door – a man. A skinny, twitchy looking guy, sort of creepy, he'd thought. But she certainly seemed to know him – kissed him when she opened the door and let him into the house. So he'd waited until near dawn, when the guy came back out again, and he'd followed him all the way back to town. He would, he promised, find out who he was, who the girl was and more importantly, whether either of them were connected to Sarah. A day had passed since then, and another meeting, too, and now here they are again.

After the last town meeting, Abernathy had been absorbed with the Faheys, and Seth was pretty sure he'd been able to slip in and out unseen before he came to meet Wick. The designated spot was in the parking lot of the grocery store. Now, Wick, for all his promises of stealth, is standing right under a security camera, a cloud of cigarette smoke swirling around his head.

"Where the fuck you been?" he growls. "I'm freezin' my fuckin' ass off." This, for Wick, is a fairly standard, even polite greeting. Seth is used to his crudeness by now, but he still flinches a little at the language.

"In the church. I thought you'd be there too?" he says. Wick snorts derisively.

"Come on. The cops don't got jack shit. I'd keep a low profile from now on if I was you, though. They gotta know you're here by now." There's a long, deliberate silence, in which he gives him a knowing look, which raises Seth's hackles. He knows they know he's here – he's not stupid – but it's not as though he hasn't been careful. He's been keeping the lowest profile possible – hardly leaving the house other than to visit Alice's grave, parking the car at the back where no one can see it – and he resents the implication that he wouldn't have thought to do that. He narrows his eyes, trying not to lose his temper.

"I know that," he says, through clenched teeth. Wick, fortunately, takes the hint.

"I, on the other hand, got big news," he says. Wick takes a deep drag on his cigarette, mouth curling just slightly at the edges. He never really smiles, Seth's noticed, just twists his mouth. He's like something out of a comic book, he thinks, and half the time, he's convinced at least some of it must be an act – all bravado and bad language, always obscured by cigarette smoke. But he trusts him. It's been long enough – years, in fact, all told – and he probably trusts this foul-mouthed, chain smoking, cantankerous ex-cop more than he's trusted anybody since Alice. He knows almost nothing about the man himself, but he's come to know that his word means something.

"Ok. What is it?" Seth asks, moving to stand on Wick's left to make sure his own face is out of reach of the security camera.

"Fuck you doin'? Ain't no fuckin' cotillion here, stand still. You wanna know or not?" Seth takes a deep breath, and coughs a little, trying not to inhale too much smoke.

"Yes. I wanna know."

"Ok. The girl is John Callaghan's daughter Mary, and the guy is some local asshole named Jimmy Murphy. He's been steppin' out on his wife with the little slut, and on top o' that, he knocked her up."

"How do you know all that?" Seth blurts. He can't help it. He simply can't fathom how Wick could possibly know so much. The detective rolls his eyes.

"Easy," he says, twisting his mouth again. "He ain't no goddamn spy. All I had to do was go to Mawhinney's right before closin'. Everybody was so fuckin' drunk, I just had to ask – didn't take long to put it together. Even better, none of 'em'll be able to swear to seein' me." He drops the remains of his cigarette on the frozen ground, stubbing it out with the toe of one scuffed shoe. "Seems this Murphy guy ain't exactly Mr. Popularity, either."

"So?" Seth dimly remembers a kid named Murphy from Sarah's class. He hadn't been up to much, he recalls: skinny back then, too, and not exactly in with the in crowd – kind of a weirdo, in fact. He'd been friends with that Gallagher kid, but nobody else that he can remember.

"So? *So?*" Wick hisses. He's building up to something. Seth knows this tactic. He's killing time, as much as anything else so he can charge him more later. He sighs.

"So?"

"*So* he was there that night. He was with Sarah the night she died. It ain't the boyfriend. It's him."

"How can you be sure?"

"Because one o' them good-for-nothin' drunks turned out to be good for somethin'. Said he saw 'em. Murphy kept callin' her Mary and when he tried to kiss her, she slapped him and ran off. He musta followed her outside. It's him. I can feel it in my gut." Until now, that would have been enough for Seth. Wick is savvy and conniving and almost always right. But now, something doesn't quite sit right about the whole thing. His lawyer's brain is kicking in and he can't shut it off. As long as they thought Sarah was alive, proof didn't matter. All that mattered was finding her. Now, they need proof.

"But that doesn't really prove anything. It just means he was with her right before she…" He can't bring himself to say it – not yet. The idea that this creep Murphy was the last person to see her alive does turn his stomach, but his own gut is telling him not to count Jacob Christie out just yet. Wick sighs and coughs, spitting on the ground.

"Fine. I'll get you your goddamn proof. And I'll throw in the boyfriend, too, if it'll make you happy." He turns to go, but stops for a second, looking back at Seth, who's uncomfortably aware that the security camera now has a clear shot at his face. "Hey. D'you ever think her high school boyfriend might have anything to do with this? You know, the one that knocked her up?" He shrugs. The idea, if he's honest with himself, has crossed his mind once or twice, but it never amounted to much. He never did find out who it was, and he couldn't find any evidence that they'd ever crossed paths again.

"No. Why don't you see if you can throw him in, too?" he says, coldly. There's a note of anger in his voice and he hopes Wick will think it's directed at him.

"Fine," Wick says, turning away. "Watch your step, McIntyre." It's something between a threat and a friendly warning and it makes him nervous. He wishes he knew what was going on already, wishes he didn't need Wick anymore, but the fact is, he does. He needs him to keep digging. He needs him to get to the truth.

Mary knew somebody had been watching them that night, but she never said anything to Jimmy. It was the middle of the night when he got there, and he was noticeably squirrelly, mumbling about people following him. Her own mind was already threatening to get the better of her – who was out there, was it because of Sarah, was it him, was he back, had he come for her, who was out there, who was out there, who was out there – but she knew better than to rile him up any more.

"Jimmy," she said, gently, once she got him to sit down with her on the couch. He's been pacing up and down her living room for what felt like hours, and she'd hardly been able to get a word in the whole time. None of it made very much sense. It was all just half-thoughts, rantings and ravings about how everybody was out to get him, everybody wanted to see him burn. It was scaring her.

"Jimmy, will you please tell me what's going on? Who's following you? Why?" she interrupted at last.

"Everybody!" he said, turning to look at her for the first time since he'd been there. "Mary, they…they think I had some'n to do with…that girl…with what happened." She stared at him, feeling all the color drain out of her face.

"What? Why?" she asked, her voice fading almost to nothing.

"Because I was there that night!" he exploded. "I was there an' I-I kissed 'er. She jus' looked so much like you and…"

"And?" she pushed, not sure she wanted to hear the answer.

"And nothin'! She left and the next thing I know she shows up dead. But the cops think 'cause I was there and I was drunk…they think it was me. They think I killed 'er."

"And...did you?" she whispered before she could stop herself. He stared at her, tears in his eyes.

"No! Mary, I...God, this is such a fuckin' nightmare." He pressed his hands over his eyes, tilting his head back for a second, like he was having a nosebleed. "Look, I'm an asshole, ok? I know it. But I'm not a fuckin' monster. I swear I didn't hurt that woman!" She nodded, giving his arm a gentle squeeze.

"Ok. Ok."

It gave her a strange, sick feeling to realize how much more easily she could believe her own father to be capable of hurting someone like that than she could believe it of Jimmy. But he didn't have it in him. Anybody could see that. He wasn't smart enough for one thing – not cold enough, not calculating enough. He was a philanderer, a weak, feckless coward. But he wasn't a killer. He was quiet for another minute, and then he grabbed her wrist, eyes wild, flashing, like a feral animal.

"Let's run away," he said, grinning manically, almost creepily. He was clutching her wrist so tightly it was starting to hurt, but she felt afraid suddenly – too afraid to struggle. "You and me. Let's go. Let's ditch this shithole and start over. Whaddaya say? We can be a real family!" He reached for her stomach, trying to touch the bump, to feel his child, and she came back to herself then. She pulled away from him and wrenched her wrist free from his other hand.

"No," she said, flatly.

"No? Why not?" He seemed genuinely surprised. She breathed in slowly.

"Because we wouldn't be a family. We'd be criminals. Come on, Jimmy, you don't think they'd find us? I don't want to spend my whole life looking over my shoulder. I don't want to be a fugitive and I sure as hell don't want that for my kid."

"But...it'd be so perfect! I could take care o' you. What could be better'n that?" he persisted. His eyes were wide, agitated, and she could see the sweat starting to bead on his forehead.

"No, Jimmy. You have to stay here and face this. You have to go home. You have to go back to her."

"But *why*?" he asked again. He was starting to get really desperate. She knew it. It broke her heart to see him looking like that. But she held firm.

"Because you don't love me." He stared at her, his breathing still a little labored, but finally, the weird manic light had gone out of his eyes. He fell silent and dropped his arms limply to his sides, like he'd physically deflated.

"Look, Jimmy, I'm just a distraction. I always was. You know that. You should be with Sally. She's the one who needs you. You have a chance here. You can do something right. Don't waste that."

"But... the baby..." Jimmy murmured, his voice small and pathetic. She shook her head.

"We'll be fine. To tell you the truth, I... I've been thinking about going back to California anyway. This... this could actually be... good for me." It was, in point of fact, the first time the thought had even occurred to her, but she needed something real and big to convince him, and two thousand miles of land seemed just real and big enough. He nodded, silently. He knew she was right. He sat there a little while longer, holding her like he did when they first met, and then he left and he never came back.

Katie finally gets up the nerve to go and talk to Sally the day after the town meeting. She didn't go – couldn't bear to. She'd been feeling a little better after her encounter with Jacob and didn't want to spoil it. For all it was over with so quickly, she'd enjoyed it. She never had gotten round to finding out what he was doing in town, but the prospect that she still might had buoyed her as well. It had given her something to think about, something to focus on. But she couldn't find him after that night. It was like he'd just disappeared. Now that she's at Sally's front door, she feels enervated, broken. She sighs as she opens the screen door, and raps at the fragile glass pane in front of her. The house itself seems bowed under the weight of something terrible. There's something rotten here, figuratively and literally – there's a foul smell coming from the garbage cans, which are overflowing onto the street. Sally answers a few seconds later and she hardly recognizes her. She's never been beautiful, but now, she looks almost inhuman. She's shrunken, hollowed out, like all the life has been pulled out of her.

"Hi," Katie whispers, trying to muster a smile.

"Katie," Sally croaks, blinking in the half light. "Come…come in."

"Jimmy," Sally says, as Katie follows her into the living room. "This is my sister – Katie."

Jimmy is sitting on the couch, head tilted back, eyes closed. He looks even worse than Sally, his skin pale and waxy. Something seems wrong about him, but she can't quite put her finger on what it is.

"Aren't you going to say hello?" Sally asks. He grunts, but he doesn't move.

"You, um...you know there's some guy out there, watching us?" Katie says, coughing a little. The air is thick with cigarette smoke and it's hard to breathe.

"'S prob'ly one o' the Mitchell brothers," Jimmy says, without opening his eyes. "They been followin' me for days."

"It...it didn't look like it...I mean, I remember the Mitchells and...well, he looked too old, for one thing," Katie says, suddenly feeling timid. She's never actually met Jimmy before, at least not that she can remember, and it's not the best of first impressions. He opens one eye and shrugs.

"Prob'ly one o' their buddies, then," he says, closing his eye again.

"What's...what's going on?" Katie asks, perching on the edge of an armchair. She hardly knows where to look and she's glad of the gloom. Jimmy sits up then, and looks at her properly for the first time.

"You mean you don't know?" She shakes her head, trying not to show how afraid she is.

"They think I killed somebody. That's what's going on," he says, his voice suddenly hard, almost threatening. He flops back again and stares up at the ceiling.

"You mean...you mean that girl they found up by the woods? Sarah something?" Phil, the desk clerk, hadn't been able to shut up about it and she'd let him talk at her a while when she couldn't find Jacob.

"McIntyre," Sally says, stiffly. "Sarah McIntyre."

"But...why?" She knows there's more than one way to read the question, but she doesn't clarify.

"Because I was the last person t'see 'er alive," Jimmy mutters. She wants to press further, to ask all the questions suddenly crowding into her head, but she stops herself. She knows now what it was that seemed off about him – he's drunk. So drunk, in fact, she's surprised he's even conscious.

"Katie, come...come to the kitchen, I'll fix us a snack," Sally says, her voice cracking. Obediently, Katie gets up and follows her into the tiny galley kitchen. It smells even worse in there than it does in the living room – of damp and of rotting food.

"Sally, what the fuck is this?" she whispers, unable to stop herself. Her sister sighs and turns her back to her, pressing her hands against the counter as though she's afraid she might fall down.

"He was with her the night she died. He tried to kiss her. Now the cops think he had something to do with...what happened." She's speaking so quietly, Katie almost can't hear her, but she can't bear to make her repeat herself.

"But you don't," she says, gently encouraging her to keep going. She knows Sally won't have said a word to anyone about what she's feeling. Their father won't have offered any support and she doesn't have any friends, Katie's sure of that. Sally shakes her head.

"No," she says, turning to look at her sister. "I think it was her father. He's back in town – I saw him in church the other day. I just can't believe that's a coincidence. You remember him, right? He was always so creepy, always watching everybody and never saying anything. I knew something had to be up." She's speaking quickly, almost manically. She's desperate. Katie can hear it in her voice.

"Oh, Sally," she breathes. She's about to put her arms around her, but Sally pulls away, making herself even smaller. She moves to try again, but a knock at the door interrupts them. Sally moves to answer it, but Jimmy's already up. Katie can see him swaying towards the door from the little serving hatch in the wall. She looks over at her sister, but her face is still turned, hidden in shadow. When she realizes what's happening, she suddenly shifts into motion, but it's too late.

"Jimmy, don't!" she yells. There's fear in her voice, Katie realizes, and she desperately wishes she'd come here sooner. Now, though, there's nothing she can do to help. When she looks again, the door is already open and little Tommy Hausmann is standing there in a police uniform. He looks so ridiculous, she almost laughs. He looks like a kid, playing dress-up, but for the gun at his side.

"Fuck d'you want?" Jimmy slurs. Tommy clears his throat and tries to make himself as tall as he can.

"We..." he begins, but he has to stop to clear his throat again as his voice hitches. "We got a complaint about the smell coming from your garbage cans."

"So? Don't hardly seem like a reason to call the cops," Jimmy says, belligerently. He's not doing himself any favors, but Sally doesn't move to stop him again. It's like she's frozen, stuck to the kitchen floor.

"Even so," Tommy says, a little more forcefully this time. "I'd like to take a look around." Jimmy shrugs.

"Whatever floats yer boat," he growls. "You wanna go diggin' through my trash, knock yerself out." Tommy, who's clearly been holding his breath, waiting for a fight from Jimmy, lets out a tiny involuntary squeak, and Katie can't help snickering just a little. He jerks his head, startled, and looks directly at her for the first time.

"Ma'am, this is no laughing – Katie!"

"Hi, Tommy. Didn't know they let kids into the force these days," she says. She knows she shouldn't be joking around, but the whole thing just seems so bizarre that she doesn't really know how she should be acting. It's like being in ninth grade again, getting hauled up in front of the principal, knowing she shouldn't be smirking, but powerless to stop herself. It's a weakness of hers: when she doesn't know what to do, that's when the giggles take over. Tommy coughs and puffs out his chest a little.

"Look, I really should…I mean, I have to…"

"Right. You've got important garbage to search."

"*Katie*," Sally hisses. It's the first word she's said since Tommy showed up and she finally seems to have come back to life.

"Sorry," Katie says, trying desperately to wipe the smile off her face. "But come on, he must be, what, fourteen?" She looks back at her sister and sees her face properly for the first time since she's been there – she's smiling too now, though she's clearly trying just as hard as Katie to stop herself. Tommy doesn't say anything else as he leaves the house, though she's sure she sees his lip tremble just a fraction, and that's the end of it. She can't hold it in anymore. Once she starts laughing, Sally joins her, and the pair of them clutch at each other, almost doubled over with hysterics. There's something wonderful in it, too. It brings the humanity back to Sally's face.

"The fuck you two laughin' at?" Jimmy yells from the living room. He sounds genuinely angry but that just makes it worse. It's all just so

181

goddamn *funny* all of a sudden. They don't even stop when Tommy Hausmann reappears, holding what looks like a filthy rag in his gloved hand. There are little bits of eggshell and lumpy, yellowish milk clinging to his sleeves, making him look even more ridiculous.

"Is this yours, Mrs. Murphy?" he asks, quietly. Sally swallows, trying to contain herself.

"No," she says, her voice still quaking. "What is it?"

"It's a dress, Mrs. Murphy. It's got blood on it." The silence that falls then is so heavy and sudden that time almost seems to stop for a moment.

"Mr. Murphy? Do you recognize it?" Tommy asks, turning to Jimmy, who's swaying violently now. He shakes his head, but he doesn't say anything. "Mr. Murphy?" Tommy says again, as Jimmy drops to his knees.

"It…it looks like the one…she was wearin'…" he whispers. All the color drains from Tommy's face as realization dawns.

"Don't move," he says, and darts back outside, slamming the door behind him.

"Jimmy? Jimmy, what the fuck did you do?" Sally yells, her hand shooting out to grab at Katie's arm with surprising force.

"Nothin'! I swear! I don't know how that dress got in our garbage!" he sobs. Katie can see Tommy outside at his car, and she can suddenly see two of the Mitchells, too. They can't know what's going on, surely. They can't have figured it out yet. They're not smart enough to do it that fast – but it won't be too long, and then all hell is going to break loose, and she won't be able to do a damn thing to stop it. Katie's heart is pounding in her chest. She knows Tommy must be radioing for help, but she doesn't see how help can get here fast enough.

Wallace Wick, like so many PIs before him, used to be a cop. He was a good cop, too. It was in his blood – had been all his life. When he was a kid and the other boys his age were dreaming of being astronauts or cowboys or firefighters, he dreamed of being a super sleuth. He wanted to be Dick Tracy. He put everything he had into getting there, and it paid off. For close to twenty years, he'd worked as a homicide detective for the Chicago PD and he loved it. He made it his business to be more devoted to the job than anybody else. It was everything to him: there was no division between Wick the cop and Wick the man.

He was great at getting results, too – so much so that his colleagues nicknamed him the bloodhound. He was relentless – smarter than he let on, methodical and wily, never using force if he didn't have to, knowing instinctively which angles to pursue and which would lead him up a blind alley. He was what a cop should be, his superiors said, and it made him swell with pride. He had more awards and commendations than anybody he knew. He lived and breathed it – would've made a great captain, they said, or even police commissioner one day. But he didn't want to end up a fat desk jockey: he wanted the glory, to get shot on the job. That was his fondest wish – to die in the line of duty. He'd been all but married to the job, and he'd have given his life to the force if he could. Women drifted in and out of his life, but none of them ever stuck around long. They all got tired of coming second in the end. But it didn't bother him. It was ok. He was ok being alone. He liked his routine, liked his privacy, and he would have made a lousy father anyway. That was ok.

It was the red tape he couldn't stand in the end – the box ticking and the form filling and the endless ways the city stood in his way when all he wanted to do was help. The judges who let truly evil people go free. The juries who made the wrong call. The bureaucrats who blocked him at every turn. So, at fifty, he made a change. He'd had enough. He was getting out on his own. With no wife and no kids, he had no one to provide for but himself. It surprised everyone who knew him. The woman he'd been half dating at the time was convinced he'd lost his mind, and left him pretty soon afterwards. They all thought he'd get what he wanted – that some thug would shoot him in the back of the head or throw him off a bridge or stab him in the gut one day and that would be that. Wallace Wick was born a cop and he was supposed to die one.

For a long time, it had felt like the right call. The only thing that stung was losing the woman, Sylvie. He'd liked her – thought maybe he could even love her. But she got spooked, and he didn't have it in him to try to fight for her. He'd lost his faith in the law, lost his faith in everything he'd been so sure of. So he started operating at the fringes of his old world, making connections with people he wouldn't have hesitated to arrest in the old days. They were scum. There was no getting around it. But they got it done. Before long, he had a cadre of shady characters on his books – hackers-for-hire, muscle-for-hire, snitches-for-hire, anybody who'd take a buck to bend the law or drop someone in it – and even though he was stuck in his tiny, filthy office, upstairs from a crappy Chinese restaurant, he still thought he was doing some good. He was still getting results, getting criminals off the street, even if he never got the credit for it. It never really bothered him that he couldn't say outright that he was one of the good guys anymore. He wasn't one of the bad guys and that was enough. Now, for the first time in nearly ten years, he wonders if he made a mistake. There's no one to back him up, no one to turn to but the stony, taciturn man who's been paying him to find out what happened to his dead stepdaughter.

It's the one case that's gotten the best of him, his whole career. He thought he'd seen it all, but this…nothing ever got under his skin like this. The whole thing was so sad. She was alive when he started looking for her and alive when he found her the first time. It was just that back then, she didn't want to be found. He never actually met the girl, but he got to know her pretty well, watching her, studying her. It was simple, really. She just wanted to be left alone. McIntyre had given up before he got a chance to tell him that, let it drop for more than two years. He never did say why he came back – an attack of conscience maybe, or some resurgent sense of family duty – and he never asked.

He was reluctant to take the case again, though. There was something that told him it couldn't end well. This girl was never going to get her happily ever after. He knew it. When he found her that first time, she already had the stench of death on her – maybe always had. He'd been doing this long enough to know it when he saw it. Some people just had limited time, and sooner or later, their numbers always came up. The real killer with this one, though, was that she did get clean. She was doing ok, had a job, had a boyfriend – pretty much a shmuck, truth be told, but he treated her well enough and he did seem like he wanted to get past his own problems. He'd thought maybe, just maybe she could outrun fate. Maybe it would even stop chasing her. Maybe she could be the exception to prove the rule. That was as far as he got when she upped and vanished. If he's honest with himself, he dropped the ball. He'd been on the point of telling McIntyre he quit – telling him she was fine, she didn't need saving anymore and he should let her live her life. But when she disappeared, all his old instincts kicked into overdrive. He knew immediately that he wasn't going to find her again – at least not alive. Now he wishes he'd never let McIntyre talk him back into the case. It had taken a lot of persuasion and the promise of an obscene bonus payment to convince him. If he hadn't given in, he wouldn't be here now. He could be chasing no-good husbands and two-bit drug dealers. He wouldn't know.

When he got here, it hit him hard. This whole town has that familiar stink. There's a cloud of death hanging over everything and it knocked him off balance. He'd gone up to Ashland under the pretense of keeping out of sight, but the truth of it was he couldn't bear to stay there. It was oppressive. It got in his lungs, in his eyes, choked him, blinded him. If he'd stayed, it would have swallowed him up, like it swallowed her. He couldn't say whether that stink was always there or Sarah brought it with her, but it's sure as hell there now, and it's not going anywhere. There's no antidote for this poison.

"We gotta get outta this place. Like, five minutes ago," Wick says, breathlessly. He'd called McIntyre in the middle of the night, leaving him a message telling him where to meet and he'd half thought he might not show. He's winded and scared. The last few days especially have taken a toll on him – more so than he realized. This town is *bad*. He knows that for sure now. There's something sick about it. He could sense it before he even set foot within its boundaries. The people here have so many secrets, even the skeletons have skeletons in their closets. He's picked up bits and pieces of it since he's been here, watching people, listening to them when they think they're alone, hiding in plain sight – it's what makes him so great at what he does and what makes him hate humanity a little bit more every day. There's Kathy Rafferty with her sham marriage, Lorelei Lefferts with her compulsive shoplifting, Andrew Mitchell who slept with his stepmother, the affairs, the wretchedness, the lies on top of lies on top of lies. Even that diner guy, Hal something. His wife didn't die. She left him. There are too many things buried here, too many people who aren't who they say they are. The whole place is resting on one big powder keg – he felt it as soon as he arrived and he feels it now. This sense of deep, unshakeable fear is new for him, though. He's just waiting for the fuse to run out, waiting for it all to go spectacularly up in smoke. He can see it unnerves McIntyre, but he can't hide it. He asked to meet in the same parking lot a day later, only this time, he outright insisted on doing it in the middle of the day, when as many people could see them as possible. He wants witnesses. He wants people to know where he is and when.

"Why?" Seth asks, blindsided.

"Because the shit's about to hit the goddamn fan," Wick wheezes.

"Why? Did you find something? Was it the high school boyfriend? Did you track him down?" Seth presses. He's speaking quickly, fearfully now, but Wick still finds himself losing patience. He shakes his head, trying to catch his breath.

"No. No, nobody remembers who she was datin' back then, much less if he's even still in town. Looks like she hid it from everybody, not just you. But listen, I don't...I don't think he's our guy. It's...I think it's Murphy." Seth's jaw tightens.

"What about the new boyfriend? Christie?" he says. Wick can already feel himself starting to lose it. McIntyre is wasting time and time is one thing he doesn't have. He shakes his head again.

"No. No, I'm tellin' you, it's Murphy, and it's about to get real fuckin' messy. We're outta time," he says, impatiently.

"You have proof?" McIntyre asks. Wick nods, rapidly. He wants to run, but he still has something of a sense of honor, and he forces himself to hold his nerve. He has to tell McIntyre the truth. The problem, of course, is that he doesn't know what will happen after the news gets out, which, inevitably, it will. People, he's long since learned, are volatile creatures, and never more so than when they think they're cornered. Here, it's even worse. It's like there's a bubble over this town, and there's pressure building underneath it all the time. Once word gets around, there'll either be a riot or a public hanging, and it won't be long, either. He knows a couple of local toughs were hanging around Murphy's place. They'll already be out for blood. People here are so afraid of being found out that they'll do anything to keep prying eyes out of their own backyards – and now they've got themselves a scapegoat. Hell, Murphy probably isn't even the worst of them. But they'll want justice, or some fucked up version of it, and they won't stop until they get it. All he knows is that he doesn't want to be around when that powder keg blows.

"Yeah. I got proof," he says. "I was sittin' on his place and the cops started sniffin' around – don't know why, didn't ask – but they found somethin' in his garbage can. They found her fuckin' clothes."

There they are, all five of them in the station, lined up like targets at the shooting range. John Callaghan, Seth McIntyre, Zachariah Fahey, Zachariah Fahey, Jr., and Jacob Christie. The two Faheys had been in after the meeting, but in the end, he'd had to wait on Christie for another day and he'd had to tell them to sit tight. At first, Abernathy thought maybe he'd bolted. He wasn't at the hotel when he'd gone to look for him, although his stuff was still there, including whatever coke hadn't found its way up his nose. He put Legler on his tail, hoping, praying he wouldn't get far. But then he'd showed up of his own accord, high as a goddamn kite, begging to be allowed into the morgue to see Sarah. He had to get Legler to restrain him until he started to come down, and then finally, he'd thrown him into the drunk tank to keep him in line until he sobered up properly. That was when the Faheys showed up, puffed up with rage, demanding to know why Christie hadn't been brought in yet, and he'd at least been able to tell them they had him, even if he obscured how it had happened.

Seth, according to Shelly, had come in just a few minutes after the Faheys, looking flushed and agitated, like he had something he needed to say, and Callaghan not long after that. In limbo, not knowing whether or not he was still a suspect, his anxiety had got the better of him, and he didn't seem wholly sure how he'd come to be there. He'd come in all wild eyed and confused, Shelly said, but Abernathy had been so busy dealing with Christie, he hadn't even realized he was there at first. Now, Callaghan, McIntyre and the Faheys are just standing there, staring at him, waiting for him to speak. It's like some sort of incredibly morbid miracle. Abernathy sighs and rests his hands on his hips. He can see Shelly Eriksen in the periphery of his vision, fidgeting nervously, and he wishes he could tell her she can go.

"All right," he says at last. "All right. Zachariah, Mr. Fahey, go with Eriksen, she'll take you to the breakroom and get you a cup of coffee. John, Seth, go with Legler, and for chrissakes, stay put 'til I'm ready to deal with you. Shelly, while you're at it, find Showalter. And where the fuck is Hausmann?" He's yelling. He doesn't want to yell – Shelly already looks like she could cry – but the whole thing is turning into one never-ending fuck-up and he can't help himself. Everyone scatters, all suddenly looking like frightened schoolchildren, and he feels himself regain a little of his authority. For his own part, he heads down to the drunk tank himself to pick Christie up. He's more or less sober now, but pale and quivering in his handcuffs. Abernathy grabs him roughly by the arm – harder than he needs to, really – but Christie doesn't flinch. Instead, he follows him meekly, silently back to his office.

"Sit," Abernathy barks. "You back on earth yet?" Christie laughs humorlessly, lowering himself gingerly into the chair opposite Abernathy's desk.

"That's the thing about coke," he says, smiling grimly. "Doesn't last long. 'S why you want more." Abernathy narrows his eyes.

"Listen, pretty boy," he hisses, through gritted teeth. "We like you for murder. So you better start taking this seriously." Christie sits up, suddenly alert.

"Wait, what? You think *I* killed Sarah?" he whispers.

"As a matter of fact, we do. We know you followed her here. We know about your record. We know about your temper, and we know you like to hit people when you lose it. How am I doing so far?" Christie is silent for a moment, staring empty-eyed ahead.

"Sarah knew all that," he says, more to himself than to Abernathy. "She knew all that, and she wanted me anyway. God, I'm such a shit." He drops his head, clasping his hands behind it. Abernathy can see he's shaking and he almost feels sorry for him.

"Yeah, that's the prevailing opinion. You got a reason why I should think otherwise?"

"Not really," Christie says, looking up. "But I didn't kill Sarah. I have an alibi. Ask Katie Weiler." Abernathy stares at him, hardly able to believe what he's hearing.

"You're telling me," he begins, "that your alibi for the night your girlfriend was murdered…is that you were sleeping with somebody else?" Christie nods. He looks like he's on the point of tears. Abernathy sighs. His only hope now is that Callaghan or McIntyre might still have something useful to say.

"Ok. We'll have to talk to Katie before we can…"He stops, though. He can see Tommy Hausmann through his window, running towards the door like he isn't even going to stop.

"Chief!" he yells, breathlessly, as he bursts inside.

"Hausmann, I'm kind of in the middle of something in here," Abernathy says, as patiently as he can. Hausmann shakes his head. Abernathy is about to kick him out, but he can see the kid is genuinely spooked. He gets up and grabs his arm – a little more gently than he did with Christie, but not much – and ushers him outside. He looks back over his shoulder, glaring.

"You," he says to Christie. "Do not move a goddamn muscle." He shuts the door and locks it behind him, resting his hands on Hausmann's shoulders. He breathes out slowly, puffing out his cheeks.

"Ok, Hausmann. This had better be the most important thing you have ever said." The kid is shaking all over – so much so, he can hardly speak, and Abernathy can see the effort he's going through just to get the words out.

"You gotta come. Showalter just arrested Murphy. He's bringin' him in now. I…I found her clothes. I found 'em in his garbage can," Hausmann gabbles.

"What? What are you talking about?" Abernathy asks. Hausmann swallows hard, briefly glancing at Christie through the door and then back at Abernathy, hesitating. The old man is losing patience. There isn't time for this.

"Come on, kid, tell me what happened!" Abernathy snaps. Hausmann colors, but manfully, he keeps going.

"Legler...Legler sent me out there to deal with some bogus call about a nuisance, sort of like a joke. I...I think he just wanted me out of the way. Some...some old busybody called us up, complaining about the smell comin' from the garbage cans and Legler said I had to...so I...I thought, hey, here's my chance. I can poke around, see what I can find, and...there it was, under a bunch of rotten eggs and old bread and stuff."

"There what was?" Abernathy asks. He's trying hard not to lose his temper, and he's acutely aware that Christie is sitting there behind his paper thin door, probably able to hear all this.

"A dress. And it had blood on it."

"So why the hell'd you wait for Showalter to come and make the collar for you?" Abernathy yells. It's too late. There's no point holding back now and he might as well take it out on Hausmann as anyone. The kid is hardly able to keep his composure, he can see that: he's never raised his voice to him before, or even in his presence, as far as he can remember, and he startles himself.

"Because...because the Mitchell brothers were there. They were hovering around and I...I couldn't hold 'em off by myself. I needed...I needed back up," Hausmann stammers, his own voice shrinking away under Abernathy's ire. Abernathy breathes in deeply and drops his arms to his sides. He scrubs his hand over his mouth and tilts his head back for a second, trying to calm down.

"Goddamn it. God*damn* it. They didn't do anything, did they?" he asks, forcing himself to take the volume down a few notches.

"No...I'm pretty sure it was all just talk. But Chief, Mrs. Murphy's still home by herself. Her sister's there, but...she can't...I mean, I don't know what they might do."

"Shit," Abernathy whispers, talking to himself as much as to Hausmann. "Shit. Ok. Here's what we're gonna do. Showalter's got Murphy, so that's a start. You're gonna go back out there and talk to the wife and the sister. I don't think they'll come after her, but...somebody should be there." He pauses, collecting himself, hoping he's not sending the kid out to get his ass kicked. He shakes himself. If Hausmann wants to be a real cop in a real city one day, then he'll have to deal with much worse. "See what you can get out of the sister especially – she's Christie's alibi. Don't stay up there any longer than you have to – you come right back here and tell me what you found out. You got that? Go, go!"

Hausmann nods rapidly and turns tail, still trembling as he leaves. Breathing out hard, Abernathy all but kicks his own door down as he goes back into his office. Still seething, surprising himself with his own strength, he grabs Christie by the collar and hauls him out of his chair, shoving him hard against the wall.

"So help me God, if you are fucking with me, I will personally see to it that you end up in the deepest, darkest hole I can find. I will cast you down with the most unimaginably evil monsters ever to walk this earth and let me tell you, they'll just *love* a pretty boy like you. They'll grind you up piece by piece 'til you're begging to be put out of your misery. Hell will seem like a fucking tea party compared with what I'll put you through. Do you understand me?"

"Yes! I mean, I'm not! I swear, I'm telling the truth! Katie'll tell you!" Christie's voice comes out high and shivering. He sounds genuinely shaken and for a split second, Abernathy feels a little sliver of satisfaction at seeing the smarmy son-of-a-bitch squirm.

"You better hope she does," he says, a little more gently. "Meantime, I'm booking you for possession and public intoxication, and you just better pray I don't decide to book you for trying to interfere with a corpse, too."

Tommy has always had a little crush on Katie. She's older than him, and she skipped town with some musician ten years back, but he never forgot her. It makes him sick to think she was with someone like Christie. As he drives back out to her sister's place, he finds himself praying it's not true. He wants her to tell him Christie was lying through his bonded teeth. He wants her to laugh at Christie the way she laughed at him. The fact of the matter is, though, guys like Christie always get girls like Katie. He's seen enough movies to know beautiful girls only ever end up with beautiful, charming, rich men. It's encoded in them from the beginning. They're told what to expect and what to aim for, and that's that. They don't settle for skinny, baby-faced guys like him. Katie is Cinderella and Christie's Prince Charming. When she ran off with that guitar player, it tore him up. She was rewriting the story, but she did it for the wrong guy. She was taking the brawny bad guy over the sweet, harmless boy who'd truly love her and take care of her. Now she's rewriting the goddamn rewrite and Prince Charming's back in the picture.

He'd all but forgotten all this until he saw her again. Things had been going so well with Shelly that he'd started to think he was finally over the fantasy. He was starting to think he was ready for the real thing, and Shelly was it. Now, though, all that teenage lust and blind hope is coming back to him, and it's clouding his judgement. He physically shakes himself as he pulls up at the Murphy house, trying to calm down.

"You can do this," he mutters, keeping his eyes on his boots for a moment. They're reassuringly large and tough-looking, and for a second, he believes they make him look tough, too. Taking a ragged breath, he pounds on the door, setting his jaw.

"Police! Open up!" he yells. It's more forceful than he's expecting and he surprises himself. It feels good – gives him a little jolt of power. Katie comes to the door after a few seconds, suddenly small and meek. She looks like the teenage girl he fell in love with again, and it's all he can do not to fold her into his arms and carry her away.

"Come in, Tommy," she says, quietly. Her eyes are red and puffy and her face looks blotchy, like she's been crying. It's the first time she's ever looked anything other than beautiful to him and it's the first time he's ever noticed she's human. Hating himself for it, he realizes it makes him love her more than ever. Silently, he follows her inside, fumbling for a light switch along the wall. It's even darker in the tiny living room now and he can only just make out Sally Murphy's shape on the couch.

"I, um...I have some questions..." he stammers, all that glorious power gone as quickly as it came. "Look, can we please turn a light on? I can't hardly see." Sally's shape seems to nod and a shadowy arm stretches out for the lamp beside her. It doesn't make much difference – it's one of those cheapo energy saving bulbs and its dim yellow glow barely lights half her face – but it's better than nothing.

"Ask your questions," she says, hoarsely.

"All right," Tommy says, swallowing hard. He knows he's about to seize up but he's come too far. He can't back away now. "Well...I need to, um...I need to ask Katie if she..."

"You wanna know if I was with Jacob Christie the night that girl died," Katie interrupts, her voice suddenly hard and angry. "Yes, I was with him. We had shitty sex and then we spent the night together. I have no reason to lie for him. I hardly know him and I don't even like him." There it is. The truth. It lands heavily, winding him. Even Sally flinches a little at the baldness of the statement. Tommy swallows again and clears his throat.

"Ok," he says, his voice hitching a little. "We'll have to check that with the hotel staff. Mrs. Murphy...do you know...is there anything you can think of...was your husband acting...differently? Has anything...changed lately?" This is going far worse than even he anticipated. He's trying to ease into it, trying to get a feel for what she knows, whether she's willing to drop her husband in it. But his voice is high and nervous now and he knows he's losing control of the situation. He's finding it hard to form a clear thought.

"He, um...he lost his job a while ago, so he's been away a lot, and he's been...I don't know, moody I guess. But it's just stress. Anybody would act different in his situation." She's already defensive. She's ready to turn on Hausmann before she'll turn on her husband, and he doesn't know how to pull it back. This was supposed to be his moment, his chance to show he could be a real cop and he's blowing it.

"Ok," he says again, trying to give himself a second to calm down. "So...what about...that night? Did he...tell you anything about...what happened?"

"He was at the goddamn bar. He saw her. You know that. But that doesn't mean he killed her!" Sally yells. That's it. She's losing it with him. It's all over now, or it might as well be.

"But...what else did he do that night?" he presses, sensing it's already too late to get anything out of her. "I mean...what about the dress?"

"What about it? Anybody could have put it in our trashcan! He-he d-didn't kill her! Why can't you believe him?" she sobs, and then she collapses again, burying her face in her sister's shoulder.

"Look, I think you'd better go," Katie says. "My sister's obviously not in any shape to be interrogated right now."

"I wasn't...I mean, I didn't mean to..." he fumbles. He hates how pathetic he sounds, how weak and childish.

"Please, Tommy," Katie says. He gets up, about to go, but something stops him. He looks at Katie's sad, beautiful face and he finds he can't leave – not yet.

"Katie," he says, finally steadying his voice. "Can I talk to you for a second – alone?" She looks at him, narrowing her eyes a little, but she nods, extricating herself from Sally's clasp. Her sister, beyond hysterical, barely seems to notice as Katie leads him into the kitchen.

"All right. What is it?" she says. Her tone is cold, hard. He wants to take her hand, to tell her he's sorry, to make everything ok. But he can't.

"Did she…did she say *anything* to you about what her husband was doing that night? Does she know something?" Tommy asks. He breathes in as he waits for her answer, and holds it.

"No," Katie replies, dropping her gaze. "Look, Tommy, you're a good kid. I know you're just trying to do your job. But if my sister says Jimmy is innocent, then he's innocent. I know it." He nods, letting his breath out through his teeth.

Kid. He feels like he's been slapped.

"Do you?" he whispers. She stares at him for a second, but her face is unreadable, and she doesn't say anything.

"Ok," he says. "Look, if you can think of anything or if she tells you anything, please – please, call." He turns to leave, but she catches him by the wrist, digging her fingernails into it as he pulls against her, hard enough to leave a mark. She looks at him pleadingly.

"Tommy," she murmurs. "You'll figure this out, right? It'll be ok?" He wants to tell her yes, to promise her that everything's going to be just fine. But the problem is, it's not going to be fine. It's never going to be fine again. All he has to offer her now is the arsenal of meaningless platitudes they taught him in training.

"We're doing everything we can." She nods, letting his wrist go.

"You'll call?" she asks, locking her eyes on his.

"Yes." She drops her gaze away again, but he keeps staring at her for another second. "I'm sorry," he mouths.

Sally went back to sitting in the dark after Tommy Hausmann left, clinging to Katie, weeping. Katie's been crying on and off too, but she hid it for her sister's sake. She'd learned, back in those early days with Donovan, that she could cry her heart out without anyone ever knowing it. So she kept her own weeping silent and she let Sally sit there, gulping and sobbing, unable to control herself, until finally, exhausted, she passed out. The thing is, though, she doesn't *know* Jimmy is innocent. She doesn't really know Jimmy at all, and she's starting to wonder whether Sally does either. All her sister ever wanted was to love and be loved. If there was something she didn't want to know, she wouldn't have asked. She would have swallowed it, locked it away, forced herself to forget. Katie desperately wants to ask her whether there's anything at all that bothers her about her husband's story, whether she has any reason to think somebody might really have planted that dress. But she doesn't. She lets her sleep. She looks like she hasn't slept in days. Katie watches her for a moment, her bony chest juddering up and down, wondering what's going on behind her flickering eyelids, wondering how much she's forced herself to ignore.

Katie wants to believe, for her sister's sake, that it could have been Seth McIntyre, to believe he could have been that cold, that calculating. It's the story Sally wants to believe, too – more than that, it's the story she's decided she does believe, to the exclusion of any other explanation, whatever the evidence seems to say. She's shutting herself down, and shutting everything else out. Katie's seen her do it before, seen her calcify a little piece of herself when she thinks she needs to. She did it after Katie left, and again after their mother died. If she needed to do it, she'd take these little parts of herself – doubt, anger, fear, sadness – and turn them to stone to keep herself safe from the things she didn't want to know or feel. She had a truly astonishing capacity to compartmentalize when she wanted to, to the point that Katie almost found it admirable.

But this is different. This isn't high school. It's not teenage bullies anymore. It's not like anything they've ever been through before. Hiding won't help, and Katie doesn't know how to make Sally wake up to what's going on right in front of her. The problem is, the story she's settled on just doesn't add up. On the outside, the guy is creepy as hell, that much is true. She saw him at the town meeting, looming at the back of the room, looking for all the world like he really was the kind of man who could have knocked his own daughter over the head and ditched her in the snow. But she just can't make the story fit together. It doesn't make sense. He couldn't have been hiding in plain sight this whole time.

He must have arrived after Sarah for one thing, and for another, she's pretty sure he'd never go near Mawhinney's. He was super religious from what she remembers, and he wouldn't have set foot in a bar. And despite the way he looks, he was always pretty much harmless. Strict, maybe, and that silent, searching stare of his could make anybody want to confess their darkest sins. It's probably what makes him a good lawyer. But he's not a killer. It's not there. It's not in him. She doesn't know what went on behind closed doors, of course, but before he moved away, he had a good reputation. People respected him, trusted him, and that doesn't come cheap. Around here, you have to *earn* that. People don't give their secrets to just anyone.

For Sally's story to work, he'd have to be a real psychopath to be able to act the way he's acting now – to stand back and watch as the town implodes around his daughter's body – and she knows the chances of that are pretty slim. There would have been signs of it before now. People would have talked about him more. But Seth never got the rumor mill going. Of course, it wouldn't take much for most people to turn on him if they thought he was guilty, she's sure of that – people like Kathy Rafferty and Lorelei Lefferts, their husbands, their kids. Speculation will be rife, and no one here has ever been especially concerned with finding proof before they turn on someone. But however quickly they might demonize him, she knows it won't stick. They'll see what she sees. They're quick to judge, but they're quick to transfer that judgement, too. They choose someone different all the time. For a while, it had been Paul Gallagher, and then when they were done with him, they moved on to that PE teacher who was accused of masturbating in the girls' locker room. She and Sally had been the subject of the gossip and the bile themselves – she for running away, Sally for her extracurricular activities in high school – but even that had faded eventually. Without Sally's intransigence, once they know he's not their guy, they'll move on from Seth. It's just a matter of time. They'll move on to Jimmy.

Jimmy. Much as she wishes it wasn't, the story is a lot easier to believe. It just makes more sense. He was drunk that night, out of control. He'd been acting weird for months, Sally said so herself. He was the last person to see her alive and he already admitted to trying to kiss her. The scene writes itself. It's easy to imagine him losing his temper, following her out back, hitting her over the head. Maybe she said something. Maybe she insulted him. Maybe he didn't mean to do it. Maybe he hit her harder than he meant to. Or maybe he pushed her and she fell. He'd have been sobering up by then. He could have panicked, and if he panicked, maybe he wasn't thinking straight. Maybe he just wanted her to disappear and the only thing he could think to do was try and make it look like someone else did it. And then the dress – that damn dress. If it weren't for that, it all might just seem like an unfortunate coincidence. But it was right there in their garbage can – must have been there for days, judging by the volume of trash on top of it – and really, who else could have put it there? It fits. The story makes sense.

Her head is spinning. She's exhausted, but she doesn't want to sleep. Sally's still passed out, slumped against the back of the couch. If she moves, she'll disturb her, and every time she closes her eyes, she sees it all happening. She sees Jimmy killing her, beating the life out of her. She stares into the silent dark, trying to come up with another story. If Sarah went somewhere else after Mawhinney's, if Jimmy was too drunk to follow her, maybe there's another explanation. But she can't make herself fill in the blanks. She knows this town, knows everybody in it. They all have their secrets and their petty jealousies and even their violent sides – the Mitchell brothers, for example, or Brian Kowalski – but the fact is, none of them tried to kiss her that night. None of them talked to her, none of them got rejected by her. Over and over again, everything keeps circling back to Jimmy.

Well, god damn if the Mitchells didn't come through. On Kowalski's instructions, Andrew, the smartest of the six of them, had called in two of his brothers and bribed them with food and booze to come with him up to Murphy's place that morning. They'd been sitting there for hours in the freezing cold, waiting, watching, just like Kowalski said, and once they saw what had happened, they hightailed it back to town to find him. They were supposed to stay there, supposed to grab Murphy for themselves and bring him with them. They didn't hang around at the house after he got picked up, though. They didn't need to, they said. They'd watched the Hausmann kid dig around in the trash for a while, watched him pull something out, watched him go back into the house, and then the next thing they knew, Dave Showalter was there, grabbing Murphy up. He was being arrested and they knew exactly why. This was it. This was what they all knew. It was him. He killed her.

This is what Kowalski was waiting for: vindication. It's proof, too, that he's still a leader of men – that he can mobilize his troops, such as they are, when he needs to. He's still the toughest of the tough guys, and on top of that, he was fucking right. He should be happy. He should be turning goddamn cartwheels right now. But he isn't. There's something about the whole thing that Kowalski doesn't like, that doesn't sit right. The thing of it is, he'd been hoping for a chance to get a little justice of his own, for an excuse to do to Murphy what he knew he deserved. But it got taken away from him. It all happened too fast. Now he's got cops protecting him and even Kowalski isn't foolhardy enough to go busting into the police station. He half thinks about finding some way to get arrested himself, get himself thrown into a holding cell with Murphy, but he thinks better of it. He can wait. It's only a matter of time. They can't keep him there forever.

The Mitchells have gone over to Mawhinney's to celebrate, but for the first time in as long as he can remember, he decided not to go with them. He stayed home. He's sitting there now, half a bottle of bourbon down, turning it all over in his mind. It makes him sick to think that little motherfucker's been sitting there this whole time after what he did, right under everybody's noses. He's got more balls than he ever thought he did, he'll give him that. He could've cut and run, but he didn't. He left that dress in his garbage can and then he just waited for the shit to come down. Kowalski's just mad it isn't him that gets to rain it down on him.

For what he did, he should get the chair. The world should get the pleasure of watching him fry. But it won't happen. The worst he'll have to face for this is spending the rest of his life in jail, and that's if he's even convicted. Something has to be done, he decides. He has to get justice if nobody else will. Those dumb fuck cops won't do it. They'll be treating him like goddamn royalty, at least compared to what he deserves. He'll get his chance, though. He'll do it. Murphy will get what he deserves in the end. This is good, he tells himself. This is right. This gives him time to plan.

He sits there, alone in his living room, with nothing but the cheap bottle of bourbon for company, but the longer he sits, the harder it is to focus. He knows what's coming. He never could stop it. Right on cue, Paul Gallagher's face drifts into his mind. Blurry, sickly, it floats in front of his eyes. There's a crackle in his head, like static, and then a little voice breaks through to tell him it's coming. Then as the voice becomes a thought, there it is. It always does this – always when he's alone, always when he least wants it to. He can't keep it at bay forever, but usually, he can dull it with the booze and he can forget for a little while longer. This time, it won't even fade. It hangs there, even when he screws his eyes shut. He knows why. He wishes like hell he didn't. But he can't hide from it.

It always starts with the day he and Gallagher really became friends, freshman year of high school. Even back then, he was a hell of an athlete. They hadn't had much to do with each other before that, but at fourteen, Gallagher would have made two of most of his classmates, and Kowalski, who'd planned to be a quarterback for the Green Bay Packers, was suddenly impressed by him. You could spot Gallagher a mile away, even then, and Kowalski has a crystal-clear memory – one of the clearest things he remembers at all – of the moment he decided they were supposed to be buddies. Something just clicked inside him. It made sense. It was high school. That was how things worked. He could tell just by looking at Gallagher that they were like each other, and for a long time, there was nothing to make him feel like he should see things any other way. They both played football. They hung out with the same guys. They skipped the same classes. Everything worked the way it was supposed to.

The only little snag, back in those early days, was Gallagher's obsession with protecting Murphy. It just didn't fit. It wasn't how things should go. Guys like Kowalski and Gallagher were supposed to beat the shit out of guys like Murphy. It was like a law of nature. But he let it slide. He let Gallagher talk him out of a lot of the ass whoopings he'd planned to unleash on Murphy, and he was even a little impressed by Gallagher's loyalty. He'd pretty much been Murphy's bodyguard since kindergarten and he was going to keep right on doing it, no matter how much Kowalski tried to talk him out of it. It was ok, though. Murphy was just a blip, a little ripple in the otherwise calm water of their friendship. He'd disappear in the end. Gallagher would see sense and cut him loose. Things would go back to how they were supposed to be.

Only Murphy didn't disappear. He hung around, like a scrawny little gnat in Kowalski's peripheral vision, and it started to make him angry. He started to lose his temper with Gallagher, started saying things that were harder to take back or laugh off. Something seismic had changed between them. He felt like the ground was moving under his feet and he couldn't keep his balance for much longer. For a while, they both tried to act like everything was the same. The idea of talking about it, of upsetting the status quo was too hard to think about. So they pretended. They pretended everything was just fine, and for a while, it worked.

Murphy was the one who started it all, the one who planted the bomb, but it was Billy Peterson who lit the fuse. All he had to do was exist. More than ten years later, the name still makes Kowalski sick to his stomach, and it's all he can do not to throw up all over his living room floor. It's something else he remembers with absolute clarity, even when he's way past halfway to wasted. The whole thing plays out in his head, in high definition, every single time.

It was a Sunday afternoon, in the summer the year after they graduated from high school. The quarterback dream had dissolved long before, when he'd blown his knee out at an away game in Pine Lake. But it was ok. He was getting over the pain and disappointment. Things had been pretty steady for a while. He had a job lined up at the autobody shop, and a little money saved from bagging groceries and fixing fences. The plan was to take a road trip some place south, maybe down to Florida, before real life had to start. Things were better with Gallagher, too. He'd been happier, easier to be around, and Kowalski figured he'd probably finally gotten laid. He'd never mentioned a name, though, so Kowalski knew it couldn't be anything serious. That had sealed it for him. They'd take the road trip together – head down where it was hot, get drunk, party, pick up as many girls as they could. Good looking as he was, with Gallagher along, it'd be like shooting fish in a barrel.

None of that ever happened, though. That Sunday, everything fell apart. They were sitting out by the river, vaguely pretending to fish, but mostly just shooting the shit, like old times. Kowalski remembers how good that felt. He remembers thinking about how things were finally going back to the way they should be. They were going to take life by the horns and live it like they were supposed to. They had a cooler full of beers and all the time in the world.

"Kowalski, I gotta tell you something," Gallagher had said. "I don' know how you're gonna take it." Kowalski felt his jaw tighten. He couldn't tell what Gallagher was going to say, but he could already feel things changing. That perfect, easy world, where everything worked the way it should, was slipping through his fingers.

"Yeah?" he said, looking out across the river. He tugged a handful of grass up by the roots and scattered it across the water. He didn't want to look back at his friend, but he couldn't stop himself. Gallagher had this dopey look on his face, all moon-eyed and sappy. Kowalski won't ever forget that face – how happy he looked. How free.

"I'm in love, man. Big time," Gallagher said, grinning. Kowalski had smiled back, much as it was already starting to hurt him. Florida was fading as fast his football career.

"Yeah? What's 'er name?" he asked. Then Gallagher had looked away, picking at the label of his empty beer bottle. He looked flushed, Kowalski remembers – sick almost.

"Billy," Gallagher whispered.

"Billy?" Kowalski snorted. Then it dawned on him. "Wait… are you sayin'…?" Gallagher nodded, and smiled, almost apologetically.

"'Fraid so," he said. "Kowalski? Say somethin'." In Kowalski's memory, the silence after that felt like it went on for years. It was like he was living his whole life all over again, but suddenly, all the colors looked two shades brighter. All the questions and doubts he'd spent so long squeezing down inside him were roiling up to the surface. But he didn't say anything. He still doesn't know what made him do what he did next, but in that second when he finally came back to himself, woozy with beer and surprise, he leaned over and kissed Gallagher hard on the mouth. But Gallagher didn't kiss him back. He pushed him away.

"Kowalski, what the *hell?*" he shouted, scrubbing his mouth with the back of his hand. His lip was bleeding, a little red jewel of liquid shining there, spilling over onto his chin.

"I gotta get outta here," Kowalski had muttered, and then he'd sprinted all the way back across town until he ran into Marty Mitchell, the oldest and meanest of his brothers. He could hear Gallagher yelling after him, but he didn't even slow down. It was like it was meant to be. Before he knew what he was doing, he was telling Marty everything, or an edited version of everything anyway, and then it was over. He couldn't take it back. It was all gone, out of his hands, and into the Mitchells'. For a little while after that, a nasty little knot of guilt settled in his gut, but it didn't last long. Quickly enough, the guilt turned to anger. That was how it was always going to be, and it's been that way ever since.

There's still a wound there, raw and real, and it's there that Gallagher lives. In that wound, all his hatred and rage and self-loathing coalesce. He can't, could never make sense of it, but that doesn't matter now. All he knows is that someone has to pay. He can't make Billy pay now so it has to be someone else. It has to be Jimmy Murphy. It's all his fault anyway.

But he finds himself hesitating. He knows why. Fucking Gallagher. He can see him plain as day, standing there, smiling, reaching out a hand. Kowalski finds himself thinking about what this must be doing to him, Murphy's best and only friend. It must be hard. It must be hurting him. Fucking Gallagher. After all this time, he's going to deny him the one thing that will give him some release. He's going to deny him the chance to exact justice on that slimy little shit – the justice he's always known he deserves. *Fucking* Gallagher.

"Lea' me alone," he says out loud, slurring. "Go'damnit. Lea' me the fuck *alone*." He hurls the empty bourbon bottle against the wall, where Gallagher's outline still hangs. It shatters, taking Gallagher with it, spraying little pieces of debris all around the room, like glittering, deadly rain. He falls forward off the couch and lands hard the floor, feeling the shards of glass embedding themselves in his skin, but he doesn't get up. He crumples, covering his face with his hands, and he weeps.

Abernathy didn't realize John Callaghan was still there until long after the hoorah with Murphy had died down. It had been chaos. Showalter had brought Murphy in, not knowing what he was walking into, and then all hell broke loose – everyone talking at once, Showalter trying to get Murphy to holding, Legler trying to re-establish some semblance of order. Zachariah Fahey, Jr., tried to take a swing at Murphy, though he wasn't much of a match for Legler, who held him off. But in the confusion, his old man had tripped, fallen, almost gotten trampled and then there was a tangle of flailing limbs as they tried to get him back to his feet. Christie, himself on his way to holding on the drug charges, was somewhere in the middle of all of that, still in handcuffs and somebody managed to hit him, thought it wasn't clear who. There was blood everywhere, screaming, cursing.

All told, it must have taken a good couple of hours to get everything squared away and take Murphy down to a cell. Once things were quiet again, Abernathy had shut himself in his office, waiting for his heart to slow down, waiting for his breathing to return to normal. Once it did, he was ready to head for home. All he wanted to hear his wife's sweet voice, to be soothed and calmed, to be told it was all over.

Everyone else was gone by then – Legler had finally kicked McIntyre and the Faheys out, despite their arguments, and a little while later, Christie, surprise, surprise, made bail. He'd just assumed Callaghan must have followed, must have gone home or gone to find Mary. He'd been caught in the middle of it all, in the frenzy and the furor along with everybody else, wanting answers just like the rest of them, but he'd been pushed to the side, kept at bay. He hadn't been a priority. But now, here he is, just...standing there.

"John!" Abernathy exclaims. "What are you still doing here?"

"Do you…do you really think you got him?" Callaghan whispers. Abernathy sighs.

"Looks that way," he says, evenly.

"That's not what I asked," Callaghan says. "I want to know. Do *you* think you got him?"

"Yes. I do." Even before the words are out of his mouth, he regrets it. It's a lie. The fact of the matter is, he isn't sure. He knows what the evidence says, but something in his gut tells him this story isn't over yet, that there's a lot more to it than there seems to be. Callaghan nods, and smiles tightly.

"Yeah. That's what I thought." It sounds like agreement, like acceptance, but there's something else in his voice.

"John?" Abernathy asks. "You got something to say?" Callaghan sighs and shakes his head.

"I don't know, it's just…it seems too tidy, don't you think?"

"Sometimes, these things are," Abernathy says, trying to invest some authority into what he's saying. "If all the evidence points to one person, there's usually a reason." Callaghan lets out a snort of laughter then, startling him.

"Come on, Frank!" he scoffs. "How would you know?" It stings at first, like a jab in the eye, but before he has time to think, he finds himself laughing, too. Suddenly, the whole horrible, ugly truth of it all lays itself out in front of him and it seems like the funniest thing in the world. Suddenly, it's all a joke. The two of them stand there, howling with laughter, gasping for breath, tears streaming. They look crazy, Abernathy thinks. They look like a pair of goddamn lunatics. But he can't stop. It must be a full five minutes before he regains enough composure to speak.

"You know what? You're goddamn right. What the hell do I know? I'm a goddamn hack!" But the laughter is subsiding now, and once it's gone, there's just the truth, hard and cold inside him. Abernathy takes a deep, shaky breath, wiping the tears from his face with the back of his hand.

"Look, John. I don't know if we've got our guy. I don't know how to do any of this – neither do you, neither does anybody. But I know what the evidence is saying. We just have to go with what we've got. We can't do anything else."

Zachariah Fahey, Jr., watches his father sleep. He's failing. He knows that. The longer this takes, the more he loses of himself. Little pieces of him break away, one by one. He's dying. His father doesn't have a lot of time left, and the little he does have, he has to spend here. Waiting. Watching him, the torture of it radiates from the old man's fragile body. They aren't waiting for the worst: it's already happening. They're already in it. This – this is the hardest thing. This is even more painful than waiting to be told she was dead. The old man is holding on, stretching out the end of his life, to find out *why*. Sarah, his beautiful, brilliant granddaughter, is gone – forever. In some ways, she'd been gone a long time, of course, but while she was alive, there was hope. Now, the thing that scared him most, the demon that visited him in the dark and whispered the truth in his ear, has been made flesh. Now, the worst of it all is that he might not get the answers he needs. There might be not be a why.

His son, unmarried, never had kids of his own. He'd wanted to. He was going to get around to it one day, he told himself, when the time was right and he found the right girl. But the right girl never did come around. Women drifted in and out of his life, but none of them were ever *right*. There was always something. This one drank too much, that one smoked, this one was an atheist, that one was a Democrat. Then suddenly he was sixty. Suddenly, it was too late.

One by one, the only family he has is disappearing. His mother was first, and then his sister, slowly and painfully, the life drained out of them by the cancer. And now, Sarah. Sarah's son is out there somewhere – he's not supposed to know about the boy, but he does. He knows why Seth took her away. He found out a little while after he and his father started looking for her. His PI had heard Seth and his own PI talking about it. But he'll never find him. He doesn't even know where to start. It's not like he can just ask. If Seth didn't want him to know about the kid, he won't just tell him what happened to him. And now his father is on his way out, too. That'll be it. He'll be the last one.

He can muster up a little sympathy for Seth, his one-time friend, and for John Callaghan to a certain extent: they both lost the same daughter. Alice never said it, but he knows what Callaghan was to her. He knows he's Sarah's real father. He'd caught them together once, although he didn't say anything at the time. He'd seen them outside the house, just standing there, looking at each other. They weren't kissing or holding hands or anything, but he could tell by the way Callaghan looked at her. He loved her. Of course, he turned out to be a cowardly little rat in the end, leaving her behind when he found out about Sarah's existence. But he did love Alice, in his own shallow, selfish way – and so did Seth. Seth is more like himself, he thinks. His is the greater tragedy. Zachariah knows that. Seth knew Sarah wasn't his, but he loved her like a daughter. It must be eating him alive, to know he could have helped her, could have stopped it before it started. Now that she's dead, he has nothing left: his parents are gone, and he has no brothers or sisters, no kids of his own. He's completely alone.

Things weren't supposed to turn out this way. Zachariah has spent his whole life being good, doing what he thought he was supposed to, abiding by the rules. He never got drunk or slept around – could count his sexual conquests on one hand, in point of fact. He studied hard. He respected his parents. He gave his students his undivided attention, made sure he helped those who were struggling. He gave to charity. He went to church, diligently, every Sunday. All that was supposed to count for something. It was supposed to mean happiness. It was supposed to mean he deserved some kind of reward. It was supposed to mean he had God's favor. He'd tried so hard. He kept believing, kept clinging on, kept hoping things would turn around. Maybe God was testing him. Maybe he was meant for more. Maybe he just had to get through this and then God's plan for him would be revealed at last.

There had to be some great, glorious light at the end of the tunnel, some reason for him to have gone through all this. There had to be. But that tunnel kept getting longer and longer, and the light kept getting dimmer and dimmer, further and further away.

Still, he didn't give up. He set his jaw and he kept holding on. It was all he had. Without it, nothing made sense. He didn't make sense. It was self-preservation as much as anything else. He didn't know where his faith ended and he began. Even his father let it go before he did. He never said it, but his son knew. He could see it. For his part, he kept it going right up until he found out Sarah was dead. That day, something died in him, too. Saving her was the only thing he had to hope for, and once he knew what had happened to her, that was it. The light went out. The immediacy of it shocked him. Someone flipped a switch and suddenly nothing was what it had been before. It was like seeing the world in different colors. Suddenly, everything was just a little bit darker. Now, sharing a room with his frail, elderly father, in this stupid, *shitty* bed and breakfast, with her *shitty* boyfriend two doors away, nursing a black eye that's a universe away from what he deserves, it's gone. It's over. The scales have fallen from his eyes. God let him down. God abandoned him. God turned his back on him. Now he's doing the same. Now there's nothing but the void.

He sits there in the viscose light of the lamp beside his bed, thinking. It swims in his head. All of it, all at once, churning until he starts to feel sick. He keeps waiting for someone to tell him it was all a mistake, or a joke, or…something. He thinks about the kids he's worked with over the years, about the chances they'll have that Sarah never will. It seems so unfair. There are the ones that rest on his conscience, too, though – the ones he could have done more for, the ones who couldn't, wouldn't be helped, the ones who slipped through his fingers even before they graduated. He wonders how many of them turned out ok, how many of them beat the odds – and how many of them ended up like her.

The cops let Christie go. They had him on the drug charges, but the stupid rich bastard made bail in hours. He saw him come back to the hotel, hiding behind a ridiculous pair of designer sunglasses. Once they had Murphy, they didn't care about Christie anymore. Zachariah still isn't sure it was him, but as far as they're concerned, they have their guy. He feels lost. He'd so believed it was Christie, so *wanted* it to be him. He'd convinced himself he was the real reason Sarah was dead – after all, he'd persuaded her to come up here, to come back to this awful town – it wasn't such a leap to assume he was the one who struck the blow that killed her. It was a trick. He'd made her think he had her interests at heart, but he was setting her up. In Chicago, he would have been caught. Here, the cops are so green, so unaccustomed to real crime, that they hardly know how to deal with it. Here, he could get away with it.

The problem, of course, is that the smarmy son-of-a-bitch has an alibi. It's new to him, this anger, this *hatred*. He's never cursed before, even inside his own head, but now the profanity comes easily. It's like a dam has broken. He sits there, on the edge of the rickety single bed and he seethes. What he wants is to break into Christie's room and kick the ever-loving shit out of him, to give him what he really deserves. Of course, he knows Christie could probably take him – he has twenty-five years on him at least – but he'd have righteous fury on his side. Maybe he could do it. Maybe he could win for once. Even if he does get the best of it, of course, underneath all the anger and the hate, he knows it won't solve anything. Not really. He slumps back on the bed and stares up at the ceiling, suddenly exhausted. There's nothing left to solve.

Gallagher doesn't know exactly what makes him go to the priest that night. If he still believed, he might have called it divine intervention. Something seemed to physically pull him up out of bed and out the door, and he finds himself halfway to the church before he even knows where he's going. In his jacket pocket is a photo. He'd been thinking about Murphy all day, trying to figure out what he could do for him, trying to come up with some way to get him out of this, and then he'd finally gone up into the attic. He didn't really know what he was looking for, but the feeling that he'd known Sarah back in high school had never really left him. It had nagged away at him, until he couldn't take it anymore. He had to look, had to find out if there was some answer or other among the piles and piles of teenage mementoes – and then there it was, plain as day, right at the top of a stack of photos. It's Sarah, the way she looked in that picture Abernathy had used back at the first town meeting, sitting in the bleachers up at the high school, sun on her smiling face – and right beside her, with his arm slung casually around her shoulders, is Daniel.

He didn't recognize him at first. His hair was still long back then, and Gallagher can just about see the top of a Metallica logo on his t-shirt. It looks wrong now – like Daniel was playing dress up. By itself, it doesn't necessarily mean anything, of course. He knows that. It's why he lay there so long, staring at the picture, resisting, trying to just go to sleep, trying to just stop thinking about it. It triggered something in him, though – an idea of an idea, never quite turning into something solid. But whatever it is, it won't go away, and then suddenly, he's out there in the snow at two in the morning. If Daniel knew her, maybe he could explain what she was doing in town. Maybe he has some answers. Maybe he could help Murphy.

Gallagher bangs his gloved hand on the door of the priest's little house out at the back of the church, clutching the picture. There's no answer at first, so he bangs harder, almost knocking the door off its hinges. Finally, the priest appears, bleary-eyed, half-awake. It's weird. He looks so small in his shabby gray robe, glasses askew, like a kid again. Gallagher blinks, shakes himself. He's here for a reason. There's no time to get sentimental.

"Paul!" Daniel croaks, his voice thick with sleep. "What're you doing here?"

"You said you didn' know 'er," Gallagher blurts, thrusting the picture into his face. Daniel closes his eyes for a second, and lets out a long, slow breath.

"Right," he says, at last. "I guess you better come in." Gallagher all but barges past him through the tiny hallway and into the living room. It takes him a second to collect himself. The last time he was here was right after Billy died, and nothing seems to have changed since then. There's still a small, plain wooden cross above the fireplace. There's still a shelf on his bookcase made over solely to a collection of hand-painted icons. There's still a picture of his parents on the table by the couch. There's still no TV. Gallagher had joked about it at the time – asked him if God had something against the boob tube. Now it just seems kind of sad. Everything in the room is a hand-me-down of some kind, with the exception of the icons maybe, and it's never occurred to Gallagher that maybe the priest just can't afford a TV. He shakes himself again. He doesn't want to allow him any sympathy.

"Sit down, Paul," Daniel says, gently, gesturing at the sagging armchair by the bookcase. "I'll make us some tea." Gallagher shakes his head.

"No," he growls. "I don' want any goddamn tea. I want you t'tell me why you lied." Daniel sighs.

"I don't know," he says, quietly. "I guess… I didn't want to have to deal with the truth."

"Hardly very Christian," Gallagher mutters. Daniel picks up the little china figurine of Christ from the mantelpiece and turns it over in his hands.

"I know. But I wasn't very Christian at the time, either. I just... didn't want to be reminded of that. It was... a dark time for me. I didn't want to think about who I was back then." Gallagher scrutinizes him for a second. Nothing's adding up yet.

"So? It was high school. It was dark for everybody," he says, trying to read Daniel's face, but it's blank – eerily so. The priest shakes his head, and looks Gallagher in the eye for the first time.

"You don't understand. I was... unhappy, and I didn't know how to handle it, so... I did things – things I'm not proud of. Drugs, booze, the whole bit." Gallagher stares. This is new for him. He's never seen Daniel like this before – never heard him say he might be anything less than perfectly sinless.

"But what about Sarah?" he whispers. Daniel takes a deep breath and lets it out shakily through his teeth.

"I... I think that was the worst of it all. We... we dated back then, and I, um... I slept with her," he says at last. Gallagher shakes his head, trying to make his thoughts stop swimming.

"So? That's not that – "

"I didn't just sleep with her," the priest interrupts, his voice suddenly, hard and strange. "She... I got her pregnant. I'm the reason her dad made her leave. Everything that happened to her after that, right up to when she got here... it's my fault." Gallagher lets his head drop forward, the weight of this news washing over him.

"So... you don' know what she was doin' here?" he asks. Daniel shakes his head.

"I'm sorry," he whispers. Gallagher gets up without another word and heads for the door. He stands there outside the church for a few more minutes, feeling more powerless than he's felt in years. For all the priest's self-flagellation, it doesn't change anything. It doesn't help Murphy.

This is the first real crime that's ever been committed in this stupid hick town and to his own dismay, Dave Showalter finds himself genuinely shocked by it. He and Chris Legler joined the force here around the same time and neither of them had ever seen it as anything other than a way station. They were on their way – Legler for narc squad or vice, himself for homicide. It didn't matter where – just not here. They'd pay their dues and then they'd be out of there and they'd never look back. He's always been good at what he does – better than Legler probably, and certainly better than Abernathy or those two local kids. He has potential. It's what his superiors have always told him. He's driven, methodical, smart. He could be one of the best.

Now, though, things are different. They're waiting for DNA tests to come back on the dress to prove it was Sarah's, to prove it was Jimmy Murphy who stripped her and ditched her in the snow. Tests on the dress she was found in were inconclusive. He hates that word. It sounds so clinical. What it means, though, is that right now, while they're waiting for the tests on her own dress, they have exactly jack shit. This is supposed to be it. This is supposed to be the last piece of the puzzle. It's supposed to solve everything.

He's not sure it will. Whoever killed her – Murphy, whoever it was – they were careful. They must have worn gloves. That white gown was pristine before they put it on her: brand new. No other DNA on it, not even detergent. Where would Murphy have even gotten it? It doesn't read the way it should. He'd met the guy once or twice, when he'd ventured into Mawhinney's for a beer, and he was no criminal mastermind – wasn't a mastermind of any kind. He was... ordinary. Twitchy, nervous, unhappy, but... ordinary. Showalter tries to put it together, to lay it out the way a lawyer would. If he was drunk, if he didn't mean to do it, he could have tried to cover it up. But how could a guy like that have had the presence of mind to even think to switch her clothes, let alone go find a box fresh white dress to put her in?

He can't help but think maybe something else is going on – maybe somebody else is involved. But there's no proof of that, and it's too late now anyway. Of course, everyone will already know. They'll know the cops have got their guy. He was less than subtle when he rolled up to the house. He knows exactly how it looked. Plenty of people would have seen him. Word will have spread. And then of course, Abernathy will have to have another one of his wretched town meetings, and after that, it'll be all over. By then, they'll already have convicted him. His death sentence will have been written.

Nobody really knows him here. He doesn't socialize with anybody in town, doesn't even spend any time here if he doesn't have to. Most weekends, when he's not working, he's at conferences or training seminars or ball games or bars in bigger towns. Anywhere but here. It was supposed to be a layover, a stop on his way to bigger things. It wasn't supposed to be like this. Things like this aren't supposed to get to him. He should be able to shrug this off. He was supposed to leave, supposed to find a nice girl and a good job, supposed to make a life for himself. Most importantly, that life was supposed to be somewhere else. Now, though, he can see all that seemingly boundless potential slipping away. He feels tied to this place, bound to it by this ugly chapter. It's part of the town's history now, and it's part of his too. He can't just leave it behind now. It'll go with him, even when he finally gets out of here. It'll always be his first murder case, his first murder arrest. It's burned into his brain. Whenever he comes across another victim, her face will be there. Whenever he makes another arrest, Murphy's face will be there. He'll never be able to shake it off.

When he goes to bed that night, it's already bothering him more than he can bear. He lies down, alone like always, but she's there. She might as well be in bed with him. He can feel her icy skin against his, turning the bed cold. The whole thing is just such a waste. He can't make her go away. She's not some faceless, nameless victim he can cast aside. She's real, human – too real, too human. He wasn't ready for this. He always knew the first one would be the hardest but it wasn't supposed to happen for months, even years yet. He had it all planned out. He'd be set up in homicide in Chicago, already part of the team. He'd have colleagues who cared about and trusted him and whom he cared about and trusted in return. He'd have people he could turn to. A call would come in and he'd go out to see the body for himself. It'd be some lowlife thug or something and he could tell himself it was no great shame. Then they'd catch the other lowlife thug that did it and that would be that. It wouldn't be somebody like Murphy. It wouldn't be like this.

There has to be another meeting. Abernathy knows that. After Showalter picked up Murphy, it was a matter of course. He doesn't have long to hold him – just long enough to have the dress sent up to Ashland to confirm the blood belongs to Sarah and to find out if there's any other DNA on it – but the town has to know. He needs them to see he hasn't let them down – not completely anyway. They need to know they have him.

He thinks about Murphy, locked up in holding, all alone, with nothing but his thoughts to keep him company. He has everybody taking turns to keep watch over him, to make sure he doesn't find a way to do something stupid, but in a way, he almost thinks it would be better if he did. Through it all, even with all the evidence they have pointing right at him, Abernathy finds he still feels a little sorry for the poor bastard. His life is already over. It's over and he doesn't even remember what he did. Maybe he really would be better off if they just left him to it. Abernathy shakes himself, trying to push the thought out, but it lingers far longer than he'd like. A few minutes go by, and it just sits there, clinging nastily at the back of his mind, like a stain inside his head, pernicious, ugly. But then there's a knock at his door, finally distracting him. He finds he's grateful for it, allowing himself to hope for some good news at last. He can see Hausmann through the window, but the boy looks anxious.

"Come in!" he calls, trying to sound friendly.

"Chief, the, uh… the lab results came back on the dress," Hausmann says, quietly. Abernathy already knows what he's about to say, but he still waits for the boy to speak, praying it'll be something else.

"And?" he asks.

"And… it was Sarah's blood… but there was no other DNA on it," Hausmann whispers, so quietly Abernathy has to strain to hear him.

"You gotta be kidding me," he breathes. This is what he was most afraid of, although he wouldn't let himself think about it. It's the worst possible outcome. They have to cut him loose. They have to turn Murphy out into the world and let him face the thugs who've been waiting for their opportunity this whole time. Even if he is guilty, he doesn't deserve that. Abernathy has always been a fervent believer in the power of the law to deliver justice, and he hates the idea of some mindless mob getting there first. That isn't right and it certainly isn't justice. It's a goddamn witch hunt. But the fact is, they haven't charged him and now they can't hold him until – unless – they find more evidence. They're right back at square one: anybody could have put that dress in his garbage can, and without something else to connect him to it or to Sarah, their case is purely circumstantial. He knows that, Murphy knows that. They all know it. They need a confession or a miracle, or both.

"So… what're you gonna do?" Hausmann asks, clearly still hoping for some comfort from the old man. "I mean… people have to know… right?" Abernathy takes a long, slow breath, and turns away. He feels sick just thinking about it, about what he'll have to say.

"I'm gonna lie."

He doesn't want to do it. He doesn't want to be responsible for this. But he knows he has to. After the meeting, he'll have to let Murphy go. But they don't need to know that. For the first time ever, he's preparing to lie to his constituents. They're all sitting there – more of them than ever – looking up at him, waiting for him to tell them what's going on. His only plan is to throw them a red herring – to tell them they've still got Murphy at the station, safely away from the baying hordes. All he has to rely on is the vague hope that nobody will go looking for him. He clears his throat, and taps the microphone.

"Ladies and gentlemen," he says, and a little part of him is suddenly five years old again, at the Circus World museum in Baraboo, where the red-coated, black-mustachioed ringmaster would start the show just like this. In that moment, he finds he almost wants to add, "boys and girls", but he checks himself just in time. "I want you to know we still have Jimmy Murphy in custody, and we plan to keep him there." It's technically true at least. Murphy is still in a holding cell for now. It's just he won't be for very much longer. There's a ripple of noise, as questions flare up. Abernathy holds up a hand, relieved to see it still has its usual effect, and the room falls quiet.

"Please be aware that we're still pursuing other lines of enquiry. We'd ask that you continue to remain calm and let us do our job," he says, hating how wooden he sounds all of a sudden. This is it. He's about to say it, and he needs it to sound convincing. "Rest assured, we will not be releasing Mr. Murphy from holding for the time being. We believe we... we believe we have enough evidence to charge him with Sarah McIntyre's murder." He stumbles, hardly able to get the words out. The moment they leave his mouth, he regrets them. No good can come of this. All he can hope for is that it's enough to buy him some time.

"You better," a voice from the back of the room calls, rising above the growing din. Abernathy peers out, looking for the source, his eyes resting on Brian Kowalski. He swallows thickly, afraid his ruse is over before it's even begun.

"What's that supposed to mean?" he asks. He wishes he sounded more threatening, but his voice is suddenly scared and small.

"It means," Kowalski says, pausing to throw a meaningful look at his buddies, eyes full of spite and hatred. "that if you let him go, whatever happens to him is on you." A roar goes up in the seats around him, and Abernathy just barely manages to silence them.

"Listen, Kowalski," Abernathy says, mustering up every last shred of authority he can find. "I hope for your sake that you're not threatening anybody right now. You ought to know better than that. And that goes for all of you clowns, too." He thrusts a finger out, pointing at Kowalski's cronies, but none of them flinch.

"If you don't give him what's comin' to him, somebody else will," Kowalski says, boldly. The roar goes up again and this time, there's no silencing it.

"Now stop this!" Abernathy yells. He didn't want to raise his voice but he can't help it. Kowalski is genuinely starting to scare him now. "Don't you realize who you're talking to? If you don't go home this minute and stay there, so help me, I'll arrest every last one of you!"

"Fine," Kowalski says, with a sneer. "We'll be good." He gestures for his crew to follow him, and they all start to get up to leave. Abernathy scowls at them, hoping his fear isn't showing.

"You'd better be."

"You can't let him go, Chief," Hausmann says. "It's for his own safety. They're callin' for his blood. You heard what Brian Kowalski said at the meeting. They'll be waiting for him. They're gonna find him." He's right. He knows he's right. It won't take much to get the Mitchells on side, and there are plenty of other thugs in town, just eager and ready to do Kowalski's bidding.

"I know. Look, Tommy, don't worry. No one's gonna know about it. We'll make sure of it. We'll get him out of here and take him over to Paul Gallagher's place. He'll be as safe there as anywhere. But I can't keep him here. You know that. I don't have enough to hold him and we just don't have the resources to take him into protective custody." Hausmann's face falls.

"Then arrest Kowalski! Take him out of the picture!" he says, desperately.

"I can't. He didn't make any direct threats and I don't have anything else to pull him up on," Abernathy replies, as evenly as he can.

"Then make something up! A busted taillight! Anything!" Hausmann pleads. His voice is shrill, childlike, and Abernathy wishes like hell there was something he could do for the poor kid.

"You know I can't do that. Besides, do you really want Kowalski in a cell with Murphy?" he asks. Hausmann drops his gaze and shakes his head.

"So we're just gonna turn him loose? We're gonna let the mob decide what happens to him?" he says, keeping his eyes on the ground. For a split second, Abernathy imagines him as Jiminy Cricket, his shrill, cricket-shaped, anthropomorphized conscience, and he almost laughs. Almost. He sighs heavily, glad not to have to meet the boy's gaze.

"These are good, decent people. We have to trust that they'll be able to keep their heads while we carry on with the investigation." He wants to believe it, wants to give Hausmann something to hold onto, but he can hear how hollow the words sound.

"Do you really believe that, sir?" Hausmann asks, quietly, looking up at last. Abernathy looks away from him, and shakes his head.

"I don't have a choice. Look, we'll put a man on his house to keep an eye on his wife – but beyond that, there's nothing we can do. We can't let anybody know where he is."

"All right," Hausmann says, sticking out his chin and puffing up his chest as far as it'll go. "I'll do it." Abernathy stares at him. He admires the kid's sense of duty, but he is still just a kid, hardly any older than Shelly. This is the force he's been tasked with leading: two kids, and two officers just waiting for their chance to move on to bigger, better things. Showalter and Legler – Showalter's already a sergeant, and Legler is well on his way up the ladder, too – spend all their time, when they aren't making Hausmann's life hell, doing everything they can to make sure they get out the minute the opportunity comes along. They're always on training weekends, and at bars or at football or hockey games in bigger towns, palling around with the officers there. They brown-nose as many decision makers as they can, knowing their talents are wasted in this tiny hamlet, knowing it's only a matter of time before they can get out. He knows they're just waiting out the clock here, that he can't stop them from moving on, and he doesn't resent them for it. But when they do eventually leave, he'll be hard pressed to replace them. Then he won't have anybody to turn to if anything like this ever happens again.

"Why don't you let Showalter or Legler do it?" he asks, gently. He has them now at least, and either one of them would be better for the job than skinny little Hausmann. Both Showalter, who wants to work homicide, and Legler, who has his sights set on narcotics, are tough and imposing, and both are gunning for positions in Chicago: they could easily see off any hot-headed moron out for Murphy's blood.

Hausmann, on the other hand, should be home in bed with Shelly, tucked up with some hot chocolate, watching the snowstorm out the window. It can't even be that long, Abernathy imagines, since the kid would have been building snowmen in his front yard.

"Because they don't care," Hausmann says, quietly. Abernathy sighs. The kid is right. He hates it, but there it is. Neither Showalter nor Legler would stick their neck out for anybody in this town the way Hausmann would.

"All right. But you call for back-up the minute you see any sign of trouble. Do you understand?" Hausmann nods.

"Yessir," he says, setting his jaw as best he can.

"Take the SUV. It's a shitty night. And Hausmann – be careful." Hausmann nods again, and turns to go.

Abernathy regrets the decision the minute the kid is out the door, but he knows this is the way it was always going to be: neither Showalter nor Legler care enough about Murphy or the town. They'd do the job as far as it went, but they wouldn't really put themselves on the line. They wouldn't be ready to give everything for this. Hausmann, on the hand, loves this place above all things. He was born and raised in the town, played softball with Murphy's wife's little sister, was taught by his mother. This is in his blood. It's more important to him than it ever would be to either of them, and he deserves the chance to prove himself. Besides, even if Abernathy hadn't given him the go ahead, he would have gone out there anyway. The look on his face told the old man that. He can only hope and pray he won't be put to the test.

To Gallagher's very great relief, the cops somehow get Murphy out of the station without a hitch. They don't explain themselves. They roll up outside his front door that night and bundle him into the house as quietly as possible, and then they're gone without a word.

"How you doin'?" he asks his friend, as they sit down on the couch. It sounds lame and stupid but it's the only thing he can think to say. Murphy shrugs, not looking at him.

"Ok, I guess," he mumbles. "Look, Paul, I... I really appreciate what you're doin' here." Gallagher smiles in spite of himself, and claps a hand on Murphy's shoulder.

"Don't mention it," he says. "Listen, um... Jimmy, I been thinkin'. Why don' you and Sally... why don'cha just... go? You could take my truck and be in Canada 'fore anybody knows you're gone." Murphy looks up then, startled, like he's remembering something he doesn't want to remember all of a sudden.

"You're not serious?" he asks, eyes widening. Gallagher takes a deep breath.

"I am," he says. "You gotta take care of 'er. She needs you." Murphy stares at him, narrowing his eyes.

"And then what? We're fugitives for the rest of our lives? That's no way to live."

"But you'd be safe. You could start over," Gallagher presses.

"I can't do it," Murphy says. His voice is quiet, but there's a determination there that his friend has never heard before. "I have to face this."

"C'mon, Jimmy! Don' be stupid! Think about Sally!" Gallagher is getting desperate now. He'd expected Murphy to jump at the idea, or at least to take it seriously – anything but this. He looks him hard in the eye, more resolute than he's ever seen him.

"I can't, Paul," he whispers. "I am thinking about Sally. I can't do it to 'er. I can't make her leave 'er whole life, make 'er go on the run. She deserves better'n that."

"She deserves to have you!" Gallagher pleads. "How can you do *that* to 'er?"

"She deserves a husband who isn't a goddamn coward!" Murphy yells. Gallagher is silent for a long moment, letting the words wash over him.

"Ok," he says at last. "Ok, I'm not gonna try'n force you." He pauses for a second and looks at his friend, trying to read his face. He feels like something else is going on inside that jumpy, twitchy brain of his but he can't figure out what it is.

"Do you wanna… talk or anything?" he asks, a little uncomfortably. For all they've been friends most of their lives, neither one of them has ever really talked about anything. They never needed to. It feels wrong now, somehow, to be trying to force that kind of a friendship after all these years. To his relief, Murphy shakes his head, with a sad smile.

"Look, I'm bushed," Gallagher says, giving Murphy's shoulder an odd, awkward little pat, almost as though he's a father and this skinny, dejected, broken man is his child. "I'm goin' to bed. The guest room's ready for you when you want it." Murphy nods, tears glinting in his eyes.

"Thank you," he murmurs.

Gallagher lies down in his big, empty bed, expecting sleep to elude him, but he really is exhausted and it doesn't take him long to drift off. But then he feels his eyes snap open. He doesn't know what woke him, but there's a cold, sick feeling in his gut. He can't be sure exactly how long he's been asleep – it feels like a few minutes, though it could have been hours – but he knows something's terribly wrong. Hastily, he rolls out of bed, heart pounding, and pads down the hallway to Murphy's room. Swallowing hard, trying to stay calm, he pushes the door open far enough to get a look at the bed, and then his stomach lurches. It's empty. Murphy is gone.

Hausmann drives as fast as he dares over along the icy streets to the Murphy house. He pulls up outside a little after ten in the evening, and peers into the small, square window, looking for signs of life. The lights are on and he can see two shadows behind the curtains. He breathes out through his nose, trying to steel himself, and he's relieved to see everything looks like its pretty much as it should be, at least for now. It must be Katie and Sally, he thinks. It's too early for them to be in bed, or for Katie to have gone back to her father's place. They're together. They're safe. It's cold in the car even though the heat is way up, and he shivers, folding his arms, half wishing his sense of duty weren't so strong. He prays Brian Kowalski won't make good on his threat, however indirect it might have been, but he doesn't have high hopes. Deep down, he's pretty sure it's just a matter of time.

The time passes far more slowly then he'd like, but as midnight approaches, he's beginning to convince himself he might just get away with it. There's hardly been a sound all night, but for the occasional owl or nighthawk, and Katie and Sally turned out the lights hours ago. Katie must have decided to stay, and he's glad of it. Her sister needs her. The ugly little house looks so peaceful in the dark. Funny, he thinks – you'd never know anything might be wrong.

Sometime around two, he decides to call the station to let Abernathy he's going to call it a night, but his hand freezes. Kowalski's face is right up against the window, an inch from the glass, his breath leaving little clouds behind. He's with maybe five or six other men, and he can't make out their faces in the dark, but he can see that they're all equally thickset, equally menacing. Worse, even in the darkness, he can see they're all carrying baseball bats, shovels, tire irons – anything that could be used to beat seven shades of shit out of Jimmy Murphy.

"Out of the car," Kowalski growls.

"Listen, fellas, you know this is a mistake. He's not even here," Hausmann says, as sternly as he can from behind the glass. "Why don't you just walk away?"

"Oh yes he is. We know the chief was lyin'," Kowalski says, raising the bat he's carrying. "Now I said get out of the goddamn car." Hausmann swallows hard, reaching for his gun as he steps down from the driver's seat.

"Don't make me use this," he stammers, trying to keep his hands from shaking. "Look, I-I swear to you. Murphy isn't here." Kowalski laughs, a rattling, mirthless sound.

"Give it up, you little pussy. We saw him come in the back," he rasps. Quickly, easily, he relieves Hausmann of his pistol, and in one swift move, he whips him hard across the face with the butt of the gun. As he crumples into the snow, Kowalski kicks him hard in the ribs, and that's the last thing Hausmann remembers clearly.

Somebody – maybe Kowalski, maybe one of his cronies, nobody can agree on it when they come to recount the story later – kicks down Murphy's door, and after that, everything is a blur of screaming and blood. So much blood. The dirty grey snow is stained with it, bright, horrible red rivers flowing out into the street under the glow of the neighbors' security light. Some of it is Hausmann's, where Kowalski broke his nose, but in the end, most of it is Murphy's. The neighbors must hear the commotion, because somebody calls the cops, but nobody comes out to see what all the noise is about. They stay safely locked inside, covering their eyes and their ears, and by the time Showalter and Legler show up, it's already too late.

Kowalski and his cronies thunder into the Murphy house, and drag him from his bed, out onto the front stoop, all roaring and grunting incoherently. He's screaming at them to stop, half naked and wild-eyed, but they don't hear him, or they don't care if they do. He tries to defend himself at first, shielding his face with his skinny arms, but he must know he doesn't stand a chance against them. Still, no one stirs from their bed. No one is coming to his rescue. This is it. This is what he knew he had to face, even if no one else did. Unchecked, in a fury of bats and shovels and fists and feet, then, they beat him – blow after blow on his head, his chest, his stomach, over and over again – while one of them holds back his hysterical wife. She's in her nightgown, shrieking and sobbing with desperate terror, and the one holding her back puts a hand over her mouth, all but smothering her while his friends finish the job. It was always there, this rage, this spite, this resentment, this pure, unadulterated hatred. Now it finally has somewhere to go. All of it is flooding out of them, destroying the man under their fists, pounding the life out of him. An animal madness seems to come over them and it's as if they're no longer men. That night, they become something else – something monstrous, demonic. They seem to grow even larger in the darkness, mouths wide and snarling, faces vicious, twisted and distorted, stained with streaks of Murphy's blood.

They finally stop when his body goes limp in front of them. He's not moving. Nothing's moving. Everything seems to freeze for a moment. They all stand there, breathless, silent, and it's only when they realize he isn't getting up that they remember where they are, what they've done. Murphy's wife breaks free at last and runs barefoot into the snow, lifting his head, wailing and sobbing, his blood soaking her flimsy nightgown. They just keep standing there, all of them frozen, like grim statues. It's as though they physically can't back away or move at all, stupefied, unable to believe their own memories. Then the stupor breaks, and they scatter, leaving her there to scream uselessly into the night.

Hausmann wakes up in the hospital with a throbbing pain behind his eyes, where Kowalski hit him. Shelly is sitting across from him, dozing, head lolling back against her chair, frizzy blonde hair in disarray.

"Shelly?" he croaks, and she stirs, smiling wanly. Stretching, she gets up to sit down beside him on the edge of the bed.

"Hey," she whispers. "How are you feeling?"

"I'm… I'm ok," he lies. "M-Murphy?" She shakes her head, tears filling her eyes.

"There wasn't anything they could do. They said… they said he was beaten so bad they didn't even recognize him."

"And…Kowalski?" he asks, not really wanting to know the answer.

"They got him," she says, reaching for his hand. "Didn't take long, thank God. Son of a bitch rolled on all five of his buddies, too." He sighs, heavily.

"That's good, I guess." She nods, squeezing his hand.

"I guess," she says, her voice hitching. She's trying to blink back the tears for his sake, but he knows she won't be able to keep it up for long. "Jesus, Tommy, I thought I lost you." She falls forward onto his chest, and starts to sob in earnest. Gently, he puts a hand on her shoulder, and gives it what he hopes is a reassuring squeeze.

"It's ok," he soothes. "I'm not going anywhere." She sits up again, and smiles feebly at him through her tears.

"I'm glad," she whispers. "I-I love you, Tommy." He tries to smile back, but the pain is too much, and he only hopes she can see it in his eyes.

"I love you, too."

A kind of queasy malaise seems to take over Father Daniel after the news of Jimmy Murphy's death spreads. Chief Abernathy didn't call a meeting after it happened – he had his hands full dealing with the aftermath, taking statements from Sally Murphy and from poor Hausmann, and arresting six men who'd been in high school with his own kids. Instead, the news got around town the old fashioned way: via the rumor mill. It spreads quickly, malignantly, like a disease. It's not long before it's all over town, and Sally – poor, plain, broken Sally – is under the microscope again. When the priest finds out, it hits him hard. He knows his parishioners can see it – he stumbles through mass, pale and shaking, hollow-eyed and sweating so much he has to stop every few minutes to wipe his forehead. Poor Father Daniel, they think. How sensitive he is. How deeply he feels.

At night, when the church is silent and empty, he clutches the picture of Sarah that Gallagher left behind to his chest, and lies prostrate at the altar, begging the heavens for strength, for mercy. But the harder he prays, the more the sickness in his soul seems to take hold. He weeps pitifully but even in the darkness, he can feel God's eyes on him. There's nowhere left for him to hide.

It doesn't surprise him when Sally Murphy comes to see him. She's looking for answers, for reassurance that somehow, everything will come right. But he can't give it to her. He just sits there, staring at her, unable to come up with the words that will help her. That's the worst part of it now: that he can't make things better for her. He can't even imagine her pain, and there's nothing he can do to ease it. The only things he can think to say sound so meaningless that he can't even bring himself to say them. She watched her husband die and there wasn't a damn thing she could do to stop it. She looks at him now, with eyes full of despair, begging him to help her find a way out of the woods.

"I don't know what to do," she whispers. "I'm... I'm so alone." He swallows hard, doing his best to look her in the eye, but he can't quite do it.

"What about your sister? Hasn't she been able to help you?" he asks. Sally drops her head and shamefully, he's relieved.

"Some," she says. "She's been helping out taking care of my dad. I just... wish there was someone to take care of me. Is that selfish?" Father Daniel sighs heavily.

"No. It isn't selfish," he says. He steadies himself, mustering up what little comfort he can, hating how feeble he sounds. "God made us to rely on each other, and to rely on Him. Ask Him for the strength you need and He will grant it to you."

"I wish I could believe that," Sally murmurs. He waits for her to say something else, but it doesn't come. Instead, she gets up, smiling tightly. "Thank you, Father."

He looks at the empty space where she was sitting for a few minutes after she leaves, wishing he believed what he'd just said himself. Until now, his faith his been his shield, his protection. It's guided him through the last ten years, of seminary training and then priesthood, of trying to be a better man. But now, it's crumbling away, rotting at the root, and he wonders how strong it really was in the first place. If he's honest with himself, he used it as a wall to hide behind – a way to exonerate himself for the sins of his youth, for Sarah, for all his sins. Slowly, slowly, it's turning to ash, and there's nothing he can do.

When Sally gets home that afternoon, to her dark, empty house, the seed has already been planted. If she's honest with herself, it's been there for a long time. The conversation with the priest only served to confirm what she already knows – her faith is gone. There's no god to pray to for the strength she needs, no one to help her, no one to love her. She sits silently in the living room, staring at the blank screen of the television that she can't even bring herself to switch on and lets it all wash over her. It's all been a lie.

She thinks of the day Jimmy proposed, the day they got married, the day they signed the deed on the house. It had all felt so perfect at the time. She'd been so relieved to have managed to carve out a life for herself that she pushed all the bad, painful feelings down inside her and simply pretended they weren't there. Now, though, she can't hide from them anymore. Now they fill up every sinew, every pore, wave after wave of agony. Even from her childhood, she can't call to mind a single moment of truly pure joy. She never felt the unfettered carelessness that her schoolmates seemed to come to so naturally. She remembers the whoosh of euphoria, at the age of six, when she'd play by herself on the swing-set in the town's tiny playground and even then, the real joy was in imagining she could swing herself so hard that she'd come away from the earth. She'd imagine she could fly off into space and be free. Then she'd come back down again and she'd be crushed by the despair of a disappointment that she couldn't then understand.

She thinks of the smiles and the birthdays and the celebrations and she realizes none of it was real. Every little piece of happiness she ever thought she'd had was built on a foundation of sand and it was only a matter of time before it all came crashing down around her. And crash it did, in truly spectacular fashion. When she stops to think about it, it amazes her just how cataclysmic the last couple of weeks have been. It's funny, she thinks. If Sarah McIntyre had never come back to town, or even if she had, and her body had never been found, she might not be where she is now. She might have gone on living this odd kind of half-life, never truly alive. But she wouldn't be here. She'd be ok, or as ok as she ever was. She'd fade away piece by piece, the way she was supposed to. Instead, it came to her all at once.

There's a part of her that knows she would have come to this point sooner or later, of course. This darkness has always been in her, all around her. These thoughts have danced through her head plenty of times – cold, frightening, malevolent, daring her to do what she's never quite worked up the nerve to do. Now, there's nothing to stop her.

Katie is at her father's house, probably making a hash of trying to cook lunch, and she's glad. She'll be there at least a few hours more. She needs to be alone to do this. Going into the bedroom she and Jimmy once shared – a room now haunted more than anywhere else by all the lies she's lived with for so many years – she sits down at her little vanity table and stares at herself in the mirror for a long time. She doesn't recognize the face looking back. It's drawn and sallow and there are deep, dark rings around her eyes. She's lost a good deal of weight and the roundness of her face has sagged away. It's as though the life has been slowly sucked out of her. She looks deflated, like a forgotten balloon, discarded at the roadside, left behind. Finally, taking a long slow breath, she sets about fishing in the left-hand drawer, where she keeps her letter paper. Using the fountain pen Jimmy gave her for their first anniversary, she takes out a piece of paper, and writes simply, "I'm sorry. Sally". She folds the piece of paper in half and writes her father and sister's names on it, swallowing hard, clenching and unclenching her fists as she tries to hold her nerve.

Feeling the tears starting to sting her eyes, trying to stay methodical, she gets down on her hands and knees to look under the bed for the box where he always kept his handgun. She'd wanted him to get rid of it – the hunting rifle, too, in point of fact, especially when they'd started to talk about having a family. But they're still there, where they've always been, the rifle in a locked cabinet in the living room, and the handgun under the bed. She finds the squat wooden box behind a pair of Jimmy's old work boots and lifts the lid, which gives a little sigh as it rises on its aged hinges. Slowly, steadying her hand, she reaches inside to touch the cold, grey metal before she picks it up. It's beautiful, in a way: sleek, heavy, ominous. Then, with more resolve than she's done anything in her entire life, she sits down on the bed, puts the barrel against her temple, squeezes her eyes shut and pulls the trigger. A second later, she opens her eyes again. The gun isn't loaded.

"You bastard," she whispers, and then screams, "You goddamn fucking bastard! You couldn't even fucking let me have that!" With an almost animal cry, she hurls the gun at the framed photo of Jimmy and her on the table. It hits the mirror instead, smashing it, and she pitches forward onto the floor, all her limbs suddenly heavy, her bones unable to hold her up. Finally letting go, she begins to weep.

"Sally?" She looks up, startled, to see Katie standing in the doorway. "What are you doing?" Sally doesn't answer. Instead, still sobbing, she turns toward the shattered glass and points.

"Oh god," Katie murmurs. Without another word, she runs to her sister and drops down to the floor to put her arms around her, clasping her as tightly as she can. "It's gonna be ok. It's all gonna be ok." She repeats it over and over again, hoping to convince herself as much as her sister.

"No," Sally says at last. "It isn't."

"Sir? Father Carmichael's here to see you," Eriksen says. It's still early and he hadn't even realized she'd come in yet. He looks up sadly at her nervous young face. She's barely out of her teens, and he can't bear to think of what this whole mess must have been doing to her these last couple of weeks. Now, with Jimmy Murphy's death to deal with on top of everything else, he's amazed she's still able to face coming into the station, especially since Hausmann is still in the hospital. He'd suggested a leave of absence, but she'd declined. She needed the routine, she said – needed the distraction.

"Did he say what he wanted?" he asks, wearily. She shakes her head.

"No, sir. Just that it was urgent." Abernathy sighs.

"All right. Send him in."

Father Daniel appears in the doorway a few seconds later, looking pale and sick. There are deep, dark circles around his eyes and his skin is grey and waxy. He looks like he hasn't slept in days. Abernathy smiles, kindly, quietly hoping the poor man doesn't keel over then and there.

"Father," he says, as brightly as he can. "You sure you wanted to see me and not a doctor? You don't look so good." The priest doesn't laugh. Instead, he falls down heavily on the chair opposite Abernathy and starts to cry.

"Father? What is it?" Abernathy asks, startled.

"It was m-me, ok? It was me. All of this... it's all m-my fault," Father Daniel gulps. Abernathy narrows his eyes, scrutinizing the priest's face.

"What was your fault?" he says, quietly.

"I killed her. I killed Sarah McIntyre." Bald, stark, the words seem to cling to the air, dark and heavy, and for a few seconds, Abernathy can't make sense of them. Then suddenly, his stomach lurches and he's afraid he might vomit all over his desk.

"What?" he whispers. The priest is still weeping, but he swallows hard, trying to control himself.

"I-I didn't mean to do it. Sh-she came to see me at the church... the same night she saw Jimmy. Th-the only reason she was talking to him was to f-find out if he knew wh-where I was."

"And... why would she want to know that?" Abernathy asks, trying to collect himself.

"Sh-she wanted to talk to me... a-about the baby," Father Daniel falters, struggling to form the words.

"What baby?" The priest swallows again, wiping his nose with the back of his hand, and lets out a slow, ragged breath before he presses on.

"Sh-she had a baby when she was sixteen. That was the reason she m-moved away. H-her f-father wouldn't let her get rid of it, b-but he made her g-give it up when it was born. Sh-she said it ruined her whole life. Sh-she was supposed to go to Harvard, but she said... sh-she got d-depressed and then... she got into b-booze, d-drugs... p-prostitution... oh God, it was all my fault."

"All right," Abernathy says, slowly. "How was it your fault?"

"Because I was the kid's father," he sobs. "I-I dated her junior year a-and I p-pressured her into s-sleeping with me and then... when I found out she was p-pregnant, I... I told her it wasn't my problem. God, I said such horrible things to her. I accused her of s-sleeping around, of b-basically being the t-town t-tramp, and... she just looked at me like..." Abernathy breathes in deeply, trying to swallow the nausea that still threatens to overwhelm him.

"Father, this doesn't make any sense. Why would she come back, fifteen years later? What did she want?"

"She f-found out I'd become a p-priest," he says, his voice cracking. "She said... she wasn't gonna let me keep l-lying. She said she-she was g-getting out of h-her old life, but... sh-she couldn't really move on until she..." He stops for a second, eyes wide and staring as he remembers. "She said I had to t-tell everybody what kind of a man I r-really am, or... or sh-she would. She k-kept saying it w-wasn't fair – th-that people should know the t-truth."

"Then what happened?" He shakes his head, covering his face with his hands as he breaks down again. "Father?" The priest doesn't look up as he continues and his voice is so muffled that Abernathy almost can't hear him.

"I-I just w-wanted her to b-be *quiet*. I kept trying to t-tell her, trying to make her s-see... that was the whole reason I b-became a priest in the f-first place – I wanted to do some g-good, to m-make up for what I did, b-but sh-she wouldn't listen. I-I didn't mean to do it, but... sh-she just wouldn't shut *up*, so... I grabbed her and... I pushed her against the wall, but... sh-she s-started crying and s-screaming, so..." He pauses for a second, clearly reliving it all in his head, stretching out both his hands to mime pushing her hard. "So... I pushed her again a-and she... she just... went down. Wh-when she didn't get up, I-I thought she was messing with me, t-trying to scare me, but...sh-she must've hit her head... then I saw the blood and... I-I knew."

"But if it was an accident, why didn't you just come and tell me?"

"B-because I knew how it would look and... I p-panicked."

"All right. So why take her body out to the woods? Why dress her up like that?" The whole thing seems like a bad dream, and Abernathy keeps waiting to wake up. He can't believe how wrong he's been about everything. The magnitude of it hits him hard, like a punch to the gut, and he only wishes he thought the priest was lying now.

"I th-thought maybe... I don't know, I could m-make it look l-like one of those r-ritual killings or s-something. God, I-I don't what I thought, I was s-so s-scared. I-I didn't want anyone to kn-know. I just-just wanted it to... go away." He stops again for a few seconds, struggling to steady his voice, but he forces himself to carry on, trying to be as definite as he can. "I-I r-remember I thought...I have to g-get r-rid of her clothes so...I put her in a b-baptismal robe, and then I drove out to the woods and...I l-left her there. I-I don't really even know why...I just...I h-had to get her out of there. I thought m-maybe…the snow…Then when you f-found her, I thought f-for sure, I…but you n-never even looked at me and…then you started l-looking at J-Jimmy, and it s-seemed so easy… all I-I had to do was p-put her c-clothes in his trash can and… oh God, Jimmy, I'm so sorry." Finally losing control, he starts sobbing again – really wailing, like a child who's been slapped – and Abernathy gets up, silently walking round his desk.

"Stand up and turn around," he says quietly, laying a hand on the priest's shoulder. Shaking and crying, he does as he's told, and for only the second time in thirty years, Abernathy reaches for his handcuffs. "Father Daniel Carmichael, you're under arrest for the murder of Sarah McIntyre. You have the right to remain silent. Anything you say can and will be used against you in a court of law. You have the right to an attorney. If you cannot afford an attorney, one will be appointed for you. Do you understand?" The priest nods and drops his head, tears still streaming down his face.

"Showalter!" Abernathy calls. "Take Father Carmichael to the interrogation room… and get him to write down his confession." Showalter duly appears in his doorway, looking intensely surprised, but he quietly takes Daniel by the arm and begins walking him out of the room.

The words sound so hollow, Abernathy thinks – and ironic, too. His confession. Abernathy lets out an audible cry of frustration. Everything that's happened, all the pain and misery, and the bastard was right under his nose the whole time. Along with the anger and the frustration of it, guilt is starting to burn in his veins. He should have known, should have figured it out. Now that he thinks of it, he even wonders if the original anonymous tip – the one that led him to Sarah's body – might have come from him. The voice sounded familiar on the recording, he remembers, and at the time, he couldn't place it, but now…

He sighs as he watches Showalter lead the priest away. What a waste, he thinks.

What a goddamn waste.

It will be his last town meeting. There can be nothing more for him to say to these people after this – nothing more for him to do. It was a scheduled meeting – one set aside weeks ago to discuss progress on the installation of a new nativity scene in the town square. It should have been completely banal. He was supposed to tell them there was a delay with the company that made the damn thing and it might not be there in time for Christmas. But none of that matters today. The tinsel hanging under the windowsills and the garlands on the altar, in place since the end of November, look wrong now. The advent wreath, duly lit every Sunday in December, is worse. He imagines Father Daniel lighting the candles and the hypocrisy of it makes him feel sick. He longs for the time when the worst thing he would have had to worry about was the ire of a couple of dozen busybodies. Now, it might as well be any other time the year. He sighs heavily, steeling himself for what lies ahead. For what seems like the millionth time in the thirty years he's been leading these meetings, he climbs up to the lectern and taps the microphone.

"Can we have some order please?" he calls, as the last few people drift in. Looking out at their sad, tired faces, he wants to turn away, to give up and go without saying anything, but his last act here can't be one of cowardice. He can't let himself fade out without even a word.

"As you all know," he begins, taking a long, slow breath. "The last few days and weeks have been among the most tragic and sordid in this town's history. Two people are dead. Seven men are in jail. Lives have been ruined beyond repair. And it's with a tremendously contrite heart that I must confirm… that James Murphy did not kill Sarah McIntyre."

There's a ripple of consternation in the room, but he holds up a hand to silence it as he always does. It's a strange jolt to think this might be the last time he makes that gesture, but he forges on.

"Today, I received a full confession from Father Daniel Carmichael. He has been taken into police custody and will be arraigned in due course."

The crowd is growing more and more agitated and he's not sure how much longer he can contain them. He holds up a hand again, willing himself to get through this. "It's because of this that I now realize I can no longer serve you, as your chief of police or as a leader in this town. I have failed you, and more importantly, I have failed James Murphy and his family. I'm no longer worthy of this role or of your trust. I'm therefore stepping down from my position and will be leaving in the coming months. I'll stay until a replacement can be found, but I will no longer be in office by the spring. I want to thank you for your faith in me as a police officer and as your leader. I can only apologize for being so unworthy of it."

Then, just as he did on that cold, hateful morning when the whole sorry unravelling of his life began, he steps down from the altar, skirts round the edge of the church, and escapes before anyone has a chance to stop him.

There are five of them there. Sally, her father, her sister, Gallagher, and Mary Callaghan. Mary stands apart from them, a few feet away from the graveside, her face hidden under a veil, but she can't hide her presence. There's nobody to hide behind. Gallagher's stomach drops when he sees her – really sees her, probably for the first time ever. Finally, it dawns on him – why Murphy wouldn't take the job with him in Ashland, why he was so secretive, why he ever tried to kiss Sarah in the first place. It's her.

Sally doesn't say anything – not at first. She stands there, keeping her eyes fixedly on the new priest. He's a skinny, earnest young man, who looks all of about twelve years old. They brought him up here right out of the seminary and it shows. He does his best, but his voice hardly even seems to have broken, and there's just something…undignified about him. Gallagher, for his part, keeps his eye on Sally, wondering if she knows already – if maybe she always knew. Or maybe it's one of those hundreds of little things she let herself pretend she'd imagined. He knows how she was with him, ignoring most things, coming up with *perfectly reasonable explanations* for the things she couldn't. He's waiting for her to blink, waiting for her to show some sign of what's going on inside her head, but she just keeps staring at the priest. The longer she stares, the more the tension seems to grow. It makes the service feel interminable.

Finally, after what feels like hours, it's over. They all stand there in silence for a minute more, and then at last, it's happening. The tension wasn't for nothing. Sally is walking over to Mary.

"Sally, don't!" Katie whispers, but her sister ignores her. Gallagher half thinks of trying to stop her too, of catching her wrist, holding her back, but he checks himself. It's not his place. She needs this. It's not up to him to take it away from her. Mary, to her credit, doesn't try to get away. She doesn't even flinch.

"It's his baby, isn't it?" Sally asks, quietly. Mary gives a little twist of her head, visibly trying to steel herself.

"Yes," she says.

"How long?" Sally goes on. There are tears standing in her eyes, for the first time all day, and she's clutching her purse so hard, Gallagher's convinced she'll tear right through the shiny black leather. Mary is silent.

"*How long?*" Sally presses, her teeth clenched. Mary takes a slow, juddering breath and lets it out over what seems an impossibly long moment.

"About six months," she says at last, her voice unsteady, afraid even. Sally nods, the tears overflowing as the full weight of it hits her.

"Six months. Right. So I guess we share an anniversary pretty much," she replies, bitterly. "How did it happen?" Mary is visibly squirming but Sally won't let her go.

"He was doing some work on my neighbor's house and...I offered him a soda one day and...well, we got to talking and...it just...happened." Sally shakes her head, with a sour little laugh.

"Right. It just *happened*. You never *meant* any of it. It was an *accident*. You piece of trash," she spits.

"I'm... I'm sorry," Mary stammers. "I just... I loved him, too."

"I think you'd better leave," Katie says, taking her sister's arm. Mary nods, covering her hand with her mouth, trying to swallow her own tears.

"I'm sorry," she says again, and she turns and all but sprints back toward the church.

"I... I wanted to say goodbye," Gallagher says feebly, as they watch her go. Sally only turns back to look at him once Mary is completely out of sight. He's been hovering the whole time, waiting for his chance, shifting awkwardly from foot to foot. "I'm going up to Duluth, and... well, I probably won't be back." She nods.

"Oh. Oh, yeah, that... that makes sense. You should be with your family," she murmurs. Then suddenly she's clutching his arm, almost as hard as she was clutching her purse. He can feel her nails even through his thick wool dress coat, surprised at how much it hurts. "Listen, do you... do you wanna come back to the house? I mean, we're not gonna have a wake or anything. My dad and Katie are going right back to his place to finish getting packed up, but... I don't know, we have... things to say, you and me."

"No. No, I can't stay. I gotta get going," he says, hoping he sounds more determined than he feels. It's getting dark already and he's stayed longer than he wanted to. He turns to leave, but she catches his arm again.

"Please stay, Paul. Just for a little while. I'm heading out west with Katie soon and... and I could really use your help with something." He's a little surprised, confused even, but he finds himself giving in to her. He nods.

"All right. Name it."

"Not yet," she says, with a strange little smile. "Come on. I'll tell you when we get there."

In silence, he follows her back to the house, wondering what on earth she could possibly need his help with, but too afraid to ask again. He doesn't even say anything when they get there. The house, for all the lives lived in it are broken beyond repair, is just the same as it always was: overstuffed and overheated, the familiar smell of cigarette smoke and air freshener hanging in the air. He lets her make him a cup of crappy coffee, lets her talk meaninglessly about old times, about how grateful she is to him for sticking by Jimmy, about how hard it'll be without him. They sit there a long time on the lumpy old couch and still she doesn't say what it is she wants him to do. She falls silent eventually, and then finally, he can't take it anymore.

"C'mon, Sal. Tell me what's up?" he asks, as gently as he can. She turns to look at him. There's a weird expression on her face, eyes narrowed, lips pursed, and he finds can't read her.

"Did you know?" she says. Her voice is hard all of a sudden, angry even.

"Know what?" he whispers, finding himself just a little scared.

"About her, about... them." She gestures vaguely, indicating Jimmy's relationship with Mary. He shakes his head.

"No. No, I swear. He never said a word." She studies his face, her eyes searching every little crack and line, reaching into him, piercing him. He feels his skin start to burn. The only person who ever made him feel so exposed was Billy. She turns away from him at last, and he lets himself breathe again. Maybe he's off the hook. But a second later, her gaze snaps back up to meet his.

"I want to destroy this place," she whispers, keeping her eyes on his. He stares, confused.

"What... what d'you mean?"

"The house – his house. I want it gone," she says, suddenly firm.

"But... how?" She smiles, a little frighteningly, he thinks, and gets up, disappearing into the tiny kitchen for a minute.

"With this," she says when she comes back. She's holding one of those big plastic jugs, the kind he and Murphy used to take camping with them – he can tell it's full of kerosene from the smell – and produces a box of matches from her pocket with a little flourish.

"Oh, Sally. Are you sure about this?" Gallagher murmurs. She nods resolutely.

"Yes. Everything important is already at my dad's place. I just... I need this. Especially after... with Mary... what he did. It's the only way." She reaches out for his hand, squeezing it more tightly than he's expecting. "Will you help me?"

"All right," Gallagher says. "All right. What do you need me to do?"

"I need you to be here with me. And I need you to call the fire department when the time comes. Then I need you to leave and never look back. But before you do all that, I need you to go outside and act normal. Can you do that?" He nods.

"Ok. Let's do this." She smiles gratefully as she ushers him out the door, and then she disappears inside the house with the kerosene. She comes back a few minutes later, pale and shivering, as if suddenly aware of the magnitude of what she's about to do. But she isn't backing down. He can see it in her eyes.

"Ready?" she asks. He nods one more time, and she lights a match, tossing it inside the door. They jump back quickly, running a few paces away to take refuge. It doesn't take long for the flames to take hold of the little wooden house. They watch in silence for a few minutes, as the fire lights up the evening sky and the last little part of Jimmy's life burns away. Gallagher knows it's time for him to play his part. He makes the call on Sally's cell phone, and then he gets in his truck and he doesn't look back.

There's always been an Abernathy. The words ring in his ears as he sets about clearing away the last of his belongings from his office at the police station. Someone else will be in this office soon. Someone else will take over his duties here and someone else will have to be elected to lead the town. His name will remain in the town hall, the last in a long list of the Abernathys who've gone before him. It's the way it has to be. There's no coming back from this. It's over for him, for his life here. He only hopes that, in the way of horrible, incomprehensible things, people will try to forget – that they'll try to scrub it from their minds, from the town's otherwise more or less uneventful history.

He looks out of the window before he leaves the building. It's almost spring and the snow is starting to melt, but it doesn't bring him the same sense of hope, of renewal as it once did. Now, all of that is over for good, too. There's nothing left for him or his family and he can no longer look at the streets or the people the way he used to. He's not their leader anymore and he can't be again. His name is tarnished now, maybe forever. Carl, his son, seemed relieved when he broke the news to him that he wouldn't have to give up his comfortable life in Milwaukee, and that hurt as much as anything. The tradition, the history – everything his ancestors had worked so hard to build and protect over the last two centuries, everything he devoted his whole existence to is gone. It's dead and buried, and there's nobody left to mourn for it.

Almost everyone who played a part in what happened is gone now, too. Even the Murphy house is gone, burned to the ground. He knows what happened – everybody does, probably, though nobody ever said it – but he let it go. He had to. Paul Gallagher was gone before the flames even went out, off to Minnesota to be closer to his sister. Katie Weiler took her father and sister with her when she went back west, the day after Jimmy's funeral. Mary Callaghan left without a word, although he suspects he knows where she's headed. Her father moved into the Ashland condo after she'd gone and hasn't been back here since. Even Tommy Hausmann, who loved the town more than anybody he'd ever met, more even than he loved it himself, went out to Iowa City, where his parents are living, a couple of months after Daniel Carmichael was arrested, and Shelly Eriksen with him. Strangely, only Showalter and Legler remain – the two people he expected to cut and run long before anybody else – but he can't imagine they'll stick around much longer. Abernathy has clung on too long himself, and it's well past time for him to bow out. He wants to make it as graceful as he can, but he knows there's not much room for that now. His sin is too great.

He and Elizabeth will drive to his sister's in Madison that night and from there, on to Dubuque. An old academy buddy found him a desk job at the police department there, where he can wait out the last couple of years until retirement. It breaks his heart to see it end this way, all the years of effort, of hard-won reputation and honor turning to dust, or worse, to paperwork, but there's no way to repair the damage to the family name. There's too much blood on his hands, too much to be forgiven. This is how it has to be.

He knows, of course, that he'll never be able to redeem himself for his cowardice, his weakness. Not even Elizabeth looks at him the same way anymore, and he hates to imagine what his daddy would think if he could see what had become of his legacy. Something somewhere along the way must have poisoned the well – maybe even some wrong he committed himself, long cast from his memory. As he thinks about it now, he wonders if maybe it doesn't go back to Billy Peterson. He had a chance to protect that poor boy and he didn't take it. At the time, his death was the worst tragedy the town had seen in decades – maybe ever. Right after it happened, he'd been able to convince himself that no one was at fault. The boy was sick. His mind was broken. No one could have saved him. But after everything that's happened in the last few months, he can't help feeling like there's some sort of punishment being wrought, and there has to be a reason for it. Someone must have failed somewhere along the way, let the poison in, and it's as likely to be him as anyone. The whole town is ailing and there's only one way for it to restore itself. It needs to start all over, cut out the rot, go back to the root, and right now, it can't do that – not while he's still there at least. Then again, maybe death simply begets death. Maybe it was already there. Maybe the roots were rotten anyway. Maybe there was no way to avoid any of this.

He won't say goodbye: there's no one left to say goodbye to, no one to be sad to see him go. Someone has already been found to take his place as the chief of police, but as of this moment, the town has no leader. He hopes it will be someone wiser, better, stronger – someone worthy of the office. Then maybe the people can start to put the pieces of their lives back together, start to heal. For the first time in the town's history, there will have to be a real election, he realizes, and it's a strange thought. Candidates will have to stand, campaigns fought, and he finds a small part of him is actually sorry he'll miss the spectacle and drama of it all.

He empties the clip from his gun, and hands it over to the unfamiliar woman at the front desk as he leaves – a stand-in from Ashland until new officers can be recruited to take over from Eriksen and Hausmann on a permanent basis. He won't get to do that either, won't get to see the eager, hopeful faces, ready to protect this place, ready to do a better job than he ever did. She doesn't say anything – probably thinks he's just retiring, smiles benignly as she watches him go, knowing nothing of the pain behind his eyes – and that's the end of it.

Mary Callaghan's baby is born in the summer, on a bright, hot day, in a San Francisco hospital, where no one knows her or her history – a little boy, already with the first hints of his father's angular features, and a full head of her own thick, dark hair. She looks out of the window at the Golden Gate bridge in the distance and thinks sadly of her own mother as she prepares to leave.

"Some day," she whispers, looking down into his big, innocent blue eyes, as she carries him out of the hospital and into the world. "Some day, I'll tell you about your daddy."

When you hit the farm that used to be the Weiler farm, you'd know you were there. You'd know you'd hit the last cornfield, after miles and miles of nothing but cornfields. There was still another mile to go before you hit the main street, such as it was, but that was the boundary. The faded red barn and the ancient silo marked the gateway. That was where it began. You saw the wide, flat streets and the wide, flat storefronts. That was when that familiar feeling would hit you. It started in your hands and feet and ran through you like a current in a wire as you got closer. It settled deep in your gut, a ball of pulsing electricity. You knew this town. You'd been there before, or maybe you never really left. Everything about it was lodged inside you. You knew the little yellow town hall, which was only open every other Tuesday. You knew the diner and the church and the bar. You knew the one sad, dusty bookstore that stayed open year after year, even though you could never figure out why. You knew the funny old guy who sat behind the counter and smiled expectantly every time somebody walked by.

Your mother grew up there. Your father passed through on his way to Iowa, or Minnesota, or Canada, or... somewhere. You had an uncle who worked at the Weiler farm the summer before college. A friend of a friend knew somebody who went to the high school, five miles out of town that served half the county's kids. You knew the guy who drove the crappy yellow school bus that took the kids there to learn and forget all the same things you learned and forgot. You knew the class clown, who used to sit at the back of the bus and yell mean things at the girls and never graduated. You knew this town. It was written into your history. It was written into everybody's history. You've found little pieces of it in every town you've ever visited. A store. A stretch of road. A church. A smile. A funny old guy looking at you with eyes full of hope and pain.

It was sewn into the fabric of every street, stitched into the stones and the earth. It was a hitch in the path, an unavoidable knot, where everybody began or ended or found themselves somewhere along the way. You'd leave it for a while, but you always circled back. It still calls out to you, even now, so many years later. It was painted onto the scenery of every stage. You've seen its shape when you looked up at the clouds. You've heard the familiar chirrup of its crickets in the creak of a door. Now, it's in the voices and the memories of everybody you know.

It was home.

Home, where you fought with your parents and told them you were leaving for good, home, where you had your first kiss, home, where you crashed your car, home, where you got drunk and stole a milk truck, home, where you first knew what it was to hate somebody, home, where you fell in love.

If you weren't born there, you knew somebody who knew somebody who knew somebody who was. You'd say its name now and wherever you were, somebody looked up. This was every town where anybody ever fooled themselves into thinking life could be simple after all. You knew these people. These were your people. You knew the places they ate, the place they got drunk, the place they prayed. You knew the playground, the river. You ate there, drank there, prayed there, played there. You hurled yourself from the ancient rope swing into the river's muddy depths, thick with algae in the summer, and for one crazy second before you hit the water, you hung there in space, flying. Or maybe your brother did, or your cousin, or your best friend from summer camp. Maybe you were too afraid to do it yourself because you heard about that kid who drowned when he hit his head on a tree branch and knocked himself out. You knew all the stories this town had to tell. You knew all its happy endings and all its regrets. You knew all the put-down-roots and all the never-quite-made-its. You knew everybody who hated this place, everybody who was torn apart by it, and everybody who, just as much as they hated it, they loved it still.

These were your people. They're half living, half ghost now, inhabiting the space between memory and flesh and blood. They were what used to be, or what you imagined used to be, or what could have been. They were those days gone by that everybody yearns for, that everybody misses, but nobody ever really had. They were perfectly imperfect. They were fragile, made up of hundreds of thousands of gossamer threads, strands drawn together from collective memory. You'd put a hand on them and they'd turn to dust. They didn't know it but they were as delicate as ancient silk. This was the town that was built of paste and sticks and paper, on hope, on vanity, on naivety. Its people were puppets, just like you. You were all players in a cosmic comedy, and this was your theatre. As much as you were a part of it, though, you were a spectator too, helpless, unable to alter the course of events. This was where it all came crashing down. This was where it all went away, stopped being what it was. Nothing can go back now. This was your ending, too. This was your part in the play. You were there to witness what happened when it couldn't be fixed. You were there to watch the show, there to see the paste and the paper turn to ash.

You knew the story of how it came to be. It was told to you from your infancy, over and over again, until it became part of you. You knew where the first house was built. You knew about the fabled first family who lived there, the Abernathys. You knew about the bright, faithful, blinkered eyes of its founder, its first king. You were there to see its last king find himself on his knees. You knew him, too. He wasn't really a king — there was no crown, no shining coat of mail — but he might as well have been. That was how everybody saw him. He was like Arthur, a golden knight in everybody's eyes. A god. You worshiped him, just like everybody else, and you never questioned it. He was your brother, your uncle, your second cousin's husband's sister's son. But heroes are never what they seem, never live up to the illusion. They're never really pure in heart, and they're never really noble in word and deed. Heroes always turn out to be human in the end.

This was your town. This was his town. It was mine and theirs and ours. We were part of its story and it was part of ours. The colors spoke of years and years of quiet. They were soft, like a fading dream, half flesh, half shadow. The image is still right there behind your eyes but it never comes into focus now. It's become muted and blurred, smudged like charcoal under your thumb.

This place swaddled you like a blanket. It pulled you to its heart, cocooned you, protected you. It swallowed you, blinded you. Everything there was always like this and everybody thought it always would be. Time went on and nothing changed. Time went on and nothing changed. Time went on and nothing changed. Nothing changed.

Nothing changed.

They were the masters of complacency. So were you. Nobody expected this. Nobody was ready for it. The town taught them not to think about what could be, not to be afraid, and not to look beyond its borders. Nothing could be better than this. Its beauty was in its immutability. But finally, nothing could be the same forever. Nothing is exactly the way you remember it now. Nothing stayed. It was a fantasy built on a foundation of lies. It was just that everybody went along with it.

Everything did change, of course. The lie was exposed, raw and open for everybody to see. Suddenly, their eyes were open. Suddenly, it all fell away underneath them. But the power of this town — that remains to this day. There's still pull in its very soil, in the roots of the trees and the corn. Its insides cracked and crumbled and collapsed, but even the dust that settled on the ruins has power. Everything you knew, or thought you knew, is gone forever now, everybody you loved, or thought you loved, is hollow-eyed and haunted. Its tragedy was your tragedy. But it still draws you in, still clutches you to its ancient heart, bathes you in the blood of its wounds, suffocates you.

You knew these winters, these bitter months, when spring seemed years away. Christmas would come and go in the blink of an eye, but the freezing weather stayed. Daylight was a fleeting thing. Some days, just for a little while, the sky would be clear and blue, as if it, too, were made of ice. You imagined it to be a vast, frozen sea, on which you could skate if you could only get there. But then the clouds would roll in. They'd fill that crystal expanse, quicker than you could ever believe. The sun would disappear and the snow would come again, in thick, blind blankets.

You knew the streets, shining and treacherous before they put salt down. You knew the bravery, the invincibility of youth. You trekked through the snow, when it was well below freezing, to get to the river. Somebody would bring beer and you'd light a fire, when it got too cold to ignore it anymore. You dared your friends to step out onto the river's frozen surface, secretly wondering what you'd do if the ice really did crack underneath your feet. The king would come, you'd tell yourself, and you'd be saved. But he can't save you now. He couldn't even save himself. He couldn't save anybody.

There's nobody left to save.

You came here at the turning point. Maybe it was designed by fate, or maybe you were the bearer of ill fortune. Maybe you brought this darkness with you. Whatever the reason, it's over now. Underneath that fragile veneer, there was always been a little whisper of something else. You knew the story – everybody did. He was an out-of-towner who came to settle down, to make a life. He was drawn in, just like everybody else. But he was different. He found himself vilified, spat upon, cast out, until it swallowed him whole. That was the first sign of it, the first crack. But you brushed it off. You pretended it didn't matter. He was an outsider, you told yourself; he didn't belong. You let it go and you carried on.

But the crack, unchecked, grew until it became a chasm, and that was the last of this town, or at least the last of the town as it always was in your memory. A light went out for good. This was the passing of everything the way it always was. You couldn't brush it off. You couldn't pretend. It was right that it should be cold, of course. Death is always cold. Nobody would guess now, but then they'd feel a little part of them freeze. Everything looked the same as it did back then, but there was nothing underneath. It was just an empty shell. The heart beat on, but the body was gone.

Eventually, the town went on. You knew it would. Slowly, it rose from the destruction and the dust. They swept the ground, collected the bones, and started again. But there's a stain now. A scar. You can't see it, but you know it's there. You can sense it, wherever you go: a shadow over everything, even when the sun shines. It's been marked out, invisibly, for the transgressions that took place within its confines. There's a dark, painful blemish, burned on its memory and your memory, and everybody else's. You've come back every now and then, when the pain faded enough, but you've felt it all over again when you got close — a throb in your temple, a tightening in your chest. You'd find yourself in the center of town, weeping without realizing the tears were flowing. The stain bleeds into everything you knew about this place. Everything is tainted. Even the most beautiful of your memories are touched with sadness. And then, when the darkness is at its deepest, you let yourself wonder if it would have been better to see it razed to the ground. Burned away. Erased from history. Nothing can ever be pure or good or free again now. Not really. Not fully. Nobody can be ok anymore.

You can't be ok anymore.

Acknowledgements

Special thanks should go to my parents, for always believing I could write a novel, to Rose and Alan, Shona Kinsella and Laurie Garrison, who all read early versions and offered support before Abernathy was finished, to Unbound, without which I'd never have realised crowdfunding wasn't for me and therefore wouldn't have got to where I am, and to the great state of Wisconsin.

Other novels, novellas and short story collections available from Stairwell Books

Carol's Christmas	N.E. David
Feria	N.E. David
A Day at the Races	N.E. David
Running With Butterflies	John Walford
Foul Play	P J Quinn
Poison Pen	P J Quinn
Rosie and John's Magical Adventure	The Children of Ryedale District Primary Schools
Wine Dark, Sea Blue	A.L. Michael
Skydive	Andrew Brown
Close Disharmony	P J Quinn
When the Crow Cries	Maxine Ridge
The Geology of Desire	Clint Wastling
Homelands	Shaunna Harper
Border 7	Pauline Kirk
Tales from a Prairie Journal	Rita Jerram
Here in the Cull Valley	John Wheatcroft
How to be a Man	Alan Smith
A Multitude of Things	David Clegg
Know Thyself	Lance Clarke
Thinking of You Always	Lewis Hill
Tyrants Rex	Clint Wastling
Rapeseed	Alwyn Marriage
A Shadow in my Life	Rita Jerram

For further information please contact rose@stairwellbooks.com

www.stairwellbooks.co.uk
@stairwellbooks